35—

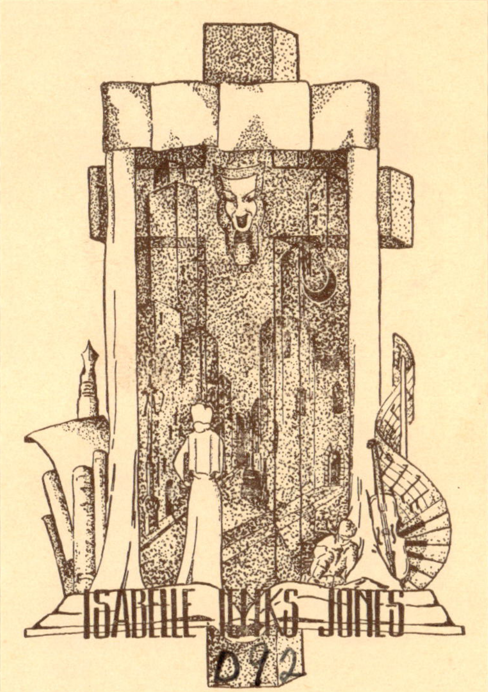

SECOND PLAYS

MODERN DRAMA
ON MR. KNOPF'S LIST

FIRST PLAYS
by A. A. Milne

LYSISTRATA
by Maurice Donnay

TWELVE THOUSAND
by Bruno Frank

CHICAGO
by Maurine Watkins

BONAPARTE
by Fritz von Unruh

These are Borzoi Books published by **Alfred A. Knopf** and for sale at the better bookshops

SECOND PLAYS

by

A·A·MILNE

NEW YORK·ALFRED·A·KNOPF·MCMXXXI

Copyright 1922, 1931, by Alfred A. Knopf, Inc.
All rights reserved—no part of this book may be reprinted in
any form without permission in writing from the publisher
Manufactured in the United States of America

To
D. M.
SO LITTLE IN RETURN FOR SO MUCH

Applications regarding Amateur Performances of the Plays in this Volume should be addressed to Samuel French, Ltd., 26 Southampton Street, Strand, London, W.C.2.

CONTENTS

MAKE-BELIEVE	*1*
MR. PIM PASSES BY	*71*
THE CAMBERLEY TRIANGLE	*143*
THE ROMANTIC AGE	*163*
THE STEPMOTHER	*249*

INTRODUCTION

Encouraged by the reviewer who announced that the Introduction to my previous collection of plays was the best part of the book, I venture to introduce this collection in a similar manner. But I shall be careful not to overdo it this time, in the hope that I may win from my critic some such tribute as, "Mr. Milne has certainly improved as a dramatist, in that his plays are now slightly better than his Introduction."

Since, then, I am trying to make this preface as distasteful as possible, in order that the plays may shine out the more pleasantly, I shall begin (how better?) with an attack on the dramatic critics. I will relate a little conversation which took place, shortly after the publication of "First Plays," between myself and a very much more eminent dramatist.

EMINENT DRAMATIST (*kindly*). Your book seems to have been well reviewed.

MYSELF (*ungratefully*). Not bad—by those who reviewed it. But I doubt if it was noticed by more than three regular dramatic critics. And considering that two of the plays in it had never been produced——

EMINENT DRAMATIST (*amused by my innocence*). My dear fellow, *you* needn't complain. I published an unproduced play a little while ago, and it didn't get a single notice from anybody.

Now I hope that, however slightly the conversations in the plays which follow may move the dramatic critic, he will at least be disturbed by this little dialogue.

All of us who are interested in the theatre are accustomed to read, and sometimes to make, ridiculous accusations against the Theatrical Manager. We condemn the mercenary fellow because he will not risk a loss of two or three thousand pounds on the intellectual masterpiece of a promising young dramatist, preferring to put on some contemptible but popular rubbish which is certain to fill his theatre. But now we see that the dramatic critic, that stern upholder of the best interests of the British Drama, will not himself risk six shillings (and perhaps two or three hours of his time) in order to read the intellectual masterpiece of the promising young dramatist, and so to be able to tell us with authority whether the Manager really *is* refusing masterpieces or no. He will not risk six shillings in order to encourage that promising young dramatist—discouraged enough already, poor devil, in his hopes of fame and fortune—by telling him that he *is* right, and that his plays *are* worth something, or (alternatively) to prevent him from wasting any more of his youth upon an art-form to which he is not suited. No, he will not risk his shillings; but he will write an important (and, let us hope, well-rewarded) article, informing us that the British Drama is going to the dogs, and that no promising young dramatist is ever given a fair chance.

Absurd, isn't it?

Let us consider this young dramatist for a moment, and ask ourselves why he goes on writing his masterpieces. I give three reasons—in their order of importance.

(1) The pleasure of writing; or, more accurately, the hell of not writing. He gets this anyhow.

(2) The appreciation of his peers; his hope of immortality; the criticism of the experts; fame, publicity, notoriety, swank, *réclame*—call it what you will. But

INTRODUCTION

it is obvious that he cannot have it unless the masterpiece is given to the world, either by manager or publisher.

(3) Money. If the masterpiece is published only, very little; if produced, possibly a great deal.

As I say, he gets his first reward anyhow. But let us be honest with ourselves. How many of us would write our masterpieces on a desert island, with no possibility of being rescued? Well, perhaps all of us; for we should feel that, even if not rescued ourselves, our manuscripts—written on bark with a burnt stick—clutched in a skeleton hand—might be recovered later by some literary sea-captain. (As it might be, Conrad.) But how many of us would write masterpieces if we had to burn them immediately afterwards, or if we were alone upon the world, the last survivors of a new flood? Could we bear to write? Could we bear not to write? It is not fair to ask us. But we can admit this much without reserve; it is the second reward which tears at us, and, lacking it, we should lose courage.

So when the promising young dramatist has his play refused by the Managers—after what weeks, months, years of hope and fear, uncertainty and bitter disappointment—he has this great consolation: "Anyway, I can always publish it." Perhaps, after a dozen refusals, a Manager offers to put on his play, on condition that he alters the obviously right (and unhappy) ending into the obviously foolish, but happy, ending which will charm the public. Does he, the artist, succumb? How easy to tell himself that he *must* get his play before the public somehow, and that, even if it is not *his* play now, yet the first two acts are as he wrote them, and that, if only to feel the thrill of the audience at that great scene between the Burglar and the Bishop (*his* creations!) he must deaden his conscience to the absurdity of a happy ending. But does he succumb? No. Heroically he tells himself: "Anyway, I can publish it; and I'm certain that the critics will agree with me that——" But the critics are too busy to bother about him. They are busy informing the world that the British Drama is going to the dogs, and that no promising young dramatist ever gets a fair chance.

Let me say here that I am airing no personal grievance. I doubt if any dramatist has less right to feel aggrieved against the critics, the managers, the public, the world, than I; and whatever right I have I renounce, in return for the good things which I have received from them. But I do not renounce the grievance of our craft. I say that, in the case of all dramatists, it is the business of the dramatic critics to review their unacted plays when published. Some of them do; most of them do not. It is ridiculous for those who do not to pretend that they take any real interest in the British Drama. But I say "review," not "praise." Let them damn, by all means, if the plays are unworthy; and, by damning, do so much of justice to the Managers who refused them.

We can now pass on safely to the plays in this volume.

We begin with a children's play. The difficulty in the way of writing a children's play is that Barrie was born too soon. Many people must have felt the same about Shakespeare. We who came later have no chance. What fun to have been Adam, and to have had the whole world of plots and jokes and stories at one's disposal. Possibly, however, one would never have thought of the things. Of course, there are still others to come after us, but our works are not immortal, and they will plagiarise us without protest. Yet I have hopes of *Make-Believe*, for it had the honour of inaugurating Mr. Nigel Playfair's

INTRODUCTION xv

management at the Lyric, Hammersmith. It is possible that the historians will remember this, long after they have forgotten my plays; more likely (alas!) that their history will be dated A.D. (After Drinkwater) and that the honour will be given to "Abraham Lincoln." I like to think that in this event my ghost will haunt them. *Make-Believe* appeared with a Prologue by the Manager, lyrics by C. E. Burton, and music by Georges Dorlay. As the title-page states that this book is, in the language of children's competitions, "my own unaided work," I print the play with a new Prologue, and without the charming lyrics. But the reader is told when he may burst into an improvisation of his own, though I warn him that he will not make such a good show of it as did my collaborators.

Mr. Pim Passes By appeared at several theatres. Let us admit cheerfully that it was a success—in spite of the warning of an important gentleman in the theatrical world, who told me, while I was writing it, that the public wouldn't stand any talk of bigamy, and suggested that George and Olivia should be engaged only, not married. (Hence the line, "Bigamy! . . . It *is* an ugly word," in the Second Act.) But, of course, nobody sees more clearly than I how largely its success was due to Mr. Dion Boucicault and Miss Irene Vanbrugh.

The Romantic Age appeared first at the Comedy, and (like *Mr. Pim*) found, in its need, a home at The Playhouse. Miss Gladys Cooper has a charming way of withdrawing into a nursing home whenever I want a theatre, but I beg her not to make a habit of it. My plays can be spared so much more easily than she. By the way, a word about Melisande. Many of the critics said that nobody behaved like that nowadays. I am terrified at the thought of arguing with them, for they can always reduce me to blushes with a scornful, "My dear man, you *can't* do that in a *play*!" And when they tell me to remember what Strindberg said in '93 (if he were alive then; I really don't know) or what Aristotle wrote in—no, I shan't even guess at Aristotle, well, then, I want to burst into tears, my ignorance is so profound. So, very humbly, I just say now that, when Melisande talks and behaves in a certain way, I do not mean that a particular girl exists (Miss Jones, of 999 Bedford Park) who talks and behaves like this, but I do mean that there is a type of girl who, in her heart, secretly, *thinks* like this. If, from your great knowledge of the most secret places of a young girl's heart, you tell me that there is no such type, then I shall only smile. But if you inform me sternly that a dramatist has no business to express an attitude in terms of an actress, then you reduce me to blushes again. For I really know nothing about play-writing, and I am only sustained by two beliefs. The first is that rules are always made for the other people; the second is that, if a play by me is not obviously by me, and as obviously not by anybody else, then (obviously) I had no business to write it.

Of the one-act plays, *The Camberley Triangle* and *The Stepmother*, nothing much need be said. The former was played at the Coliseum; the latter, written for Miss Winifred Emery, was deemed by the management too serious for that place of amusement. This, however, was to the great advantage of the play, for now it has appeared only at Charity *matinées* with an "all-star" cast.

As before, the plays are printed in the order in which they were written; in this case between October 1918 and June 1920. May the reader get as much enjoyment from them as I had in their writing. But no; that is plainly impossible.

A. A. MILNE.

MAKE-BELIEVE

A CHILDREN'S PLAY IN A PROLOGUE
AND THREE ACTS

Make-Believe was first produced at the Lyric Theatre, Hammersmith, on December 24, 1918. The chief parts were played by Marjory Holman, Jean Cadell, Rosa Lynd, Betty Chester, Roy Lennol, John Barclay, Kinsey Peile, Stanley Drewitt, Ivan Berlyn, and Herbert Marshall—several parts each.

MAKE-BELIEVE

PROLOGUE

The playroom of the HUBBARD FAMILY—*nine of them. Counting* MR. *and* MRS. HUBBARD, *we realize that there are eleven* HUBBARDS *in all, and you would think that one at least of the two people we see in the room would be a* HUBBARD *of sorts. But no. The tall manly figure is* JAMES, *the* HUBBARDS' *butler, for the* HUBBARDS *are able to afford a butler now. How different from the time when Old Mother Hubbard—called "old" because she was at least twenty-two, and "mother" because she had a passion for children—could not even find a bone for her faithful terrier; but, of course, that was before* HENRY *went into work. Well, the tall figure is* JAMES, *the butler, and the little one is* ROSEMARY, *a friend of the* HUBBARD FAMILY. ROSEMARY *is going in for literature this afternoon, as it's raining, and* JAMES *is making her quite comfortable first with pens and ink and blotting-paper—always so important when one wants to write. He has even thought of a stick of violet sealing-wax; after that there can be no excuse.*

ROSEMARY. Thank you, James. (*She sits down.*) If any one calls I am not at home.
JAMES. Yes, Miss.

ROSEMARY. You may add that I am engaged in writing my auto—autobiography.

JAMES. Yes, Miss.

ROSEMARY. It's what every one writes, isn't it, James?

JAMES. I believe so, Miss.

ROSEMARY. Thank you. (*He goes to the door.*) Oh, James?

JAMES. Yes, Miss?

ROSEMARY. What *is* an autobiography?

JAMES. Well, I couldn't rightly say, Miss—not to explain it properly.

ROSEMARY (*dismayed*). Oh, James! . . . I thought you knew everything.

JAMES. In the ordinary way, yes, Miss, but every now and then——

ROSEMARY. It's very upsetting.

JAMES. Yes, Miss. . . . How would it be to write a play instead? Very easy work, they tell me.

ROSEMARY (*nodding*). Yes, that's much better. I'll write a play. Thank you, James.

JAMES. Not at all, Miss. [*He goes out.*
(ROSEMARY *bites her pen, and thinks deeply. At last the inspiration comes.*)

ROSEMARY (*as she writes*). Make-Believe. M-a-k-e hyphen B-e-l—— (*she stops and frowns*) Now which way *is* it? (*She tries it on the blotting paper*) *That* looks wrong. (*She tries it again*) So does that. Oh, dear! (*She rings the bell* . . . JAMES *returns.*)

JAMES. Yes, Miss?

ROSEMARY. James, I have decided to call my play Make-Believe.

JAMES. Yes, Miss.

ROSEMARY (*carelessly*). When you spell "believe," it *is* "i-e," isn't it?

JAMES. Yes, Miss.

MAKE-BELIEVE

ROSEMARY. I thought at first it was "e-i."

JAMES. Now you mention it, I think it is, Miss.

ROSEMARY (*reproachfully*). Oh, James! Aren't you certain?

JAMES. M-a-k-e, make, B-e-l—— (*He stops and scratches his whiskers.*)

ROSEMARY. Yes. *I* got as far as that.

JAMES. B-e-l——

ROSEMARY. You see, James, it spoils the play if you have an accident to the very first word of it.

JAMES. Yes, Miss. B-e-l—— I've noticed sometimes that if one writes a word careless-like on the blotting-paper, and then looks at it with the head on one side, there's a sort of instinct comes over one, as makes one say (*with a shake of the head*) "Rotten." One can then write it the other way more hopeful.

ROSEMARY. I've tried that.

JAMES. Then might I suggest, Miss, that you give it another name altogether? As it might be, "Susan's Saturday Night," all easy words to spell, or "Red Revenge," or——

ROSEMARY. I *must* call it Make-Believe, because it's all of the play I've thought of so far.

JAMES. Quite so, Miss. Then how would it be to spell it wrong on purpose? It comes funnier that way sometimes.

ROSEMARY. Does it?

JAMES. Yes, Miss. Makes 'em laugh.

ROSEMARY. Oh! . . . Well, which *is* the wrong way?

JAMES. Ah, there you've got me again, Miss.

ROSEMARY (*inspired*). I know what I'll do. I'll spell it "i-e"; and if it's right, then I'm right, and if it's wrong, then I'm funny.

JAMES. Yes, Miss. That's the safest.

ROSEMARY. Thank you, James.

JAMES. Not at all, Miss. [*He goes out.*

ROSEMARY (*writing*). Make-Believe. A Christmas Entertainment—— (*She stops and thinks, and then shakes her head.*) No, play—a Christmas Play in three acts. Er—— (*She is stuck.*)

Enter JAMES.

JAMES. Beg pardon, Miss, but the Misses and Masters Hubbard are without, and crave admittance.

ROSEMARY. All nine of them?

JAMES. Without having counted them, Miss, I should say that the majority of them were present.

ROSEMARY. Did you say that I was not at home?

JAMES. Yes, Miss. They said that, this being their house, and you being a visitor, if you *had* been at home, then you wouldn't have been here. Yumour on the part of Master Bertram, Miss.

ROSEMARY. It's very upsetting when you're writing a play.

JAMES. Yes, Miss. Perhaps they could help you with it. The more the merrier, as you might say.

ROSEMARY. What a good idea, James. Admit them.

JAMES. Yes, Miss. (*He opens the door and says very rapidly*) The Misses Ada, Caroline, Elsie, Gwendoline, and Isabel Hubbard, The Masters Bertram, Dennis, Frank, and Harold Hubbard. (*They come in.*)

ROSEMARY. How do you do?

ADA. Rosemary, darling, what *are* you doing?

BERTRAM. It's like your cheek, bagging our room.

CAROLINE (*primly*). Hush, Bertram. We ought always to be polite to our visitors when they stay with us. I am sure, if Rosemary wants our room——

DENNIS. Oh, chuck it!

ADA (*at* ROSEMARY's *shoulder*). Oh, I say, she's writing a play!

(*Uproar and turmoil, as they all rush at* ROSE-
MARY.)

THE BOYS. Coo! I say, shove me into it. What's it about? Bet it's awful rot.

THE GIRLS. Oh, Rosemary! Am *I* in it? Do tell us about it. Is it for Christmas?

ROSEMARY (*in alarm*). James, could you——?

JAMES (*firmly*). Quiet, there, quiet! Down, Master Dennis, down! Miss Gwendoline, if you wouldn't mind—— (*He picks her up and places her on the floor.*) Thank you. (*Order is restored.*)

ROSEMARY. Thank you, James. . . . Yes, it's a play for Christmas, and it is called "Make-Believe," and that's all I'm certain about yet, except that we're all going to be in it.

BERTRAM. Then I vote we have a desert island——

DENNIS. And pirates——

FRANK. And cannibals——

HAROLD (*gloatingly*). Cannibals eating people—Oo!

CAROLINE (*shocked*). Harold! How would *you* like to be eaten by a cannibal?

DENNIS. Oh, chuck it! How would *you* like to be a cannibal and have nobody to eat? (CAROLINE *is silent, never having thought of this before.*)

ADA. Let it be a fairy-story, Rosemary, darling. It's so much *prettier*.

ELSIE. With a lovely princess——

GWENDOLINE. And a humble woodcutter who marries her——

ISABEL (*her only contribution*). P'itty P'incess.

BERTRAM. Princesses are rot.

ELSIE (*with spirit*). So are pirates! (*Deadlock.*)

CAROLINE. *I* should like something about Father Christmas, and snow, and waits, and a lovely ball, and everybody getting nice presents and things.

DENNIS (*selfishly, I'm afraid*). Bags I all the presents.
(*Of course, the others aren't going to have that. They all say so together.*)

ROSEMARY (*above the turmoil*). James, I *must* have silence.

JAMES. Silence, all!

ROSEMARY. Thank you. . . . You will be interested to hear that I have decided to have a Fairy Story *and* a Desert Island *and* a Father Christmas.

ALL. Good! (*Or words to that effect.*)

ROSEMARY (*biting her pen*). I shall begin with the Fairy Story. (*There is an anxious silence. None of them has ever seen anybody writing a play before. How does one do it? Alas,* ROSEMARY *herself doesn't know. She appeals to* JAMES.) James, how *do* you begin a play? I mean when you've *got* the title.

JAMES (*a man of genius*). Well, Miss Rosemary, seeing that it's to be called "Make-Believe," why not make-believe as it's written already?

ROSEMARY. What a good idea, James!

JAMES. All that is necessary is for the company to think very hard of what they want, and—there we are! Saves all the bother of writing and spelling and what not.

ROSEMARY (*admiringly*). James, how clever you are!

JAMES. So-so, Miss Rosemary.

ROSEMARY. Now then, let's all think together. Are you all ready?

ALL. Yes! (*They clench their hands.*)

ROSEMARY. Then one, two, three—Go!

(*They think. . . . The truth is that* JAMES, *who wasn't really meant to be in it, thinks too. If there is anything in the play which you don't like, it is* JAMES *thinking.*)

ACT I.—THE PRINCESS AND THE WOODCUTTER

The WOODCUTTER *is discovered singing at his work, in a glade of the forest outside his hut. He is tall and strong, and brave and handsome; all that a woodcutter ought to be. Now it happened that the* PRINCESS *was passing, and as soon as his song is finished, sure enough, on she comes.*)

PRINCESS. Good morning, Woodcutter.

WOODCUTTER. Good morning. (*But he goes on with his work.*)

PRINCESS (*after a pause*). Good morning, Woodcutter.

WOODCUTTER. Good morning.

PRINCESS. Don't you ever say anything except good morning?

WOODCUTTER. Sometimes I say good-bye.

PRINCESS. You *are* a cross woodcutter to-day.

WOODCUTTER. I have work to do.

PRINCESS. You are still cutting wood? Don't you ever do anything else?

WOODCUTTER. Well, you are still a Princess; don't *you* ever do anything else?

PRINCESS (*reproachfully*). Now, that's not fair, Woodcutter. You can't say I was a Princess yesterday, when I came and helped you stack your wood. Or the day before, when I tied up your hand where you had cut it. Or the day before that, when we had our meal together on the grass. Was I a Princess then?

WOODCUTTER. Somehow I think you were. Somehow

I think you were saying to yourself, "Isn't it sweet of a Princess to treat a mere woodcutter like this?"

PRINCESS. I think you're perfectly horrid. I've a good mind never to speak to you again. And—and I would, if only I could be sure that you would notice I wasn't speaking to you.

WOODCUTTER. After all, I'm just as bad as you. Only yesterday I was thinking to myself how unselfish I was to interrupt my work in order to talk to a mere Princess.

PRINCESS. Yes, but the trouble is that you *don't* interrupt your work.

WOODCUTTER (*interrupting it and going up to her with a smile*). Madam, I am at your service.

PRINCESS. I wish I thought you were.

WOODCUTTER. Surely you have enough people at your service already. Princes and Chancellors and Chamberlains and Waiting Maids.

PRINCESS. Yes, that's just it. That's why I want your help. Particularly in the matter of the Princes.

WOODCUTTER. Why, has a suitor come for the hand of her Royal Highness?

PRINCESS. Three suitors. And I hate them all.

WOODCUTTER. And which are you going to marry?

PRINCESS. I don't know. Father hasn't made up his mind yet.

WOODCUTTER. And this is a matter which father— which His Majesty decides for himself?

PRINCESS. Why, of course! You should read the History Books, Woodcutter. The suitors to the hand of a Princess are always set some trial of strength or test of quality by the King, and the winner marries his daughter.

WOODCUTTER. Well, I don't live in a Palace, and I

ACT I] MAKE-BELIEVE 11

think my own thoughts about these things. I'd better
get back to my work. (*He goes on with his chopping.*)

PRINCESS (*gently, after a pause*). Woodcutter!

WOODCUTTER (*looking up*). Oh, are you there? I
thought you were married by this time.

PRINCESS (*meekly*). I don't want to be married.
(*Hastily*) I mean, not to any of those three.

WOODCUTTER. You can't help yourself.

PRINCESS. I know. That's why I wanted *you* to help
me.

WOODCUTTER (*going up to her*). Can a simple woodcutter help a Princess?

PRINCESS. Well, perhaps a simple one couldn't, but a
clever one might.

WOODCUTTER. What would his reward be?

PRINCESS. His reward would be that the Princess,
not being married to any of her three suitors, would
still be able to help him chop his wood in the mornings.
. . . I *am* helping you, aren't I?

WOODCUTTER (*smiling*). Oh, decidedly.

PRINCESS (*nodding*). I thought I was.

WOODCUTTER. It is kind of a great lady like yourself
to help so humble a fellow as I.

PRINCESS (*meekly*). I'm not *very* great. (*And she isn't.
She is the smallest, daintiest little Princess that ever
you saw.*)

WOODCUTTER. There's enough of you to make a hundred men unhappy.

PRINCESS. And one man happy?

WOODCUTTER. And one man very, very happy.

PRINCESS (*innocently*). I wonder who he'll be. . . .
Woodcutter, if *you* were a Prince, would you be my
suitor?

WOODCUTTER (*scornfully*). One of three?

PRINCESS (*excitedly*). Oo, would you kill the others? With that axe?

WOODCUTTER. I would not kill them, in order to help His Majesty make up his mind about his son-in-law. But if the Princess had made up her mind—and wanted me——

PRINCESS. Yes?

WOODCUTTER. Then I would marry her, however many suitors she had.

PRINCESS. Well, she's only got three at present.

WOODCUTTER. What is that to me?

PRINCESS. Oh, I just thought you might want to be doing something to your axe.

WOODCUTTER. My axe?

PRINCESS. Yes. You see, she *has* made up her mind.

WOODCUTTER (*amazed*). You mean—— But—but I'm only a woodcutter.

PRINCESS. That's where you'll have the advantage of them, when it comes to axes.

WOODCUTTER. Princess! (*He takes her in his arms*) My Princess!

PRINCESS. Woodcutter! My woodcutter! My, oh so very slow and uncomprehending, but entirely adorable woodcutter!

> (*They sing together. They just happen to feel like that.*)

WOODCUTTER (*the song finished*). But what will His Majesty say?

PRINCESS. All sorts of things. . . . Do you really love me, woodcutter, or have I proposed to you under a misapprehension?

WOODCUTTER. I adore you!

PRINCESS (*nodding*). I thought you did. But I wanted to hear you say it. If I had been a simple peasant, I suppose you would have said it a long time ago?

WOODCUTTER. I expect so.

PRINCESS (*nodding*). Yes. . . . Well, now we must think of a plan for making Mother like you.

WOODCUTTER. Might I just kiss you again before we begin?

PRINCESS. Well, I don't quite see how I am to stop you.

> (*The* WOODCUTTER *picks her up in his arms and kisses her.*)

WOODCUTTER. There!

PRINCESS (*in his arms*). Oh, woodcutter, woodcutter, why didn't you do that the first day I saw you? Then I needn't have had the bother of proposing to you. (*He puts her down suddenly*) What is it?

WOODCUTTER (*listening*). Somebody coming. (*He peers through the trees and then says in surprise*) The King!

PRINCESS. Oh! I must fly!

WOODCUTTER. But you'll come back?

PRINCESS. Perhaps.

> [*She disappears quickly through the trees.*
> (*The* WOODCUTTER *goes on with his work and is discovered at it a minute later by the* KING *and* QUEEN.)

KING (*puffing*). Ah! and a seat all ready for us. How satisfying. (*They sit down, a distinguished couple—reading from left to right, "*KING, QUEEN*"—on a bench outside the* WOODCUTTER'S *hut.*)

QUEEN (*crossly—she was like that*). I don't know why you dragged me here.

KING. As I told you, my love, to be alone.

QUEEN. Well, you aren't alone. (*She indicates the* WOODCUTTER.)

KING. Pooh, he doesn't matter. . . . Well now, about these three Princes. They are getting on my mind rather. It is time we decided which one of them is to marry our beloved child. The trouble is to choose between them.

QUEEN. As regards appetite, there is nothing to choose between them. They are three of the heartiest eaters I have met for some time.

KING. You are right. The sooner we choose one of them, and send the other two about their business, the better. (*Reflectively*) There were six peaches on the breakfast-table this morning. Did I get one? No.

QUEEN. Did *I* get one? No.

KING. Did our darling child get one—not that it matters? No.

QUEEN. It is a pity that the seven-headed bull died last year.

KING. Yes, he had a way of sorting out competitors for the hand of our beloved one that was beyond all praise. One could have felt quite sure that, had the three competitors been introduced to him, only one of them would have taken any further interest in the matter.

QUEEN (*always the housekeeper*). And even he mightn't have taken any interest in his meals.

KING (*with a sigh*). However, those days are over. We must think of a new test. Somehow I think that, in a son-in-law, moral worth is even more to be desired than mere brute strength. Now my suggestion is this: that you should disguise yourself as a beggar woman and approach each of the three princes in turn, supplicating their charity. In this way we shall discover which of the three has the kindest heart. What do you say, my dear?

QUEEN. An excellent plan. If you remember, I suggested it myself yesterday.

KING (*annoyed*). Well, of course, it had been in my mind for some time. I don't claim that the idea is original; it has often been done in our family. (*Getting up*) Well then, if you will get ready, my dear, I will go and find our three friends and see that they come this way. [*They go out together.*

(*As soon as they are out of sight the* PRINCESS *comes back.*)

PRINCESS. Well, Woodcutter, what did I tell you?

WOODCUTTER. What did you tell me?

PRINCESS. Didn't you listen to what they said?

WOODCUTTER. I didn't listen, but I couldn't help hearing.

PRINCESS. Well, *I* couldn't help listening. And unless you stop it somehow, I shall be married to one of them to-night.

WOODCUTTER. Which one?

PRINCESS. The one with the kindest heart—whichever that is.

WOODCUTTER. Supposing they all three have kind hearts?

PRINCESS (*confidently*). They won't. They never have. In our circles when three Princes come together, one of them has a kind heart and the other two haven't. (*Surprised*) Haven't you read any History at all?

WOODCUTTER. I have no time for reading. But I think it's time History was altered a little. We'll alter it this afternoon.

PRINCESS. What do you mean?

WOODCUTTER. Leave this to me. I've got an idea.

PRINCESS (*clapping her hands*). Oh, how clever of you! But what do you want me to do?

WOODCUTTER (*pointing*). You know the glade over there where the brook runs through it? Wait for me there.

PRINCESS. I obey my lord's commands.

[*She blows him a kiss and runs off.*

(*The* WOODCUTTER *resumes his work. By and by the* RED PRINCE *comes along. He is a—well, you will see for yourself what he is like.*)

RED PRINCE. Ah, fellow. . . . Fellow! . . . I said fellow! (*Yes, that sort of man.*)

WOODCUTTER (*looking up*). Were you speaking to me, my lord?

RED PRINCE. There is no other fellow here that I can see.

(*The* WOODCUTTER *looks round to make sure, peers behind a tree or two, and comes back to the* PRINCE.)

WOODCUTTER. Yes, you must have meant me.

RED PRINCE. Yes, of course I meant you, fellow. Have you seen the Princess come past this way? I was told she was waiting for me here.

WOODCUTTER. She is not here, my lord. (*Looking round to see that they are alone*) My lord, are you one of the Princes who is seeking the hand of the Princess?

RED PRINCE (*complacently*). I am, fellow.

WOODCUTTER. His Majesty the King was here a while ago. He is to make his decision between you this afternoon. (*Meaningly*) I think I can help you to be the lucky one, my lord.

RED PRINCE. You suggest that I take an unfair advantage over my fellow-competitors?

WOODCUTTER. I suggest nothing, my lord. I only say that I can help you.

RED PRINCE (*magnanimously*). Well, I will allow you to help me.

WOODCUTTER. Thank you. Then I will give you this advice. If a beggar woman asks you for a crust of bread this afternoon, remember—it is the test!

RED PRINCE (*staggered*). The test! But I haven't *got* a crust of bread!

WOODCUTTER. Wait here and I will get you one.

(*He goes into the hut.*)

RED PRINCE (*speaking after him as he goes*). My good fellow, I am extremely obliged to you, and if ever I can do anything for you, such as returning a crust to you of similar size, or even lending you another slightly smaller one, or—— (*The* WOODCUTTER *comes back with the crust.*) Ah, thank you, my man, thank you.

WOODCUTTER. I would suggest, my lord, that you should take a short walk in this direction (*pointing to the opposite direction to that which the* PRINCESS *has taken*), and stroll back casually in a few minutes' time when the Queen is here.

RED PRINCE. Thank you, my man, thank you.

(*He puts the crust in his pocket and goes off.*)
(*The* WOODCUTTER *goes on with his work. The* BLUE PRINCE *comes in and stands watching him in silence for some moments.*)

WOODCUTTER (*looking up*). Hullo!

BLUE PRINCE. Hullo!

WOODCUTTER. What do you want?

BLUE PRINCE. The Princess.

WOODCUTTER. She's not here.

BLUE PRINCE. Oh!

(*The* WOODCUTTER *goes on with his work and the* PRINCE *goes on looking at him.*)

WOODCUTTER (*struck with an idea*). Are you one of the Princes who is wooing the Princess?

BLUE PRINCE. Yes.

WOODCUTTER (*coming towards him*). I believe I could help your Royal Highness.

BLUE PRINCE. Do.

WOODCUTTER (*doubtfully*). It would perhaps be not quite fair to the others.

BLUE PRINCE. Don't mind.

WOODCUTTER. Well then, listen. (*He pauses a moment and looks round to see that they are alone.*)

BLUE PRINCE. I'm listening.

WOODCUTTER. If you come back in five minutes, you will see a beggar woman sitting here. She will ask you for a crust of bread. You must give it to her, for it is the way His Majesty has chosen of testing your kindness of heart.

BLUE PRINCE (*feeling in his pockets*). No bread.

WOODCUTTER. I will give you some.

BLUE PRINCE. Do.

WOODCUTTER (*taking a piece from his pocket*). Here you are.

BLUE PRINCE. Thanks.

WOODCUTTER. Not at all, I'm very glad to have been able to help you.

> (*He goes on with his work. The* BLUE PRINCE *remains looking at him.*)

BLUE PRINCE (*with a great effort*). Thanks.

> (*He goes slowly away. A moment later the* YELLOW PRINCE *makes a graceful and languid entry.*)

YELLOW PRINCE. Ah, come hither, my man, come hither.

WOODCUTTER (*stopping his work and looking up*). You want me, sir?

YELLOW PRINCE. Come hither, my man. Tell me, has her Royal Highness the Princess passed this way lately?

WOODCUTTER. The Princess?

YELLOW PRINCE. Yes, the Princess, my bumpkin. But perhaps you have been too much concerned in your own earthy affairs to have noticed her. You—ah—cut wood, I see.

WOODCUTTER. Yes, sir, I am a woodcutter.

YELLOW PRINCE. A most absorbing life. Some day

ACT I] MAKE-BELIEVE 19

we must have a long talk about it. But just now I have other business waiting for me. With your permission, good friend, I will leave you to your faggots. (*He starts to go.*)

WOODCUTTER. Beg your pardon, sir, but are you one of those Princes that want to marry our Princess?

YELLOW PRINCE. I had hoped, good friend, to obtain your permission to do so. I beg you not to refuse it.

WOODCUTTER. You are making fun of me, sir.

YELLOW PRINCE. Discerning creature.

WOODCUTTER. All the same, I *can* help you.

YELLOW PRINCE. Then pray do so, log-chopper, and earn my everlasting gratitude.

WOODCUTTER. The King has decided that whichever of you three Princes has the kindest heart shall marry his daughter.

YELLOW PRINCE. Then you will be able to bear witness to him that I have already wasted several minutes of my valuable time in condescending to a mere faggot-splitter. Tell him this and the prize is mine. (*Kissing the tips of his fingers*) Princess, I embrace you.

WOODCUTTER. The King will not listen to me. But if you return here in five minutes, you will find an old woman begging for bread. It is the test which their Majesties have arranged for you. If you share your last crust with her——

YELLOW PRINCE. Yes, but do I look as if I carried a last crust about with me?

WOODCUTTER. But see, I will give you one.

YELLOW PRINCE (*taking it between the tips of his fingers*). Yes, but——

WOODCUTTER. Put it in your pocket, and when——

YELLOW PRINCE. But, my dear bark-scraper, have you no feeling for clothes at all? How can I put a thing like this in my pocket? (*Handing it back to him*) I beg you

to wrap it up. Here, take this. (*Gives him a scarf*)
Neatly, I pray you. (*Taking an orange ribbon out of his
pocket*) Perhaps a little of this round it would make it
more tolerable. You think so? I leave it to you. I
trust your taste entirely. . . . Leaving a loop for the
little finger, I entreat you . . . so. (*He hangs it on his
little finger*) In about five minutes, you said? We will
be there. (*With a bow*) We thank you.

> (*He departs delicately. The* WOODCUTTER *smiles
> to himself, puts down his axe and goes off to
> the* PRINCESS. *And just in time. For behold!
> the* KING *and* QUEEN *return. At least we
> think it is the* QUEEN, *but she is so heavily
> disguised by a cloak which she wears over
> her court dress, that for a moment we are
> not quite sure.*)

KING. Now then, my love, if you will sit down on that
log there—(*placing her*)—excellent—I think perhaps
you should remove the crown. (*Removes it*) There!
Now the disguise is perfect.

QUEEN. You're sure they are coming? It's a very
uncomfortable seat.

KING. I told them that the Princess was waiting for
them here. Their natural disappointment at finding
I was mistaken will make the test of their good nature
an even more exacting one. My own impression is that
the Yellow Prince will be the victor.

QUEEN. Oh, I hate that man.

KING (*soothingly*). Well, well, perhaps it will be the
Blue one.

QUEEN. If anything, I dislike him *more* intensely.

KING. Or even the Red.

QUEEN. Ugh! I can't bear him.

KING. Fortunately, dear, you are not called upon
to marry any of them. It is for our darling that we

are making the great decision. Listen! I hear one coming. I will hide in the cottage and take note of what happens.

> (*He disappears into the cottage as the* BLUE PRINCE *comes in.*)

QUEEN. Oh, sir, can you kindly spare a crust of bread for a poor old woman? Please, pretty gentleman!

BLUE PRINCE (*standing stolidly in front of her and feeling in his pocket*). Bread . . . Bread . . . Ah! Bread! (*He offers it.*)

QUEEN. Oh, thank you, sir. May you be rewarded for your gentle heart.

BLUE PRINCE. Thank you.

> (*He stands gazing at her. There is an awkward pause.*)

QUEEN. A blessing on you, sir.

BLUE PRINCE. Thank you. (*He indicates the crust*) Bread.

QUEEN. Ah, you have saved the life of a poor old woman——

BLUE PRINCE. Eat it.

QUEEN (*embarrassed*). I—er—you—er—— (*She takes a bite and mumbles something.*)

BLUE PRINCE. What?

QUEEN (*swallowing with great difficulty*). I'm almost too happy to eat, sir. Leave a poor old woman alone with her happiness, and——

BLUE PRINCE. Not too happy. Too weak. Help you eat. (*He breaks off a piece and holds it to her mouth. With a great effort the* QUEEN *disposes of it.*) Good! . . . Again! (*She does it again.*) Now! (*She swallows another piece.*) Last piece! (*She takes it in. He pats her kindly on the back, and she nearly chokes.*) Good. . . . Better now?

QUEEN (*weakly*). Much.

22   MAKE-BELIEVE   [ACT I

BLUE PRINCE. Good day.

QUEEN (*with an effort*). Good day, kind gentleman.

[*He goes out.*

(*The* KING *is just coming from the cottage, when he returns suddenly. The* KING *slips back again.*)

BLUE PRINCE. Small piece left over. (*He gives it to her. She looks hopelessly at him.*) Good-bye.

[*He goes.*

QUEEN (*throwing the piece down violently*). Ugh! What a man!

KING (*coming out*). Well, well, my dear, we have discovered the winner.

QUEEN (*from the heart*). Detestable person!

KING. The rest of the competition is of course more in the nature of a formality——

QUEEN. Thank goodness.

KING. However, I think that it will prevent unnecessary discussion afterwards if we—— Take care, here is another one. (*He hurries back.*)

Enter the RED PRINCE.

QUEEN (*with not nearly so much conviction*). Could you spare a crust of bread, sir, for a poor hungry old woman?

RED PRINCE. A crust of bread, madam? Certainly. As luck will have it, I have a crust on me. My last one, but—your need is greater than mine. Eat, I pray.

QUEEN. Th-thank you, sir.

RED PRINCE. Not at all. Come, eat. Let me have the pleasure of seeing you eating.

QUEEN. M-might I take it home with me, pretty gentleman?

RED PRINCE. (*firmly*). No, no. I must see you eating. Come! I will take no denial.

ACT I] MAKE-BELIEVE 23

QUEEN. Th-thank you, sir. (*Hopefully*) Won't you share it with me?

RED PRINCE. No, I insist on your having it all. I am in the mood to be generous. Oblige me by eating it now for I am in a hurry; yet I will not go until you have eaten. (*She does her best.*) You eat but slowly. (*Sternly*) Did you deceive me when you said you were hungry?

QUEEN. N-no. I'm very hungry. (*She eats.*)

RED PRINCE. That's better. Now understand—however poor I am, I can always find a crust of bread for an old woman. Always! Remember this when next you are hungry. . . . You spoke? (*She shakes her head and goes on eating.*) Finished?

QUEEN (*with great difficulty*). Yes, thank you, pretty gentleman.

RED PRINCE. There's a piece on the ground there that you dropped. (*She eats it in dumb agony.*) Finished?

QUEEN (*huskily*). Yes, thank you, pretty gentleman.

RED PRINCE. Then I will leave you, madam. Good morning. [*He goes out.*

(*The* QUEEN *rises in fury. The* KING *is about to come out of the cottage, when the* YELLOW PRINCE *enters. The* QUEEN *sits down again and mumbles something. It is certainly not an appeal for bread, but the* YELLOW PRINCE *is not to be denied.*)

YELLOW PRINCE (*gallantly*). My poor woman, you are in distress. It pains me to see it, madam, it pains me terribly. Can it be that you are hungry? I thought so, I thought so. Give me the great pleasure, madam, of relieving your hunger. See (*holding up his finger*), my own poor meal. Take it! It is yours.

QUEEN (*with difficulty*). I am not hungry.

YELLOW PRINCE. Ah, madam, I see what it is. You

do not wish to deprive me. You tell yourself, perchance, that it is not fitting that one in your station of life should partake of the meals of the highly born. You are not used, you say, to the food of Princes. Your rougher palate——

QUEEN (*hopefully*). Did you say food of princes?

YELLOW PRINCE. Where was I, madam? You interrupted me. No matter—eat. (*She takes the scarf and unties the ribbon.*) Ah, now I remember. I was saying that your rougher palate——

QUEEN (*discovering the worst*). No! No! Not bread!

YELLOW PRINCE. Bread, madam, the staff of life. Come, madam, will you not eat? (*She tries desperately.*) What can be more delightful than a crust of bread by the wayside?

> (*The* QUEEN *shrieks and falls back in a swoon. The* KING *rushes out to her.*)

KING (*to* YELLOW PRINCE). Quick, quick, find the Princess.

YELLOW PRINCE. The Princess—find the Princess!

> (*He goes vaguely off and we shall not see him again. But the* WOODCUTTER *and the* PRINCESS *do not need to be found. They are here.*)

WOODCUTTER (*to* PRINCESS). Go to her, but don't show that you know me.

> (*He goes into the cottage, and the* PRINCESS *hastens to her father.*)

PRINCESS. Father!

KING. Ah, my dear, you're just in time. Your mother——

PRINCESS. My mother?

KING. Yes, yes. A little plan of mine—of hers—your poor mother. Dear, dear!

PRINCESS. But what's the matter?

KING. She is suffering from a surfeit of bread, and——

ACT I]   MAKE-BELIEVE   25

(*The* WOODCUTTER *comes up with a flagon of wine.*)

WOODCUTTER. Poor old woman! She has fainted from exhaustion. Let me give her some——

QUEEN (*shrieking*). No, no, not bread! I will *not* have any more bread.

WOODCUTTER. Drink this, my poor woman.

QUEEN (*opening her eyes*). Did you say drink? (*She seizes the flagon and drinks.*)

PRINCESS. Oh, sir, you have saved my mother's life!

WOODCUTTER. Not at all.

KING. I thank you, my man, I thank you.

QUEEN. My deliverer! Tell me who you are!

PRINCESS. It is my mother, the Queen, who asks you.

WOODCUTTER (*amazed, as well he may be*). The Queen!

KING. Yes, yes. Certainly, the Queen.

WOODCUTTER (*taking off his hat*). Pardon, your Majesty. I am a woodcutter, who lives alone here, far away from courts.

QUEEN. Well, you've got more sense in your head than any of the Princes that *I've* seen lately. You'd better come to court.

PRINCESS (*shyly*). You will be very welcome, sir.

QUEEN. And you'd better marry the Princess.

KING. Isn't that perhaps going a *little* too far, dear?

QUEEN. Well, you wanted kindness of heart in your son-in-law, and you've got it. And he's got common sense too. (*To* WOODCUTTER) Tell me, what do you think of bread as—as a form of nourishment?

WOODCUTTER (*cautiously*). One can have too much of it.

QUEEN. Exactly my view. (*To* KING) There you are, you see.

KING. Well, if you insist. The great thing, of course, is that our darling child should be happy.

PRINCESS. I will do my best, father. (*She takes the* WOODCUTTER'S *hand.*)

KING. Then the marriage will take place this evening. (*With a wave of his wand*) Let the revels begin.

(*They begin.*)

ACT II.—OLIVER'S ISLAND

Scene I.—*The Schoolroom* (*Ugh!*)

OLIVER *is discovered lying flat on his*——*well, lying flat on the floor, deep in a book. The* CURATE *puts his head in at the door.*

CURATE. Ah, our young friend, Oliver! And how are we this morning, dear lad?

OLIVER (*mumbling*). All right, thanks.

CURATE. That's well, that's well. Deep in our studies, I see, deep in our studies. And what branch of Knowledge are we pursuing this morning?

OLIVER (*without looking up*). "Marooned in the Pacific," or "The Pirate's Bride."

CURATE. Dear, dear, what will Miss Pinniger say to this interruption of our studies?

OLIVER. Silly old beast.

CURATE. Tut-tut, dear lad, that is not the way to speak of our mentors and preceptors. So refined and intelligent a lady as Miss Pinniger. Indeed I came here to see her this morning on a little matter of embroidered vestments. Where is she, dear lad?

OLIVER. It isn't nine yet.

CURATE (*looking at his watch*). Past nine, past nine.

OLIVER (*jumping up*). Je-hoshaphat!

CURATE. Oliver! Oliver! My dear lad! Swearing at *your* age! Really, I almost feel it my duty to inform your aunt——

OLIVER. Fat lot of swearing in just mentioning one of the Kings of Israel.

CURATE. Of Judah, dear boy, of Judah. To be ignorant on such a vital matter makes it even more reprehensible. I cannot believe that our dear Miss Pinniger has so neglected your education that——

Enter our dear MISS PINNIGER, *the Governess.*

GOVERNESS. Ah, Mr. Smilax; how pleasant to see you!

CURATE. My dear Miss Pinniger! You will forgive me for interrupting you in your labours, but there is a small matter of—ah!——

GOVERNESS. Certainly, Mr. Smilax. I will walk down to the gate with you. Oliver, where is Geraldine?

OLIVER. Aunt Jane wanted her.

GOVERNESS. Well, you should be at your lessons. It's nine o'clock. The fact that I am momentarily absent from the room should make no difference to your zeal.

OLIVER (*without conviction*). No, Miss Pinniger. (*He sits down at his desk, putting "Marooned in the Pacific" inside it.*)

CURATE (*playfully*). For men must work, Oliver, men must work. How doth the little busy bee—— Yes, Miss Pinniger, I am with you. [*They go out.*

OLIVER (*opening his poetry book and saying it to himself*). It was a summer evening—It was a summer evening—(*He stops, refers to the book, and then goes on to himself*) Old Kaspar's work was done. It was a summer evening, Old Kaspar's work was done——

Enter GERALDINE—*or* JILL.

JILL. Where's Pin?

OLIVER. Hallo, Jill. Gone off with Dearly Belovéd. Her momentary absence from the room should make no difference to your zeal, my dear Geraldine. And what are we studying this morning, dear child? (*To himself*) It was a summer evening, Old Kaspar's work was done.

JILL (*giggling*). Is that Pin?

OLIVER. Pin and Dearly Belovéd between them. She's a bit batey this morning.

JILL (*at her desk*). And all my sums have done themselves wrong. (*Hard at it with paper and pencil*) What's nine times seven, Oliver?

OLIVER. Fifty-six. Old Kaspar's work was done. Jolly well wish mine was. And he before his cottage door. Fat lot of good my learning this stuff if I'm going to be a sailor. I bet Beatty didn't mind what happened to rotten old Kaspar when he saw a German submarine.

JILL. Six and carry five. Aunt Jane has sent for the doctor to look at my chest.

OLIVER. What's the matter with your chest?

JILL. I blew my nose rather loud at prayers this morning.

OLIVER. I say, Jill, you *are* going it!

JILL. It wasn't my fault, Oliver. Aunt Jane turned over two pages at once and made me laugh, so I had to turn it into a blow.

OLIVER. Bet you what you like she knew.

JILL. Of course she did, and she'll tell the doctor, and he'll be as beastly as he can. What did she say to you for being late?

OLIVER. I said somebody had bagged my sponge, and she wouldn't like me to come down to prayers all unsponged, and she said, "Excuses, Oliver, *always* excuses! Leave me. I will see you later." Suppose that means I've got to go to bed this afternoon. Jill, if I do, be sporty and bring me up "Marooned in the Pacific."

JILL. They'll lock the door. They always do.

OLIVER. Then I shall jolly well go up for a handkerchief this morning, and shove it in the bed, just in case. Cavé—here's Pin.

MISS PINNIGER *returns to find them full of zeal.*

GOVERNESS (*sitting down at her desk*). Well, Oliver, have you learnt your piece of poetry?

OLIVER (*nervously*). I—I think so, Miss Pinniger.

GOVERNESS. Close the book, and stand up and say it. (*Oliver takes a last despairing look, and stands up.*) Well?

OLIVER. It was a summer evening——

GOVERNESS. The title and the author first, Oliver. Everything in its proper order.

OLIVER. Oh, I say, I didn't know I had to learn the title.

JILL (*in a whisper*). After Blenheim.

GOVERNESS. Geraldine, kindly attend to your own work.

OLIVER. After Blenheim. It was a summer evening.

GOVERNESS. After Blenheim, by Robert Southey. One of our greatest poets.

OLIVER. After Blenheim, by Robert Southey, one of our greatest poets. It was a summer evening, Old Kaspar's work was done—er—Old Kaspar's work was done—er—work was done, er. . . .

GOVERNESS. And he before——

OLIVER. Oh yes, of course. And he before—er—and he before—er—It was a summer evening, Old Kaspar's work was done, and he before—er—and he before—— Er, it *was* a summer evening——

GOVERNESS. So you have already said, Oliver.

OLIVER. I just seem to have forgotten this bit, Miss Pinniger. And he before——

GOVERNESS. Well, what was he before?

ACT II] MAKE-BELIEVE 31

OLIVER (*hopefully*). Blenheim? Oh no, it was *after* Blenheim.

GOVERNESS (*wearily*). His cottage door.

OLIVER. Oo, yes. And he before his cottage door was sitting in the sun. (*He clears his throat*) Was sitting in the sun. Er—(*He coughs again*)—er——

GOVERNESS. You have a cough, Oliver. Perhaps the doctor had better see you when he comes to see Geraldine.

OLIVER. It was just something tickling my throat, Miss Pinniger. Er—it was a summer evening.

GOVERNESS. You haven't learnt it, Oliver?

OLIVER. Yes, I have, Miss Pinniger, only I can't quite remember it. And he before his cottage door——

GOVERNESS. Is it any good, Geraldine, asking you if you have got any of your sums right?

JILL. I've got one, Miss Pinniger . . . nearly right . . . except for some of the figures.

GOVERNESS. Well, we shall have to spend more time at our lessons, that's all. This afternoon—ah—er——

(*She stands up as* AUNT JANE *and the* DOCTOR *come in.*)

AUNT JANE. I'm sorry to interrupt lessons, Miss Pinniger, but I have brought the Doctor to see Geraldine. (*To* DOCTOR) You will like her to go to her room?

DOCTOR. No, no, dear lady. There is no need. Her pulse—(*He feels it*)—dear, dear! Her tongue—(*She puts it out*)—tut-tut! A milk diet, plenty of rice-pudding, and perhaps she would do well to go to bed this afternoon.

AUNT JANE. I will see to it, doctor.

JILL (*mutinously*). I *feel* quite well.

DOCTOR (*to* AUNT JANE). A dangerous symptom. *Plenty* of rice-pudding.

GOVERNESS. Oliver was coughing just now.

OLIVER (*to himself*). Shut up!

DOCTOR (*turning to* OLIVER). Ah! His pulse—(*Feels it*)—tut-tut! His tongue—(OLIVER *puts it out*) Dear, dear! The same treatment, dear lady, as prescribed in the other case.

OLIVER (*under his breath*). Beast!

AUNT JANE. Castor-oil, liquorice-powder, ammoniated quinine—anything of that nature, doctor?

DOCTOR. *As* necessary, dear lady, *as* necessary. The system must be stimulated. Nature must be reinforced.

AUNT JANE (*to* GOVERNESS). Which do they dislike least?

OLIVER *and* JILL (*hastily*). Liquorice-powder!

DOCTOR. Then concentrate on the other two, dear lady.

AUNT JANE. Thank you, doctor. [*They go out.*

GOVERNESS. We will now go on with our lessons. Oliver, you will have opportunities in your bedroom this afternoon of learning your poetry. By the way, I had better have that book which you were reading when I came in just now.

OLIVER (*trying to be surprised*). Which book?

JILL (*nobly doing her best to save the situation*). Miss Pinniger, if you're multiplying rods, poles, or perches by nine, does it matter if——

GOVERNESS. I am talking to Oliver, Geraldine. Where is that book, Oliver?

OLIVER. Oh, *I* know the one you mean. I must have put it down somewhere. (*He looks vaguely about the room.*)

GOVERNESS. Perhaps you put it in your desk.

OLIVER. My desk?

JILL (*going up to* MISS PINNIGER *with her work*). You see, it's all gone wrong here, and I think I must have multiplied—— (*Moving in front of her as she moves*) I think I must have multiplied——

> (*Under cover of this,* OLIVER *makes a great effort to get the book into* JILL's *desk, but it is no good.*)

GOVERNESS (*brushing aside* JILL *and advancing on* OLIVER). Thank you, *I* will take it.

OLIVER (*looking at the title*). Oh yes, this is the one.

GOVERNESS. And I will speak to your aunt at *once* about the behaviour of both of you. [*She goes out.*

OLIVER (*gallantly*). *I* don't care.

JILL. I did try to help you, Oliver.

OLIVER. You wait. Won't I jolly well bag something of hers one day, just when she wants it.

JILL. I'm afraid you'll find the afternoon rather tiring without your book. What will you do?

OLIVER. I suppose I shall have to think.

JILL. What shall you think about?

OLIVER. I shall think I'm on my desert island.

JILL. Which desert island?

OLIVER. The one I always pretend I'm on when I'm thinking.

JILL. Isn't there any one else on it ever?

OLIVER. Oo, lots of pirates and Dyaks and cannibals and—other people.

JILL. What sort of other people?

OLIVER. I shan't tell you. This is a special think I thought last night. As soon as I thought of it, I decided to keep it for (*impressively*) a moment of great emergency.

JILL (*silenced*). Oh! . . . Oliver?

OLIVER. Yes?

JILL. Let me be on your desert island this time. Because I did try to help you.

OLIVER. Well—well— (*Generously*) Well, you can if you like.

JILL. Oh, thank you, Oliver. Won't you tell me what it's about, and then we can both think it together this afternoon.

OLIVER. I expect you'll think all sorts of silly things that *never* happen on a desert island.

JILL. I'll try not to, Oliver, if you tell me.

OLIVER. All right.

JILL (*coming close to him*). Go on.

OLIVER. Well, you see, I've been wrecked, you see, and the ship has foundered with all hands, you see, and I've been cast ashore on a desert island, you see.

JILL. Haven't I been cast ashore too?

OLIVER. Well, you will be this afternoon, of course. Well, you see, we land on the island, you see, and it's a perfectly ripping island, you see, and—and we land on it, you see, and . . .

. . . .

But we are getting on too fast. When the good ship crashed upon the rock and split in twain, it seemed like that all aboard must perish. Fortunately OLIVER *was made of stern mettle. Hastily constructing a raft and placing the now unconscious* JILL *upon it, he launched it into the seething maelstrom of waters and pushed off. Tossed like a cockle-shell upon the mountainous waves, the tiny craft with its precious freight was in imminent danger of foundering. But* OLIVER *was made of stern mettle. With dauntless courage he rigged a jury-mast, and placed a telescope to his eye. "Pull for the lagoon,* JILL," *cried the dauntless* OLIVER, *and in another moment.* . . .

As the raft glides into the still waters beyond the reef, we can see it more clearly. Can it be JILL's *bed, with*

OLIVER *in his pyjamas perched on the rail, and holding up his bath-towel? Does he shorten sail for a moment to thump his chest and say, "But* OLIVER *was made of stern mettle"? Or is it*——

But the sun is sinking behind the swamp where the rattlesnakes bask. For a moment longer the sail gleams like copper in its rays, and then—fizz-z—we have lost it. See! Is that speck on the inky black waters the dauntless Oliver? It is. Let us follow to the island and see what adventures befall him.

SCENE II.—*It is the island which we have dreamed about all our lives. But at present we cannot see it properly, for it is dark. In one of those tropical darknesses which can be felt rather than seen* OLIVER *hands* JILL *out of the boat.*

OLIVER. Tread carefully, Jill, there are lots of deadly rattlesnakes about.

JILL (*stepping hastily back into the boat*). Oli-ver!

OLIVER. You hear the noise of their rattles sometimes when the sun is sinking behind the swamp. (*The deadly rattle of the rattlesnake is heard*) There!

JILL. Oh, Oliver, are they very deadly? Because if they are, I don't think I shall like your island.

OLIVER. Those aren't. I always have their teeth taken out when ladies are coming. Besides, it's daylight now.

(*With a rapidity common in the tropics—although it may just be* OLIVER's *gallantry—the sun climbs out of the sea, and floods the island.* JILL, *no longer frightened, steps out of the boat, and they walk up to the clearing in the middle.*)

JILL (*looking about her*). Oh, what a lovely island! I think it's lovely, Oliver.

OLIVER (*modestly*). It's pretty decent, isn't it? Won't you lie down? I generally lie down here and watch the turtles coming out of the sea to deposit their eggs on the sand.

JILL (*lying down*). How many do they de-deposit usually, Oliver?

OLIVER. Oh, three—or a hundred. Just depends how hungry I am. Have a bull's-eye, won't you?

JILL (*excitedly*). Oh, did you bring some?

OLIVER (*annoyed*). Bring some? (*Brightening up*) Oh, you mean from the wreck?

JILL (*hastily*). Yes, from the wreck. I mean besides the axe and the bag of nails and the gunpowder.

OLIVER. Couldn't. The ship sank with all hands before I could get them. But it doesn't matter, because (*going up to one of the trees*) I recognise this as the bull's-eye tree. (*He picks a couple of bull's-eyes and gives one to her.*)

JILL. Oh, Oliver, how lovely! Thank you. (*She puts it in her mouth.*)

OLIVER (*sucking hard*). There was nothing but bread-fruit trees here the first time I was marooned on it. Rotten things to have on a decent island. So I planted a bull's-eye tree, and a barley-sugar-cane grove, and one or two other things, and made a jolly ripping place of it.

JILL (*pointing*). What's that tree over there?

OLIVER. That one? Rice-pudding tree.

JILL (*getting up indignantly*). Oliver! Take me back to the boat at once.

OLIVER. I say, shut up, Jill. You didn't think I meant it for *you*, did you?

JILL. But there's only you and me on the island.

OLIVER. What about the domestic animals? I suppose *they've* got to eat.

JILL. Oh, how lovely! Have we got a goat and a parrot, and a—a ——

OLIVER. Much better than that. Look in that cage there.

JILL. Oh, is that a cage? I never noticed it. What do I do?

OLIVER (*going to it*). Here, I'll show you. (*He draws the blind, and the* DOCTOR *is exposed sitting on a stump of wood and blinking at the sudden light*) What do you think of that?

JILL. Oliver!

OLIVER (*proudly*). I thought of that in bed one night. Spiffing idea, isn't it? I've got some other ones in the plantation over there. Awfully good specimens. I feed 'em on rice-pudding.

JILL. Can this one talk?

OLIVER. I'm teaching it. (*Stirring it up with a stick*) Come up there.

DOCTOR (*mumbling*). Ninety-nine, ninety-nine . . .

OLIVER. That's all it can say at present. I'm going to give it a swim in the lagoon to-morrow. I want to see if there are any sharks. If there aren't, then we can bathe there afterwards.

(*The* DOCTOR *shudders.*)

JILL. Have you given it a name yet? I think I should like to call it Fluffkins.

OLIVER. Righto! Good night, Fluffkins. Time little doctors were in bed. (*He pulls down the blind.*)

JILL (*lying down again*). Well, I think it's a lovely island.

OLIVER (*lying beside her*). If there's anything you want, you know, you've only got to say so. Pirates or anything like that. There's a ginger-beer well if you're thirsty.

JILL (*closing her eyes*). I'm quite happy, Oliver, thank you.

OLIVER (*after a pause, a little awkwardly*). Jill, you didn't ever want to marry a pirate, did you?

JILL (*still on her back with her eyes shut*). I hadn't thought about it much, Oliver dear.

OLIVER. Because I can get you an awfully decent pirate, if you like, and if I was his brother-in-law it would be ripping. I've often been marooned with him, of course, but never as his brother-in-law.

JILL. Why don't you marry his daughter and be his son-in-law?

OLIVER. He hasn't got a daughter.

JILL. Well, you could think him one.

OLIVER. I don't want to. If ever I'm such a silly ass as to marry, which I'm jolly well not going to be, I shall marry a—a dusky maiden. Jill, be sporty. All girls have to get married some time. It's different with men.

JILL. Very well, Oliver. I don't want to spoil your afternoon.

OLIVER. Good biz. (*He stands up, shuts his eyes and waves his hands about.*)

Enter the PIRATE CHIEF

PIRATE CHIEF (*with a flourish*). Gentles, your servant. Commodore Crookshank, at your service. Better known on the Spanish Main as One-eared Eric.

OLIVER. Glad to meet, you, Commodore. I'm—er—Two-toed Thomas, the Terror of the Dyaks. But you may call me Oliver, if you like. This is my sister Jill—the Pride of the Pampas.

PIRATE CHIEF (*with another bow*). Charmed!

JILL (*politely*). Don't mention it, Commodore.

OLIVER. My sister wants to marry you. Er—carry on. (*He moves a little away from them and lies down.*)

JILL (*sitting down and indicating a place beside her*). Won't you sit down, Commodore?

PIRATE CHIEF. Thank you, madam. The other side if I may. I shall hear better if you condescend to accept me. (*He sits down on the other side of her.*)

JILL. Oh, I'm so sorry! I was forgetting about your ear.

PIRATE CHIEF. Don't mention it. A little discussion in the La Plata river with a Spanish gentleman. At the end of it I was an ear short and he was a head short. It was considered in the family that I had won.

(*There is an awkward pause.*)

JILL (*shyly*). Well, Commodore?

PIRATE CHIEF. Won't you call me Eric?

JILL. I am waiting, Eric.

PIRATE CHIEF. Madam, I am not a marrying man, not to any extent, but if you would care to be Mrs. Crookshank, I'd undertake on my part to have the deck swabbed every morning, and to put a polish on the four-pounder that you could see your pretty face in.

JILL. Eric, how sweet of you. But I think you must speak to my brother in the library first. Oli-ver!

OLIVER (*coming up*). Hallo! Settled it?

JILL. It's all settled, Oliver, between Eric and myself, but you will want to ask him about his prospects, won't you?

OLIVER. Yes, yes, of course.

PIRATE. I shall be very glad to tell you anything I can, sir. I think I may say that I am doing fairly well in my profession.

OLIVER. What's your ship? A sloop or a frigate?

PIRATE. A brigantine.

JILL (*excited*). Oh, that's what Oliver puts on his hair when he goes to a party.

OLIVER (*annoyed*). Shut up, Jill! A brigantine? Ah yes, a rakish craft, eh, Commodore?

PIRATE (*earnestly*). Extremely rakish.

OLIVER. And how many pieces of eight have you?

PIRATE. Nine thousand.

OLIVER. Ah! (*To* JILL) What's nine times eight?

JILL (*to herself*). Nine times eight.

OLIVER (*to himself*). Nine times eight.

PIRATE (*to himself*). Nine times eight.

JILL. Seventy-two.

PIRATE. I made it seventy-one, but I expect you're right.

OLIVER. Then you've seventy-two thousand pieces altogether?

PIRATE. Yes, sir, about that.

OLIVER. Any doubloons?

PIRATE. Hundreds of 'em.

OLIVER. Ingots of gold?

PIRATE. Lashings of 'em.

JILL. And he's going to polish up the four-pounder until I can see my face in it.

OLIVER. I was just going to ask you about your guns. You've got 'em fore and aft of course?

PIRATE. Yes, sir. A four-pounder fore and a half-pounder haft.

OLIVER (*a little embarrassed*). And do you ever have brothers-in-law in your ship?

PIRATE. Well, I never have had yet, but I have always been looking about for one.

JILL. Oh, Oliver, isn't Eric a *nice* man?

OLIVER (*casually*). I suppose the captain's brother-in-law is generally the first man to board the Spaniard with his cutlass between his teeth?

PIRATE. You might almost say always. Many a ship on the Spanish Main I've had to leave unboarded through want of a brother-in-law. They're touchy about it somehow. Unless the captain's brother-in-law comes first they get complaining.

OLIVER (*bashfully*). And there's just one other thing. If the brigantine happened to put in at an island for water, and the captain's brother-in-law happened— just happened—to be a silly ass and go and marry a dusky maiden, whom he met on the beach——

PIRATE. Bless you, it's always happening to a captain's brother-in-law.

OLIVER (*in a magnificent manner*). Then, Captain Crookshank, you may take my sister!

JILL. Thank you, Oliver.

(*It is not every day that* ONE-EARED ERIC, *that famous chieftain, marries into the family of the* TERROR OF THE DYAKS. *Naturally the occasion is celebrated by the whole pirate crew with a rousing chorus, followed by a dance in which the dusky maidens of the Island join. At the end of it,* JILL *finds herself alone with* TUA-HEETA, *the Dusky Princess.*)

JILL (*fashionably*). I'm so pleased to meet my brother's future wife. It's so nice of you to come to see me. You will have some tea, won't you? (*She puts out her hand and presses an imaginary bell*) I wanted to see you, because I can tell you so many little things about my brother, which I think you ought to know. You see, Eric—my husband——

TUA-HEETA. Ereec?

JILL. Yes. I wish you could see him. He's so nice-looking. But I'm afraid he won't be home to tea. That's the worst of marrying a sailor. They are away so much. Well, I was telling you about Oliver. I think it would be better if you knew at once that—he doesn't like rice-pudding.

TUA-HEETA. Rice-poodeeng?

JILL. Yes, he hates it. It is very important that you should remember that. Then there's another thing— (*An untidy looking servant comes in. Can it be—can it possibly be* AUNT JANE? *Horrors!*) He dislikes —— Oh, there you are, Jane. You've been a very long time answering the bell.

AUNT JANE. I'm so sorry, ma'am, I was just dressing.

JILL. Excuses, Jane, always excuses. Leave me. Take a week's notice. (*To* TUA-HEETA) You must excuse my maid. She's very stupid. Tea at once, Jane. (AUNT JANE *sniffs and goes off.*) What was I saying? Oh yes, about Oliver. He doesn't care for cod-liver oil in the way that some men do. You would be wise not to force it on him just at first. . . . Have you any idea where you are going to live?

TUA-HEETA. Live? (*These dusky maidens are no conversationalists.*)

JILL. I expect Oliver will wish to reside at Hammersmith, so convenient for the City. You'll like Hammersmith. You'll go to St. Paul's Church, I expect. The Vicar will be sure to call. (*Enter* AUNT JANE *with small tea-table.*) Ah, here's tea. (*To* JANE) You're very slow, Jane.

AUNT JANE. I'm sorry, ma'am.

JILL. It's no good being sorry. Take another week's notice. (*To* TUA-HEETA) You must forgive my talking to my maid. She wants such a lot of looking after. (JANE *puts down the table*) That will do, Jane. (JANE *bumps against the table*) Dear, dear, how clumsy you are. What wages am I giving you now?

AUNT JANE. A shilling a month, ma'am.

JILL. Well, we'd better make it ninepence. (JANE *goes out in tears.*) Servants are a great nuisance, aren't

ACT II]   MAKE-BELIEVE   43

they? Jane is a peculiarly stupid person. She used to be aunt to my brother, and I have only taken her on out of charity. (*She pours out from an imaginary teapot*) Milk? Sugar? (*She puts them in and hands the imaginary cup to* TUA-HEETA.)

TUA-HEETA. Thank you. (*Drinks.*)

JILL (*pouring herself a cup*). I hope you like China. (*She drinks, and then rings an imaginary bell*) Well, as I was saying—— (*Enter* AUNT JANE.) You can clear away, Jane.

AUNT JANE. Yes, ma'am.

> (*She clears away the tea and* TUA-HEETA *and—very quickly—herself, as* OLIVER *comes back.* OLIVER *has been discussing boarding-tactics with his brother-in-law.* CAPTAIN CROOKSHANK *belongs to the now old-fashioned Marlinspike School;* OLIVER *is for well-primed pistols.*)

JILL. Oh, Oliver, I love your island. I've been thinking things all by myself. You're married to Tua-heeta. You don't mind, do you?

OLIVER. Not at all, Jill. Make yourself at home. I've just been trying the doctor in the lagoon. There *were* sharks there, after all, so we'll have to find another place for bathing. Oh, and I shot an elephant. What would you like to do now?

JILL. Just let's lie here and see what happens. (*What happens is that a cassowary comes along.*) Oh, what a lovely bird! Is it an ostrich?

> (*The cassowary sniffs the air, puts its beak to the ground and goes off again.*)

OLIVER. Silly! It's a cassowary, of course.

JILL. What's a cassowary?

OLIVER. Jill! Don't you remember the rhyme?

I wish I were a cassowary
Upon the plains of Timbuctoo
And then I'd eat a missionary—
And hat and gloves and hymn-book too!

JILL. Is that all they're for?

OLIVER. Well, what else would you want them for?

(*A* MISSIONARY, *pith-helmet, gloves, hymn-book, umbrella, all complete—creeps cautiously up. He bears a strong likeness to the curate, the* REVEREND MR. SMILAX.)

MISSIONARY. I am sorry to intrude upon your privacy, dear friends, but have you observed a cassowary on this island, apparently looking for something?

OLIVER. Yes, we saw one just now.

MISSIONARY (*shuddering*). Dear, dear, dear. You didn't happen to ask him what was the object of his researches?

JILL. He went so quickly.

MISSIONARY (*coming out of the undergrowth to them*). I wonder if you have ever heard of a little rhyme which apparently attributes to the bird in question, when residing in the level pastures of Timbuctoo, an unholy lust for the body and appurtenances thereto of an unnamed clerical gentleman?

OLIVER
and   } (*shouting* together). Yes! Rather!
JILL

MISSIONARY. Dear, dear! Fortunately—I say fortunately—this is not Timbuctoo! (OLIVER *slips away and comes back with a notice-board "Timbuctoo," which he places at the edge of the trees, unseen by the* MISSIONARY, *who goes on talking to* JILL) I take it that a cassowary residing in other latitudes is of a more temperate habit. His appetite, I venture to suggest, dear lady, would be under better restraint. That being so, I may perhaps safely—— (*He begins to move off, and comes suddenly up to the notice-board*) Dear, dear, dear, dear, dear! This is terrible! You said, I think, that the—ah—bird in question was moving in *this* direction?

OLIVER. That's right.

MISSIONARY. Then I shall move, hastily yet with all due precaution, in *that* direction. (*He walks off on tiptoe, looking over his shoulder in case the cassowary should reappear. Consequently, he does not observe the enormous* CANNIBAL *who has appeared from the trees on the right, until he bumps into him*) I beg your—— (*He looks up*) Dear, dear, dear, dear, dear!

CANNIBAL. Boria, boria, boo!

MISSIONARY. Yes, my dear sir, it is as you say, a beautiful morning.

CANNIBAL. Boria, boria, boo!

MISSIONARY. But I was just going a little walk—in this direction—if you will permit me.

CANNIBAL (*threateningly*). Boria, boria, boo!

MISSIONARY. I have noticed it, my dear sir, I have often made that very observation to my parishioners.

CANNIBAL (*very threateningly*). Boria, boria, boo!

MISSIONARY. Oh, what's he saying?

OLIVER. He says it's his birthday to-morrow.

CANNIBAL. Wurra, wurra wug!

OLIVER. And will you come to the party?

MISSIONARY (*to* CANNIBAL). My dear sir, it is most kind of you to invite me, but a prior engagement in a different part of the country—a totally unexpected call upon me in another locality—will unfortunately——

(*While he is talking, the cassowary comes back, sidles up to him, and taps with his beak on the* MISSIONARY'S *pith-helmet.*)

MISSIONARY (*absently, without looking round*). Come in! . . . As I was saying, my dear sir—— (*The bird taps again. The* MISSIONARY *turns round annoyed*) Can't you see I'm engaged—— Oh dear, dear, dear, dear, dear!

> (*He clasps the* CANNIBAL *in his anguish, recoils from the* CANNIBAL *and clasps the cassowary. The three of them go off together,* OLIVER *and* JILL *following eagerly behind to see who gets most.*)
>
> (*The* PIRATES *come back, each carrying a small wooden ammunition-box, and sit round in a semicircle, the* PIRATE CHIEF *in the middle.*)

PIRATE. Steward! Steward!

STEWARD (*hurrying in*). Yes, sir, coming, sir.

CHIEF. Now then, tumble up, my lad. I would carouse. Circulate the dry ginger.

STEWARD (*hurrying out*). Yes, sir, going, sir.

CHIEF. Look lively, my lad, look lively.

STEWARD (*hurrying in*). Yes, sir, coming, sir. (*He hands round mugs to them all.*)

CHIEF (*rising*). Gentlemen! (*They all stand up*) The crew of the *Cocktail* will carouse—— (*They all take one step to the right, one back, and one left—which brings them behind their boxes—and then place their right feet on the boxes together*) One! (*They raise their mugs*) Two! (*They drink*) Three! (*They bang down their mugs*) Four! (*They wipe their mouths with the backs of their hands*) So! . . . Steward!

STEWARD. Yes, sir, here, sir.

CHIEF. The carouse is over.

STEWARD. Yes, sir. (*He collects the mugs and goes out.*)

> (*The* PIRATES *sit down again.*)

CHIEF (*addressing the men*). Having passed an hour thus in feasting and song——

(*Hark! is it the voice of our dear* MISS PINNIGER? *It is.*)

GOVERNESS (*off*). Oliver! Oliver! Jill! You may get up now and come down to tea.

CHIEF. Having, as I say, slept off our carouse——

GOVERNESS (*off*). Oliver! Jill! (*She comes in*) Oh, I beg your pardon, I—er——

(*All the* PIRATES *rise and draw their weapons.*)

CHIEF. Pray do not mention it. (*Polishing his pistol lovingly*) You were asking——

GOVERNESS. I—I was l-looking for a small boy—Oliver——

CHIEF. Oliver? (*To* 1ST PIRATE) Have we any Olivers on board?

1ST PIRATE. No, Captain. Only Bath Olivers.

CHIEF (*to* GOVERNESS). You cannot be referring to my brother-in-law, hight Two-Toed Thomas, the Terror of the Dyaks?

GOVERNESS. Oh no, no—— Just a small boy and his sister—Jill.

CHIEF (*to* 2ND PIRATE). Have we any Jills on board?

2ND PIRATE. No, Captain. Only gills of rum.

CHIEF (*to* GOVERNESS). You cannot be referring to Mrs. Crookshank, styled the Pride of the Pampas?

GOVERNESS. Oh no, no, I am so sorry. Perhaps I—er——

CHIEF. Wait, woman. (*To* 6TH PIRATE) Ernest, offer your seat to the lady.

(*The* 6TH PIRATE *stands up.*)

GOVERNESS (*nervously*). Oh please don't trouble, I'm getting out at the next station—I mean I——

6TH PIRATE (*thunderously*). Sit down!

(*She sits down tremblingly and he stands by her with his pistol.*)

CHIEF. Thank you. (*To* 1ST PIRATE) Cecil, have you your pencil and notebook with you?

1ST PIRATE (*producing them*). Ay, ay, Captain.

CHIEF. Then we will cross-examine the prisoner. (*To* GOVERNESS) Name?

GOVERNESS. Pinniger.

1ST PIRATE (*writing*). Pincher.

CHIEF. Christian names, if any?

GOVERNESS. Letitia.

1ST PIRATE (*writing*). Letisher—how would you spell it, Captain?

CHIEF. Spell it like a sneeze. Age?

GOVERNESS. Twenty-three.

CHIEF (*to* 1ST PIRATE). Habits—untruthful. Appearance—against her. Got that?

1ST PIRATE. Yes, sir.

CHIEF (*to* GOVERNESS). And what are you for?

GOVERNESS. I teach. Oliver and Jill, you know.

CHIEF. And what do you teach them?

GOVERNESS. Oh, everything. Arithmetic, French, Geography, History, Dancing——

CHIEF (*holding up his hand*). A moment! I would take counsel with Percy. (*To* 2ND PIRATE) Percy, what shall we ask her in Arithmetic? (*The* 2ND PIRATE *whispers to him.*) Excellent. (*To her*) If you really are a teacher as you say, answer me this question. The brigantine *Cocktail* is in longitude 40° 39′ latitude 22° 50′, sailing closehauled on the port tack at 8 knots in a 15-knot nor'-nor' westerly breeze—how soon before she sights the Azores?

GOVERNESS. I—I—I'm afraid I—— You see—I——

CHIEF (*to* 1ST PIRATE). Arithmetic rotten.

1ST PIRATE (*writing*). Arithmetic rotten.

CHIEF (*to* 3RD PIRATE). Basil, ask her a question in French.

ACT II] MAKE-BELIEVE 49

3RD PIRATE. What would the mate of a French frigate say if he wanted to say in French, "Avast there, ye lubbering swab" to a friend like?

GOVERNESS. Oh, but I hardly—I——

CHIEF (*to* 1ST PIRATE). French futile.

1ST PIRATE (*writing*). French futile.

CHIEF (*to* 4TH PIRATE). I don't suppose it's much use, Francis. But try her in Geography.

4TH PIRATE. Well now, lady. If you was wanting a nice creek to lay up cosy in, atween Dago Point and the Tortofitas, where would you run to?

GOVERNESS. R-run to? But that isn't—of course I——

CHIEF (*to* 1ST PIRATE). Geography ghastly.

1ST PIRATE (*writing*). Geography ghastly.

CHIEF (*to* 5TH PIRATE). Give her a last chance, Mervyn. See if she knows any history.

5TH PIRATE. I suppose you couldn't tell me what year it was when old John Cann took the *Saucy Codfish* over Black Tooth Reef and laid her alongside the Spaniard in the harbour there, and up comes the Don in his nightcap. "Shiver my timbers," he says in Spanish, "but there's only one man in the whole of the Spanish Main," he says, "and that's John Cann," he says, "who could——"

(*The* GOVERNESS *looks dumbly at him.*)

CHIEF. She couldn't. History hopeless.

1ST PIRATE. History hopeless.

CHIEF (*to* GOVERNESS). What else do you teach?

GOVERNESS. Music, dancing—er—but I don't think——

CHIEF. Steward!

STEWARD (*coming in*). Yes, sir, coming, sir.

CHIEF. Concertina.

STEWARD (*going out*). Yes, sir, going, sir.

CHIEF (*to* GOVERNESS). Can you dance a hornpipe?

GOVERNESS. No, I——

CHIEF. Dancing dubious.

1ST PIRATE (*writing*). Dancing dubious.

STEWARD (*coming in*). Concertina, sir.

CHIEF. Give it to the woman. (*He takes it to her.*)

GOVERNESS. I'm afraid I—— (*She produces one ghastly noise and drops the concertina in alarm.*)

1ST PIRATE (*writing*). What shall I say, sir? Music mouldy or music measly?

CHIEF (*standing up*). Gentlemen, I think you will agree with me that the woman Pinniger has proved that she is utterly incapable of teaching anybody anything. Twenty-five years, man and boy, I have sailed the Spanish Main, and with the possible exception of a dumb and half-witted negro whom I shipped as cook in '64, I have never met any one so profoundly lacking in intellect. I propose, therefore, that for the space of twenty-four hours the woman Pinniger should be incarcerated in the smuggler's cave, in the company of a black beetle of friendly temperament.

GOVERNESS. Mercy! Mercy!

1ST PIRATE. I should like to second that.

CHIEF. Those in favour—ay! (*They all say "Ay."*) Contrary—No! (*The* GOVERNESS *says "No."*) The motion is carried.

> (*One of the Pirates opens the door of the cave. The* GOVERNESS *rushes to the* CHIEF *and throws herself at his feet.* OLIVER *and* JILL *appear in the nick of time.*)

OLIVER. A maiden in distress! I will rescue her. (*She looks up and* OLIVER *recognizes her*) Oh! Carry on, Commodore.

> (*The* GOVERNESS *is lowered into the cave and the door is shut.*)

CHIEF (*to his men*). Go, find that black beetle, and

ACT II] MAKE-BELIEVE 51

having found it, introduce it circumspectly by the back door.

PIRATES. Ay, ay, sir. [*They go out.*

OLIVER. All the same, you know, I jolly well should like to rescue somebody.

JILL (*excitedly*). Oo, rescue me, Oliver.

CHIEF (*solemnly*). Two-toed Thomas, Terror of the Dyaks, and Pest of the North Pacific, truly thou art a well-plucked one. Wilt fight me for the wench? (*He puts an arm round* JILL.)

OLIVER. I will.

CHIEF. Swords?

OLIVER. Pistols.

CHIEF. At twenty paces?

OLIVER. Across a handkerchief.

CHIEF. Done! (*Feeling in his pockets*) Have you got a handkerchief? I think I must have left mine on the dressing-table.

OLIVER (*bringing out his and putting it hastily back again*). Mine's rather—— Jill, haven't you got one?

JILL (*feeling*). I know I had one, but I——

CHIEF. This is an ill business. Five-and-thirty duels have I fought—and never before been delayed for lack of a handkerchief.

JILL. Ah, here it is. (*She produces a very small one and lays it on the ground. They stand one each side of it, pistols ready.*)

OLIVER. Jill, you must give the word.

JILL. Are you ready?

(*The sound of a gong is heard.*)

CHIEF. Listen! (*The gong is heard again*) The Spanish Fleet is engaged!

JILL. *I* thought it was our tea gong.

CHIEF. Ah, perhaps you're right.

OLIVER. I say, we oughtn't to miss tea. (*Holding out his hand to her*) Come on, Jill.

CHIEF. But you'll come back? We shall always be waiting here for you whenever you want us.

JILL. Yes, we'll come back, won't we, Oliver?

OLIVER. Oo, rather.

> (*The whole population of the Island, Animals, Pirates, and Dusky Maidens, come on. They sing as they wave good-bye to the children who are making their way to the boat.*)

JILL (*from the boat*). Good-bye, good-bye.

OLIVER. Good-bye, you chaps.

JILL (*politely*). And thank you all for a very pleasant afternoon.

> [*They are all singing as the boat pushes off. Night comes on with tropical suddenness. The singing dies slowly down.*

ACT III.—FATHER CHRISTMAS AND THE HUBBARD FAMILY

Scene I.—*The drawing-room of the* HUBBARDS *before Fame and Prosperity came to them. It is simply furnished with a deal table and two cane chairs.*

MR. *and* MRS. HUBBARD, *in faultless evening dress, are at home,* MR. HUBBARD *reading a magazine,* MRS. HUBBARD *with her hands in her lap. She sighs.*

MR. HUBBARD (*impetuously throwing down his magazine*). Dearest, you sighed?

MRS. HUBBARD (*quickly*). No, no, Henry. In a luxurious and well-appointed home such as this, why should I sigh?

MR. HUBBARD. True, dear. Not only is it artistically furnished, as you say, but it is also blessed with that most precious of all things—(*he lifts up the magazine*)—a library.

MRS. HUBBARD. Yes, yes, Henry, we have much to be thankful for.

MR. HUBBARD. We have indeed. But I am selfish. Would you care to read? (*He tears out a page of the magazine and hands it to her.*)

MRS. HUBBARD. Thank you, thank you, Henry.

(*They both sit in silence for a little. She sighs again.*)

MR. HUBBARD. Darling, you did sigh. Tell me what grieves you.

MRS. HUBBARD. Little Isabel. Her cough troubles me.

MR. HUBBARD (*thoughtfully*). Isabel?

MRS. HUBBARD. Yes, dear, our youngest. Don't you remember, she comes after Harold?

MR. HUBBARD (*counting on his fingers*). A, B, C, D, E, F, G, H, I—dear me, have we got nine already?

MRS. HUBBARD (*imploringly*). Darling, say you don't think it's too many.

MR. HUBBARD. Oh no, no, not at all, my love. . . . After all, it isn't as if they were real children.

MRS. HUBBARD (*indignantly*). Henry! How can you say they are not real?

MR. HUBBARD. Well, I mean they're only the children we thought we'd like to have if Father Christmas gave us any.

MRS. HUBBARD. They are just as real to me as if they were here in the house. Ada, Bertram, Caroline, the high-spirited Dennis, pretty Elsie with the golden ringlets, dear little fair-haired Frank——

MR. HUBBARD (*firmly*). Darling one, Frank has curly brown hair. It was an understood thing that you should choose the girls, and *I* should choose the boys. When we decided to take—A, B, C, D, E, F—a sixth child, it was my turn for a boy, and I selected Frank. He has curly brown hair and a fondness for animals.

MRS. HUBBARD. I dare say you're right, dear. Of course it is a little confusing when you never see your children.

MR. HUBBARD. Well, well, perhaps some day Father Christmas will give us some.

MRS. HUBBARD. Why does he neglect us so, Henry? We hang up our stockings every year, but he never seems to notice them. Even a diamond necklace or a few oranges or a five-shilling postal order would be something.

MR. HUBBARD. It is very strange. Possibly the fact that the chimney has not been swept for some years may have something to do with it. Or he may have forgotten our change of address. I cannot help feeling that if he knew how we had been left to starve in this way he would be very much annoyed.

MRS. HUBBARD. And clothes. I have literally nothing but what I am standing up in—I mean sitting down in.

MR. HUBBARD. Nor I, my love. But at least it will be written of us in the papers that the Hubbards perished in faultless evening dress. We are a proud race, and if Father Christmas deliberately cuts us off in this way, let us go down proudly. . . . Shall we go on reading or would you like to walk up and down the room? Fortunately these simple pleasures are left to us.

MRS. HUBBARD. I've finished this page.

MR. HUBBARD (*tearing out one*). Have another, my love.

(*They read for a little while, until interrupted by a knock at the door.*)

MRS. HUBBARD. Some one at the door! Who could it be?

MR. HUBBARD (*getting up*). Just make the room look a little more homey, dear, in case it's any one important.

(*He goes out, leaving her to alter the position of the chairs slightly.*)

MRS. HUBBARD. Well?

MR. HUBBARD (*coming in*). A letter. (*He opens it.*)

MRS. HUBBARD. Quick!

MR. HUBBARD (*whistling with surprise*). Father Christmas! An invitation to Court! (*Reading*) "Father Christmas at Home, 25th December. Jollifications, 11.59 P.M." My love, he has found us at last! (*They embrace each other.*)

MRS. HUBBARD. Henry, how gratifying!

MR. HUBBARD. Yes. (*Sadly, after a pause*) But we can't go.

MRS. HUBBARD (*sadly*). No, I have no clothes.

MR. HUBBARD. Nor I.

MRS. HUBBARD. How can I possibly go without a diamond necklace? None of the Montmorency-Smythe women has ever been to Court without a diamond necklace.

MR. HUBBARD. The Hubbards are a proud race. No male Hubbard would dream of appearing at Court without a gentleman's gold Albert watch-chain. . . . Besides, there is another thing. There will be many footmen at Father Christmas's Court, who will doubtless require coppers pressed into their palms. My honour would be seriously affected, were I compelled to whisper to them that I had no coppers.

MRS. HUBBARD. It is very unfortunate. Father Christmas may have hundreds of presents waiting for us.

MR. HUBBARD. True. But how would it be to hang up our stockings again this evening—now that we know he knows we are here? I would suggest tied on to the door-knocker, to save him the trouble of coming down the chimney.

MRS. HUBBARD (*excitedly*). Henry, I wonder! But of course we will.

(*They begin to take off—the one a sock, the other a stocking.*)

MR. HUBBARD. I almost wish now that my last suit had been a knickerbocker one. However, we must do what we can with a sock.

MRS. HUBBARD (*holding up her stocking and looking at it a little anxiously*). I hope Father Christmas won't give me a bicycle. A stocking never sets so well after it has had a bicycle in it.

MR. HUBBARD (*taking it from her*). Now, dear, I will go down and put them in position. Let us hope that fortune will be kind to us.

MRS. HUBBARD. Let us hope so, darling. And quickly. For (*picking up her page of the magazine*) it is a trifle cold.

[*He goes out and she is left reading.*

SCENE II.—*Outside the house the snow lies deep. The stocking and sock are tied on to the door-knocker. There is a light in the window.*
A party of carol-singers, with lanterns, come by and halt in the snow outside the house.

PETER ABLEWAYS. Friends, are we all assembled?

JONAS HUMPHREY. Ay, ay, Peter Ableways, assembled and met together in a congregation, for the purpose of lifting up our voices in joyous thanksgiving, videlicet the singing of a carol or other wintry melody.

JENNIFER LING. Keep your breath for your song, Master Humphrey. That last "Alleluia" of yours was a poor windy thing, lacking grievously in substance.

JONAS (*sadly*). It is so. I never made much of an Alleluia. It is not in my nature somehow. 'Tis a vain boastful thing an Alleluia.

MARTHA PORRITT. Are we to begin soon, Master Ableways? My feet are cold.

JONAS. What matter the feet, Martha Porritt, if the heart be warm with loving-kindness and seasonable emotions?

MARTHA. Well, nothing of me will be warm soon.

JENNIFER. Ay, let's begin, Peter Ableways, while we carry the tune in our heads. It is ill searching for the notes in the middle of the carol, as some singers do.

PETER. Well spoken, Mistress Jennifer. Now listen

all, while I unfold the nature of the entertainment. *Item*—A carol or birth song to draw the attention of all folk to the company here assembled and the occasion celebrated. *Item*—Applause and the clapping of hands. *Item*—A carol or song of thanksgiving. *Item*—A collection.

JONAS. An entertainment well devised, Master Ableways, sobeit the words of the second song remain with me after I am delivered of the first.

MARTHA. Are we to begin soon, Master Ableways? My feet are cold.

PETER. Are we all ready, friends? I will say one—two—three—and at "three" I pray you all to give it off in a hearty manner from the chest. One—two——

JONAS. Hold, hold, Master Ableways! Does it begin—No, that's the other one. (JENNIFER *whispers the first line to him*) Ay, ay—I have it now—and bursting to get out of me. Proceed, Peter Ableways.

PETER. One—two—three—— (*They carol.*)

PETER. Well sung, all.

HUMPHREY. The applause followed, good Master Peter, as ordained. Moreover, I have the tune of the second song ready within me. Likewise a la-la-la or two to replace such words as I have forgotten.

MARTHA. Don't forget the collection, Master Ableways

PETER. Ay, the collection. (*He takes off his hat and places it on the ground.*)

HUMPHREY. Nay, not so fast, Master Peter. It would be ill if the good folk thought that our success this night were to be estimated by an empty hat. Place some of our money in it, Master Ableways. Where money is, money will come.

JENNIFER. Ay, it makes a pleasing clink.

PETER. True, Mistress Jennifer. Master Humphrey

speaks true. (*He pours some coppers from his pockets into his hat.*)

MARTHA. Are we to go on, Master Ableways? My feet are cold.

PETER (*shaking the hat*). So, a warning noise.

HUMPHREY. To it again, gentles.

PETER. Are all ready? One—two—three! (*They carol.*)

PETER. Well sung, all.

HUMPHREY. Have you the hat, Master Peter?

PETER (*picking it up*). Ay, friend, all is ready.

> (*The door opens and* MR. HUBBARD *appears at the entrance.*)

MR. HUBBARD. Good evening, friends.

PETER. Good evening, sir. (*He holds out the hat.*)

MR. HUBBARD (*looking at it*). What is this? (PETER *shakes it*) Aha! Money!

PETER. Remember the carol singers, sir.

MR. HUBBARD (*helping himself*). My dear friends, I will always remember you. This is most generous. I shall never forget your kindness. This is most unexpected. But not the less welcome, not the less—— I think there's a ha'penny down there that I missed— thank you. As I was saying, unexpected but welcome. I thank you heartily. Good evening, friends.

[*He goes in and shuts the door.*

PETER (*who has been too surprised to do anything but keep his mouth open*). Well! . . . Well! . . . Well, friends, let us to the next house. We have got all that we can get here.

[*They trail off silently.*

MARTHA (*as they go off*). Master Ableways!

PETER. Ay, lass!

MARTHA. My feet aren't so cold now.

(*But this is to be an exciting night. As soon as
they are gone, a Burglar and a Burglaress
steal into view.*)

BILL. Wotcher get, Liz? (*She holds up a gold watch
and chain. He nods and holds up a diamond necklace*)
'Ow's that?

LIZ (*starting suddenly*). H'st!

BILL (*in a whisper*). What is it?

LIZ. Copper!

BILL (*desperately*). 'Ere, quick, get rid of these. 'Ide
'em in the snow, or——

LIZ. Bill! (*He turns round*) Look! (*She points to the
stocking and sock hanging up*) We can come back for
'em as soon as 'e's gone.

(BILL *looks at them, and back at her, and grins.
He drops the necklace into one and the
watch into the other. As the* POLICEMAN *approaches they strike up,* "*While shepherds
watched their flock by night,*" *with an air
of great enthusiasm.*)

POLICEMAN. Now then, move along there.

(*They move along. The* POLICEMAN *flashes his
light on the door to see that all is well. The
stocking and sock are revealed. He beams
sentimentally at them.*)

SCENE III.—*We are inside the house again.* MRS. HUBBARD *is still reading a page of the magazine. In
dashes* MR. HUBBARD *with the sock and stocking.*

MR. HUBBARD. My darling, what do you think? Father
Christmas has sent you a little present. (*He hands her
the stocking.*)

MRS. HUBBARD. Henry! Has he sent you one too?

MR. HUBBARD (*holding up his sock*). Observe!

ACT III] MAKE-BELIEVE 61

MRS. HUBBARD. How sweet of him! I wonder what mine is. What is yours, darling?

MR. HUBBARD. I haven't looked yet, my love. Perhaps just a few nuts or something of that sort, with a card attached saying, "To wish you the old, old wish." We must try not to be disappointed, whatever it is, darling.

MRS. HUBBARD. Of course, Henry. After all, it is the kindly thought which really matters.

MR. HUBBARD. Certainly. All the same, I hope—— Will you look in yours, dear, first, or shall I?

MRS. HUBBARD. I think I should like to, darling. (*Feeling it*) It feels so exciting. (*She brings out a diamond necklace*) Henry!

MR. HUBBARD. My love! (*They embrace*) Now you will be able to go to Court. You must say that your husband is unfortunately in bed with a bad cold. You can tell me all about it when you come home. I shall be able to amuse myself with—— (*He is feeling in his sock while talking, and now brings out the watch and chain.*)

MRS. HUBBARD. Henry! My love!

MR. HUBBARD. A gentleman's gold hunter and Albert watch-chain. My darling!

(*They put down their presents on the table and embrace each other again.*)

MRS. HUBBARD. Let's put them on at once, Henry, and see how they suit us.

MR. HUBBARD. Allow me, my love. (*He fastens her necklace.*)

MRS. HUBBARD (*happily*). Now I feel really dressed again! Oh, I wish we had a looking-glass.

MR. HUBBARD (*opening his gold watch*). Try in here, my darling.

MRS. HUBBARD (*surveying herself*). How perfectly sweet! . . . Now let me put your watch-chain on for you, dear. (*She arranges it for him*—HENRY *very proud.*)

MR. HUBBARD. Does it suit me, darling?

MRS. HUBBARD. You look fascinating, Henry!

(*They strut about the room with an air.*)

MR. HUBBARD (*taking out his watch and looking at it ostentatiously*). Well, well, we ought to be starting. My watch makes it 11.58. (*He holds it to her ear*) Hasn't it got a sweet tick?

MRS. HUBBARD. Sweet! But starting where, Henry? Do you mean we can really—— But you haven't any money.

MR. HUBBARD. Money? (*Taking out a handful*) Heaps of it.

MRS. HUBBARD. Father Christmas?

MR. HUBBARD. Undoubtedly, my love. Brought round to the front door just now by some of his messengers. By the way, dear—(*indicating the sock and stocking*)—hadn't we better put these on before we start?

MRS. HUBBARD. Of course. How silly of me!

(*They sit down and put them on.*)

MR. HUBBARD. Really this is a very handsome watch-chain.

MRS. HUBBARD. It becomes you admirably, Henry.

MR. HUBBARD. Thank you, dear. There's just one little point. Father Christmas is sometimes rather shy about acknowledging the presents he gives. He hates being thanked. If, therefore, he makes any comment on your magnificent necklace or my handsome watch-chain, we must say that they have been in the family for some years.

MRS. HUBBARD. Of course, dear. (*They get up.*)

MR. HUBBARD. Well, now we're ready.

MRS. HUBBARD. Darling one, don't you think we might bring the children?

MR. HUBBARD. Of course, dear! How forgetful of me! . . . Children—'shun! (*Listen! Their heels click as they come to attention*) Number! (*Their voices— alternate boy and girl, one to nine—are heard*) Right turn!

MRS. HUBBARD. Darling one, I almost seem to hear them!

MR. HUBBARD. Are you ready, my love?

MRS. HUBBARD. Yes, Henry.

MR. HUBBARD. Quick march!

> (*The children are heard tramping off. Very proudly* MR. *and* MRS. HUBBARD *bring up the rear.*)

SCENE IV.—*The Court of* FATHER CHRISTMAS. *Shall we describe it? No. But there is everything there which any reasonable person could want, from ices to catapults. And the decorations, done in candy so that you can break off a piece whenever you are hungry, are superb.*

1ST USHER (*from the back*). Father Christmas!

SEVERAL USHERS (*from the front*). Father Christmas! (*He comes in.*)

FATHER CHRISTMAS (*genially*). Good evening, everybody.

I ought to have said that there are already some hundreds of people there, though how some of them got invitations—but, after all, that is not our business. Wishing to put them quite at their ease, FATHER CHRISTMAS, *who has a very creditable baritone, gives them a song. After the applause which follows it, he retires to the throne at the back, and awaits his more important guests. The* USHERS *take up their places, one at the entrance, one close to the throne.*

1ST USHER. Mr. and Mrs. Henry Hubbard! (*They come in.*)

MR. HUBBARD (*pressing twopence into his palm*). Thank you, my man, thank you.

2ND USHER. Mr. and Mrs. Henry Hubbard.

MR. HUBBARD (*handing out another twopence*). Not at all, my man, not at all.

>(MRS. HUBBARD *curtsies and* MR. HUBBARD *bows to* FATHER CHRISTMAS.)

FATHER CHRISTMAS. I am delighted to welcome you to my Court. How are you both?

MR. HUBBARD. Very well, thank you, sir. My wife has a slight cold in one foot, owing to——

MRS. HUBBARD (*hastily*). A touch of gout, sir, inherited from my ancestors, the Montmorency-Smythes.

FATHER CHRISTMAS. Dear me, it won't prevent you dancing, I hope?

MRS. HUBBARD. Oh no, sir.

FATHER CHRISTMAS. That's right. We shall have a few more friends coming in soon. You have been giving each other presents already, I see. I congratulate you, madam, on your husband's taste.

MRS. HUBBARD (*touching her necklace*). Oh no, this is a very old heirloom of the Montmorency-Smythe family.

MR. HUBBARD. An ancestress of Mrs. Hubbard's—a lady-in-waiting at the Tottenham Court—at the Tudor Court—was fortunate enough to catch the eye of—er——

MRS. HUBBARD. Elizabeth.

MR. HUBBARD. Queen Elizabeth, and—er——

FATHER CHRISTMAS. I see. You are lucky, madam, to have such beautiful jewels. (*Turning to* MR. HUBBARD) And this delightful gold Albert watch-chain——

MR. HUBBARD. Presented to an ancestor of mine, Sir Humphrey de Hubbard, at the battle of—er——

MRS. HUBBARD. Agincourt.

MR. HUBBARD. As you say, dear, Agincourt. By King Richard the—I should say William the—well, by the King.

FATHER CHRISTMAS. How very interesting.

MR. HUBBARD. Yes. My ancestor clove a scurvy knave from the chaps to the chine. I don't quite know how you do that, but I gather that he inflicted some sort of a scratch upon his adversary, and the King rewarded him with this handsome watch-chain.

USHERS (*announcing*). Mr. Robinson Crusoe! (*He comes in.*)

FATHER CHRISTMAS. How do you do?

CRUSOE (*bowing*). I'm a little late, I'm afraid, sir. My raft was delayed by adverse gales.

> (FATHER CHRISTMAS *introduces him to the* HUBBARDS, *who inform him that the weather is very seasonable.*)

USHERS. Miss Riding Hood! (*She comes in.*)

FATHER CHRISTMAS. How do you do?

RIDING HOOD (*curtseying*). I hope I am in time, sir. I had to look in on my grandmother on the way here.

> (FATHER CHRISTMAS *makes the necessary introductions.*)

MRS. HUBBARD (*to* CRUSOE). Do come and see me, Mr. Crusoe. Any Friday. I should like your advice about my parrot. He's moulting in all the wrong places.

MR. HUBBARD. (*to* RED RIDING HOOD). I don't know if you're interested in wolves at all, Miss Hood. I heard a very good story about one the other day. (*He begins to tell it, but she has hurried away before he can remember whether it was Thursday or Friday.*)

USHERS. Baron Bluebeard! (*He comes in.*)

FATHER CHRISTMAS. How do you do?

BLUEBEARD (*bowing*). I trust you have not been waiting for me, sir. I had a slight argument with my wife before starting, which delayed me somewhat.

(FATHER CHRISTMAS *forgives him.*)

USHERS. Princess Goldilocks!

FATHER CHRISTMAS. How do you do?

GOLDILOCKS (*curtseying*). I brought the youngest bear with me—do you mind? *She introduces the youngest bear to* FATHER CHRISTMAS *and the other guests*) Say, how do you do, darling? (*To an* USHER) Will you give him a little porridge, please, and if you have got a nice bed where he could rest a little afterwards—he gets tired so quickly.

USHER. Certainly, your Royal Highness.

(*Music begins.*)

GOLDILOCKS (*to* FATHER CHRISTMAS). Are we going to dance? How lovely!

FATHER CHRISTMAS (*to the* HUBBARDS). You will dance, won't you?

MRS. HUBBARD. I think not just at first, thank you.

GOLDILOCKS (*to* CRUSOE). Come along!

CRUSOE. I am a little out of practice—er—but if you don't mind—er—— (*He comes.*)

BLUEBEARD (*to* RIDING HOOD). May I have the pleasure?

MRS. HUBBARD (*to* RIDING HOOD). Be careful, dear; he has a very bad reputation.

RIDING HOOD (*to* BLUEBEARD). You don't eat people, do you?

BLUEBEARD (*pained by this injustice*). Never!

RIDING HOOD. Oh then, I don't mind. But I do hate being eaten.

Now we can't possibly describe the whole dance to

ACT III]   MAKE-BELIEVE   67

you, for in every corner of the big ballroom couples were revolving and sliding, and making small talk with each other. So we will just take two specimen conversations.

CRUSOE (*nervous, poor man*). Princess Goldilocks, may I speak to you on a matter of some importance to me?

GOLDILOCKS. I wish you would.

CRUSOE (*looking across at* BLUEBEARD *and* RED RIDING HOOD, *who are revolving close by*). Alone.

GOLDILOCKS (*to* BLUEBEARD). Do you mind? You can have your turn afterwards.

BLUEBEARD (*to* RIDING HOOD). Shall we adjourn to the Buffet?

RIDING HOOD. Oh, do let's.   [*They adjourn.*

CRUSOE (*bravely*). Princess, I am a lonely man.

GOLDILOCKS (*encouragingly*). Yes, Robinson?

CRUSOE. I am not much of a one for society, and I don't quite know how to put these things, but—er—if you would like to share my island, I—I should so love to have you there.

GOLDILOCKS. Oh. Robbie!

CRUSOE (*warming to it*). I have a very comfortable house, and a man-servant, and an excellent view from the south windows, and several thousands of acres of good rough-shooting, and—oh, do say you'll come!

GOLDILOCKS. May I bring my bears with me?

CRUSOE. Of course! I ought to have said that. I have a great fondness for animals.

GOLDILOCKS. How sweet of you! But perhaps I ought to warn you that we all like porridge. Have you——

CRUSOE. I have a hundred acres of oats.

GOLDILOCKS. Then, Robinson, I am yours. (*They embrace*) There! Now tell me—did you make all your clothes yourself?

CRUSOE (*proudly*). All of them.

GOLDILOCKS (*going off with him*). How wonderful of you! Really you hardly seem to want a wife.

[*They go out. Now it is the other couple's turn.*

Enter, then, BLUEBEARD *and* RIDING HOOD

BLUEBEARD. Perhaps I ought to tell you at once, Miss Riding Hood, that I have been married before.

RIDING HOOD. Yes?

BLUEBEARD. My last wife unfortunately died just before I started out here this evening.

RIDING HOOD (*calmly*). Did you kill her?

BLUEBEARD (*taken aback*). I—I—I——

RIDING HOOD. Are you quite a nice man, Bluebeard?

BLUEBEARD. W-what do you mean? I am a very *rich* man. If you will marry me, you will live in a wonderful castle, full of everything that you want.

RIDING HOOD. That will be rather jolly.

BLUEBEARD (*dramatically*). But there is one room into which you must never go. (*Holding up a key*) Here is the key of it. (*He offers it to her.*)

RIDING HOOD (*indifferently*). But if I'm never to go into it, I shan't want the key.

BLUEBEARD (*upset*). You—you *must* have the key.

RIDING HOOD. Why?

BLUEBEARD. The—the others all had it.

RIDING HOOD (*coldly*). Bluebeard, you aren't going to talk about your *other* wives all the time, are you?

BLUEBEARD. N—no.

RIDING HOOD. Then don't be silly. And take this key, and go and tidy up that ridiculous room of yours, and when it's nice and clean, and when you've shaved off that absurd beard, perhaps I'll marry you.

BLUEBEARD (*furiously drawing his sword*). Madam!

RIDING HOOD. Don't do it here. You'll want some hot water.

ACT III] MAKE-BELIEVE 69

BLUEBEARD (*trying to put his sword back*). This is too much, this is——

RIDING HOOD. You're putting it in the wrong way round.

BLUEBEARD (*stiffly*). Thank you. (*He manages to get it in.*)

RIDING HOOD. Well, do you want to marry me?

BLUEBEARD. Yes!

RIDING HOOD. Sure?

BLUEBEARD (*admiringly*). More than ever. You're the first woman I've met who hasn't been afraid of me.

RIDING HOOD (*surprised*). Are you very alarming? Wolves frighten me sometimes, but not just silly men. . . . (*Giving him her hand*) All right then. But you'll do what I said?

BLUEBEARD. Beloved one, I will do anything for you.

> (CRUSOE *and* GOLDILOCKS *come back. Probably it will occur to the four of them to sing a song indicative of the happy family life awaiting them. On the other hand they may prefer to dance.* . . .)

But enough of this. Let us get on to the great event of the evening. Ladies and gentlemen, are you all assembled? Then silence, please, for FATHER CHRISTMAS.

FATHER CHRISTMAS. Ladies and gentlemen, it gives me great pleasure to see you here at my Court this evening; and in particular my friends Mr. and Mrs. Hubbard, of whom I have been too long neglectful. However, I hope to make up for it to-night. (*To an* USHER) Disclose the Christmas Tree!

The Christmas Tree is disclosed, and—what do you think? Children disguised as crackers are hanging from every branch! Well, I never!

FATHER CHRISTMAS (*quite calmly*). Distribute the presents!

> (*An* USHER *takes down the children one by one and places them in a row, reading from the labels on them,* "MRS. HUBBARD, MR. HUBBARD" *alternately.*)

USHER (*handing list to* MR. HUBBARD). Here is the nominal roll, sir.

MR. HUBBARD (*looking at it in amazement*). What's this? (MRS. HUBBARD *looks over his shoulder*) Ada, Bertram, Caroline—My darling one!

MRS. HUBBARD. Henry! Our children at last! Oh, are they all—*all* there?

MR. HUBBARD. We'll soon see, dear. Ada!

ADA (*springing to attention*). Father! (*She stands at ease.*)

MR. HUBBARD. Bertram! . . . (*And so on up to* ELSIE) . . . Frank!

FRANK. Father!

MR. HUBBARD. There you are darling, I told you he had curly brown hair. . . . Gwendoline! (*And so on.*)

MRS. HUBBARD (*to* FATHER CHRISTMAS). Oh thank you so much. It is sweet of you.

MR. HUBBARD (*to* FATHER CHRISTMAS). We are slightly overcome. Do you mind if we just dance it off? (FATHER CHRISTMAS *nods genially.*) Come on, children!

> (*He holds out his hands, and he and his wife and the children dance round in a ring singing, "Here we go round the Christmas Tree, all on a Christmas evening."* . . .

And then—— But at this moment JAMES *and* ROSEMARY *and the* HUBBARD *children stopped thinking, so of course the play came to an end. And if there were one or two bits in it which the children didn't quite understand, that was* JAMES's *fault. He never ought to have been thinking at all, really.*

MR. PIM PASSES BY

A COMEDY IN THREE ACTS

CHARACTERS

GEORGE MARDEN, J.P.
OLIVIA (*his wife*).
DINAH (*his niece*).
LADY MARDEN (*his aunt*).
BRIAN STRANGE.
CARRAWAY PIM.
ANNE.

THE first performance of this play in London took place at the New Theatre on January 5, 1920, with the following cast:

George Marden	BEN WEBSTER.
Olivia	IRENE VANBRUGH.
Dinah	GEORGETTE COHAN.
Lady Marden	ETHEL GRIFFIES.
Brian Strange	LESLIE HOWARD.
Carraway Pim	DION BOUCICAULT.
Anne	ETHEL WELLESLEY.

MR. PIM PASSES BY

ACT I

The morning-room at Marden House (Buckinghamshire) decided more than a hundred years ago that it was all right, and has not bothered about itself since. Visitors to the house have called the result such different adjectives as "mellow," "old-fashioned," "charming"—even "baronial" and "antique"; but nobody ever said it was "exciting." Sometimes OLIVIA *wants it to be more exciting, and last week she let herself go over some new curtains. At present they are folded up and waiting for her; she still has the rings to put on. It is obvious that the curtains alone will overdo the excitement; they will have to be harmonised with a new carpet and cushions.* OLIVIA *has her eye on just the things, but one has to go carefully with* GEORGE. *What was good enough for his great-great-grandfather is good enough for him. However, we can trust* OLIVIA *to see him through it, although it may take time.*

There are two ways of coming into the room; by the open windows leading from the terrace or by the door. On this pleasant July morning MR. PIM *chooses the latter way—or rather* ANNE *chooses it for him; and old* MR. PIM, *wistful, kindly, gentle, little* MR. PIM, *living in some world of his own whither we cannot follow, ambles after her.*

ANNE. I'll tell Mr. Marden you're here, sir. Mr. Pim, isn't it?

PIM (*coming back to this world*). Yes—er—Mr. Carraway Pim. He doesn't know me, you understand, but if he could just see me for a moment—er—— (*He fumbles in his pockets*) I gave you that letter?

ANNE. Yes, sir, I'll give it to him.

PIM (*bringing out a letter which is not the one he was looking for, but which reminds him of something else he has forgotten*). Dear me!

ANNE. Yes, sir?

PIM. I ought to have sent a telegram, but I can do it on my way back. You have a telegraph office in the village?

ANNE. Oh yes, sir. If you turn to the left when you get outside the gates, it isn't more than a hundred yards down the hill.

PIM. Thank you, thank you. Very stupid of me to have forgotten.

[ANNE *goes out.*

(MR. PIM *wanders about the room humming to himself, and looking vaguely at the pictures. He has his back to the door as* DINAH *comes in. She is nineteen, very pretty, very happy, and full of boyish high spirits and conversation.*)

DINAH. Hullo!

PIM (*turning round*). Ah, good morning, Mrs. Marden. You must forgive my—er——

DINAH. Oh I say, I'm not Mrs. Marden. I'm Dinah.

PIM (*with a bow*). Then I will say, Good morning, Miss Diana.

DINAH (*reproachfully*). Now, look here, if you and I are going to be friends you mustn't do that. Dinah *not* Diana. Do remember it, there's a good man, because I get so tired of correcting people. Have you come to stay with us?

PIM. Well no, Miss—er—Dinah.

DINAH (*nodding*). That's right. I can see I shan't have to speak to *you* again. Now tell me *your* name, and I bet you I get it right first time. And do sit down.

PIM (*sitting down*). Thank you. My name is—er—Pim, Carraway Pim——

DINAH. Pim, that's easy.

PIM. And I have a letter of introduction to your father——

DINAH. Oh no; now you're going wrong again, Mr. Pim. George isn't my father; he's my uncle. *Uncle George*—he doesn't like me calling him George. Olivia doesn't mind—I mean she doesn't mind being called Olivia, but George is rather touchy. You see, he's been my guardian since I was about two, and then about five years ago he married a widow called Mrs. Telworthy—that's Olivia—so she became my Aunt Olivia, only she lets me drop the Aunt. Got that?

PIM (*a little alarmed*). I—I think so, Miss Marden.

DINAH (*admiringly*). I say, you *are* quick, Mr. Pim. Well, if you take my advice, when you've finished your business with George, you will hang about a bit and see if you can't see Olivia. She's simply devastating. I don't wonder George fell in love with her.

PIM. It's only the merest matter of business—just a few minutes with your uncle—I'm afraid I shall hardly——

DINAH. Well, you must please yourself, Mr. Pim. I'm just giving you a friendly word of advice. Naturally, I was awfully glad to get such a magnificent aunt, because, of course, marriage *is* rather a toss up, isn't it, and George might have gone off with anybody. It's different on the stage, where guardians always marry their wards, but George couldn't marry *me* because I'm his niece. Mind you, I don't say that I should have had him, because between ourselves he's a little bit old-fashioned.

PIM. So he married—er—Mrs. Marden instead.

DINAH. Mrs. Telworthy—don't say you've forgotten already, just when you were getting so good at names. Mrs. Telworthy. You see, Olivia married the Telworthy man and went to Australia with him, and he drank himself to death in the bush, or wherever you drink yourself to death out there, and Olivia came home to England, and met my uncle, and he fell in love with her and proposed to her, and he came into my room that night—I was about fourteen—and turned on the light and said, "Dinah, how would you like to have a beautiful aunt of your very own?" And I said: "Congratulations, George." That was the first time I called him George. Of course, I'd seen it coming for *weeks*. Telworthy, isn't it a funny name?

PIM. Very singular. From Australia, you say?

DINAH. Yes, I always say that he's probably still alive, and will turn up here one morning and annoy George, because that's what first husbands always do in books, but I'm afraid there's not much chance.

PIM (*shocked*). Miss Marden!

DINAH. Well, of course, I don't really *want* it to happen, but it *would* be rather exciting, wouldn't it? However, things like that never seem to occur down here, somehow. There was a hay-rick burnt last year about a mile away, but that isn't quite the same thing, is it?

PIM. No, I should say that that was certainly different.

DINAH. Of course, something very, very wonderful

did happen last night, but I'm not sure if I know you well enough—— (*She looks at him hesitatingly.*)

PIM (*uncomfortably*). Really, Miss Marden, I am only a—a passer-by, here to-day and gone to-morrow. You really mustn't——

DINAH. And yet there's something about you, Mr. Pim, which inspires confidence. The fact is—(*in a stage whisper*)—I got engaged last night!

PIM. Dear me, let me congratulate you.

DINAH. I expect that's why George is keeping you such a long time. Brian, my young man, the well-known painter—only nobody has ever heard of him—he's smoking a pipe with George in the library and asking for his niece's hand. Isn't it exciting? You're really rather lucky, Mr. Pim—I mean being told so soon. Even Olivia doesn't know yet.

PIM (*getting up*). Yes, yes. I congratulate you, Miss Marden. Perhaps it would be better——

[ANNE *comes in.*

ANNE. Mr. Marden is out at the moment, sir—— Oh, I didn't see you, Miss Dinah.

DINAH. It's all right, Anne. *I'm* looking after Mr. Pim.

ANNE. Yes, Miss.

[*She goes out.*

DINAH (*excitedly*). That's me. They can't discuss me in the library without breaking down, so they're walking up and down outside, and slashing at the thistles in order to conceal their emotion. *You* know. I expect Brian——

PIM (*looking at his watch*). Yes, I think, Miss Marden, I had better go now and return a little later. I have a telegram which I want to send, and perhaps by the time I came back——

DINAH. Oh, but how disappointing of you, when we were getting on together so nicely. And it was just going to be your turn to tell me all about *yours*elf.

PIM. I have really nothing to tell, Miss Marden. I have a letter of introduction to Mr. Marden, who in turn will give me, I hope, a letter to a certain distinguished man whom it is necessary for me to meet. That is all. (*Holding out his hand*) And now, Miss Marden——

DINAH. Oh, I'll start you on your way to the post office. I want to know if you're married, and all that sort of thing. You've got heaps to tell me, Mr. Pim. Have you got your hat? That's right. Then we'll—hullo, here's Brian.

> (BRIAN STRANGE *comes in at the windows. He is what* GEORGE *calls a damned futuristic painter-chap, aged twenty-four. To look at, he is a very pleasant boy, rather untidily dressed.*)

BRIAN (*nodding*). How do you do?

DINAH (*seizing him*). Brian, this is Mr. Pim. Mr. Carraway Pim. He's been telling me all about himself. It's so interesting. He's just going to send a telegram, and then he's coming back again. Mr. Pim, this is Brian —*you* know.

BRIAN (*smiling and shaking hands*). How do you do?

DINAH (*pleadingly*). You *won't* mind going to the post office by yourself, will you, because, you see, Brian and I—(*she looks lovingly at* BRIAN).

PIM (*because they are so young*). Miss Dinah and Mr. —er—Brian, I have only come into your lives for a moment, and it is probable that I shall now pass out of them for ever, but you will allow an old man——

DINAH. Oh, not old!

PIM (*chuckling happily*). Well, a middle-aged man— to wish you both every happiness in the years that you have before you. Good-bye, good-bye.

[*He disappears gently through the windows.*

DINAH. Brian, he'll get lost if he goes that way.

BRIAN (*going to the windows and calling after him*). Round to the left, sir. . . . That's right. (*He comes back into the room*) Rum old bird. Who is he?

DINAH. Darling, you haven't kissed me yet.

BRIAN (*taking her in his arms*). I oughtn't to, but then one never ought to do the nice things.

DINAH. Why oughtn't you?

(*They sit on the sofa together.*)

BRIAN. Well, we said we'd be good until we'd told your uncle and aunt all about it. You see, being a guest in their house——

DINAH. But, darling child, what *have* you been doing all this morning *except* telling George?

BRIAN. *Trying* to tell George.

DINAH (*nodding*). Yes, of course, there's a difference.

BRIAN. I think he guessed there was something up, and he took me down to see the pigs—he said he had to see the pigs at once—I don't know why; an appointment perhaps. And we talked about pigs all the way, and I couldn't say, "Talking about pigs, I want to marry your niece——"

DINAH (*with mock indignation*). Of course you couldn't.

BRIAN. No. Well, you see how it was. And then when we'd finished talking about pigs, we started talking *to* the pigs——

DINAH (*eagerly*). Oh, *how* is Arnold?

BRIAN. The little black-and-white one? He's very jolly, I believe, but naturally I wasn't thinking about him much. I was wondering how to begin. And then Lumsden came up, and wanted to talk pig-food, and the atmosphere grew less and less romantic, and—and I gradually drifted away.

DINAH. Poor darling. Well, we shall have to approach him through Olivia.

BRIAN. But I always wanted to tell her first; she's so much easier. Only you wouldn't let me.

DINAH. That's your fault, Brian. You would tell Olivia that she ought to have orange-and-black curtains.

BRIAN. But she *wants* orange-and-black curtains.

DINAH. Yes, but George says he's not going to have any futuristic nonsense in an honest English country house, which has been good enough for his father and his grandfather and his great-grandfather, and—and all the rest of them. So there's a sort of strained feeling between Olivia and George just now, and if Olivia were to—sort of recommend you, well, it wouldn't do you much good.

BRIAN (*looking at her*). I see. Of course I know what *you* want, Dinah.

DINAH. What do I want?

BRIAN. You want a secret engagement, and notes left under door-mats, and meetings by the withered thorn, when all the household is asleep. *I* know you.

DINAH. Oh, but it is such fun! I love meeting people by withered thorns.

BRIAN. Well, I'm not going to have it.

DINAH (*childishly*). Oh, George! Look at us being husbandy!

BRIAN. You babe! I adore you. (*He kisses her and holds her away from him and looks at her*) You know, you're rather throwing yourself away on me. Do you mind?

DINAH. Not a bit.

BRIAN. We shall never be rich, but we shall have lots of fun, and meet interesting people, and feel that we're doing something worth doing, and not getting paid nearly enough for it, and we can curse the Academy together and the British Public, and—oh, it's an exciting life.

DINAH (*seeing it*). I shall love it.

BRIAN. I'll make you love it. You shan't be sorry, Dinah.

DINAH. You shan't be sorry either, Brian.

BRIAN (*looking at her lovingly*). Oh, I know I shan't. . . . What will Olivia think about it? Will she be surprised?

DINAH. She's never surprised. She always seems to have thought of things about a week before they happen. George just begins to get hold of them about a week *after* they've happened. (*Considering him*) After all, there's no reason why George *shouldn't* like you, darling.

BRIAN. I'm not his sort, you know.

DINAH. You're more Olivia's sort. Well, we'll tell Olivia this morning.

OLIVIA (*coming in*). And what are you going to tell Olivia this morning? (*She looks at them with a smile*) Oh, well, I think I can guess.

Shall we describe OLIVIA? *But you will know all about her before the day is over.*

DINAH (*jumping up*). Olivia, darling!

BRIAN (*following*). Say you understand, Mrs. Marden.

OLIVIA. Mrs. Marden, I am afraid, is a very dense person, Brian, but I think if you asked Olivia if she understood——

BRIAN. Bless you, Olivia. I knew you'd be on our side.

DINAH. Of course she would.

OLIVIA. I don't know if it's usual to kiss an aunt-in-law, Brian, but Dinah is such a very special sort of niece that——(*she inclines her cheek and* BRIAN *kisses it*).

DINAH. I say, you *are* in luck to-day, Brian.

OLIVIA (*going over to her chair by the work-table and getting to business with the curtains*). And how many people have been told the good news?

BRIAN. Nobody yet.

DINAH. Except Mr. Pim.

BRIAN. Oh, does *he*——

OLIVIA. Who's Mr. Pim?

DINAH. Oh, he just happened—I say, are those *the* curtains? Then you're going to have them after all?

OLIVIA (*with an air of surprise*). After all what? But I decided on them long ago. (*To* BRIAN) You haven't told George yet?

BRIAN. I began to, you know, but I never got any farther than "Er—there's just—er——"

DINAH. George *would* talk about pigs all the time.

OLIVIA. Well, I suppose you want me to help you.

DINAH. Do, darling.

BRIAN. It would be awfully decent of you. Of course, I'm not quite his sort really——

DINAH. You're *my* sort.

BRIAN. But I don't think he objects to me, and——

(GEORGE *comes in, a typical, narrow-minded, honest country gentleman of forty odd.*)

GEORGE (*at the windows*). What's all this about a Mr. Pim? (*He kicks some of the mud off his boots*) Who is he? Where is he? I had most important business with Lumsden, and the girl comes down and cackles about a Mr. Pim, or Ping, or something. Where did I put his card? (*Bringing it out*) Carraway Pim. Never heard of him in my life.

DINAH. He said he had a letter of introduction, Uncle George.

GEORGE. Oh, *you* saw him, did you? Yes, that reminds me, there *was* a letter—(*he brings it out and reads it*).

DINAH. He had to send a telegram. He's coming back.

ACT I] MR. PIM PASSES BY 83

OLIVIA. Pass me those scissors, Brian.

BRIAN. These? (*He picks them up and comes close to her.*)

OLIVIA. Thank you. (*She indicates* GEORGE's *back. "Now?" says* BRIAN *with his eyebrows. She nods.*)

GEORGE (*reading*). Ah well, a friend of Brymer's. Glad to oblige him. Yes, I know the man he wants. Coming back, you say, Dinah? Then I'll be going back. Send him down to the farm, Olivia, when he comes. (*To* BRIAN) Hallo, what happened to *you*?

OLIVIA. Don't go, George, there's something we want to talk about.

GEORGE. Hallo, what's this?

BRIAN (*to* OLIVIA). Shall I——?

OLIVIA. Yes.

BRIAN (*stepping out*). I've been wanting to tell you all this morning, sir, only I didn't seem to have an opportunity of getting it out.

GEORGE. Well, what is it?

BRIAN. I want to marry Dinah, sir.

GEORGE. You want to marry Dinah? God bless my soul!

DINAH (*rushing to him and putting her cheek against his coat*). Oh, do say you like the idea, Uncle George.

GEORGE. Like the idea! Have you heard of this nonsense, Olivia?

OLIVIA. They've just this moment told me, George. I think they would be happy together.

GEORGE (*to* BRIAN). And what do you propose to be happy together *on*?

BRIAN. Well, of course, it doesn't amount to much at present, but we shan't starve.

DINAH. Brian got fifty pounds for a picture last March!

GEORGE (*a little upset by this*). Oh! (*Recovering gamely*) And how many pictures have you sold since?

BRIAN. Well, none, but——

GEORGE. None! And I don't wonder. Who the devil is going to buy pictures with triangular clouds and square sheep? And they call that Art nowadays! Good God, man, (*waving him to the windows*) go outside and *look* at the clouds!

OLIVIA. If he draws round clouds in future, George, will you let him marry Dinah?

GEORGE. What—what? Yes, of course, you *would* be on his side—all this Futuristic nonsense. I'm just taking these clouds as an example. I suppose I can see as well as any man in the county, and I say that clouds *aren't* triangular.

BRIAN. After all, sir, at my age one is naturally experimenting, and trying to find one's (*with a laugh*)— well, it sounds priggish, but one's medium of expression. I shall find out what I want to do directly, but I think I shall always be able to earn enough to live on. Well, I have for the last three years.

GEORGE. I see, and now you want to experiment with a wife, and you propose to start experimenting with *my* niece?

BRIAN (*with a shrug*). Well, of course, if you——

OLIVIA. You could help the experiment, darling, by giving Dinah a good allowance until she's twenty-one.

GEORGE. Help the experiment! I don't *want* to help the experiment.

OLIVIA (*apologetically*). Oh, I thought you did.

GEORGE. You will talk as if I was made of money. What with taxes always going up and rents always going down, it's as much as we can do to rub along as we are, without making allowances to everybody who thinks she wants to get married. (*To* BRIAN) And that's thanks to you, my friend.

BRIAN (*surprised*). To me?

OLIVIA. You never told me, darling. What's Brian been doing?

DINAH (*indignantly*). He hasn't been doing anything.

GEORGE. He's one of your Socialists who go turning the country upside down.

OLIVIA. But even Socialists must get married sometimes.

GEORGE. I don't see any necessity.

OLIVIA. But you'd have nobody to damn after dinner, darling, if they all died out.

BRIAN. Really, sir, I don't see what my politics and my art have got to do with it. I'm perfectly ready not to talk about either when I'm in your house, and as Dinah doesn't seem to object to them——

DINAH. I should think she doesn't.

GEORGE. Oh, you can get round the women, I daresay.

BRIAN. Well, it's Dinah I want to marry and live with. So what it really comes to is that you don't think I can support a wife.

GEORGE. Well, if you're going to do it by selling pictures, I don't think you can.

BRIAN. All right, tell me how much you want me to earn in a year, and I'll earn it.

GEORGE (*hedging*). It isn't merely a question of money. I just mention that as one thing—one of the important things. In addition to that, I think you are both too young to marry. I don't think you know your own minds, and I am not at all persuaded that, with what I venture to call your outrageous tastes, you and my niece will live happily together. Just because she thinks she loves you, Dinah may persuade herself now that she agrees with all you say and do, but she has been properly brought up in an honest English country household, and—er—she—well, in short, I cannot at all approve of any engagement between you. (*Getting up*) Olivia, if this Mr.—er—Pim comes, I shall be down at the farm. You might send him along to me.

(*He walks towards the windows.*)

BRIAN (*indignantly*). Is there any reason why I shouldn't marry a girl who has been properly brought up?

GEORGE. I think you know my views, Strange.

OLIVIA. George, wait a moment, dear. We can't quite leave it like this.

GEORGE. I have said all I want to say on the subject.

OLIVIA. Yes, darling, but I haven't begun to say all that *I* want to say on the subject.

GEORGE. Of course, if you have anything to say, Olivia, I will listen to it; but I don't know that this is quite the time, or that you have chosen—(*looking darkly at the curtains*)—quite the occupation likely to—er—endear your views to me.

DINAH (*mutinously*). I may as well tell you, Uncle George, that *I* have got a good deal to say, too.

OLIVIA. I can guess what you are going to say, Dinah, and I think you had better keep it for the moment.

DINAH (*meekly*). Yes, Aunt Olivia.

OLIVIA. Brian, you might take her outside for a walk. I expect you have plenty to talk about.

GEORGE. Now mind, Strange, no love-making. I put you on your honour about that.

BRIAN. I'll do my best to avoid it, sir.

DINAH (*cheekily*). May I take his arm if we go up a hill?

OLIVIA. I'm sure you'll know how to behave—both of you.

BRIAN. Come on, then, Dinah.

DINAH. Righto.

GEORGE (*as they go*). And if you do see any clouds, Strange, take a good look at them. (*He chuckles to himself*) Triangular clouds—I never heard of such nonsense. (*He goes back to his chair at the writing-table*) Futuristic rubbish. . . . Well, Olivia?

OLIVIA. Well, George?

GEORGE. What are you doing?

OLIVIA. Making curtains, George. Won't they be rather sweet? Oh, but I forgot—you don't like them.

GEORGE. I don't like them, and what is more, I don't mean to have them in my house. As I told you yesterday, this is the house of a simple country gentleman, and I don't want any of these new-fangled ideas in it.

OLIVIA. Is marrying for love a new-fangled idea?

GEORGE. We'll come to that directly. None of you women can keep to the point. What I am saying now is that the house of my fathers and forefathers is good enough for me.

OLIVIA. Do you know, George, I can hear one of your ancestors saying that to his wife in their smelly old cave, when the new-fangled idea of building houses was first suggested. "The Cave of my Fathers is——"

GEORGE. That's ridiculous. Naturally we must have progress. But that's just the point. (*Indicating the curtains*) I don't call this sort of thing progress. It's —ah—retrogression.

OLIVIA. Well, anyhow, it's pretty.

GEORGE. There I disagree with you. And I must say once more that I will not have them hanging in my house.

OLIVIA. Very well, George. (*But she goes on working.*)

GEORGE. That being so, I don't see the necessity of going on with them.

OLIVIA. Well, I must do something with them now

I've got the material. I thought perhaps I could sell them when they're finished—as we're so poor.

GEORGE. What do you mean—so poor?

OLIVIA. Well, you said just now that you couldn't give Dinah an allowance because rents had gone down.

GEORGE (*annoyed*). Confound it, Olivia! Keep to the point! We'll talk about Dinah's affairs directly. We're discussing our own affairs at the moment.

OLIVIA. But what is there to discuss?

GEORGE. Those ridiculous things.

OLIVIA. But we've finished that. You've said you wouldn't have them hanging in your house, and I've said, "Very well, George." Now we can go on to Dinah and Brian.

GEORGE (*shouting*). But put these beastly things away.

OLIVIA (*rising and gathering up the curtains*). Very well, George. (*She puts them away, slowly, gracefully. There is an uncomfortable silence. Evidently somebody ought to apologise.*)

GEORGE (*realising that he is the one*). Er—look here, Olivia, old girl, you've been a jolly good wife to me, and we don't often have rows, and if I've been rude to you about this—lost my temper a bit perhaps, what?—I'll say I'm sorry. May I have a kiss?

OLIVIA (*holding up her face*). George, darling! (*He kisses her.*) Do you love me?

GEORGE. You know I do, old girl.

OLIVIA. As much as Brian loves Dinah?

GEORGE (*stiffly*). I've said all I want to say about that. (*He goes away from her.*)

OLIVIA. Oh, but there must be lots you want to say —and perhaps don't like to. Do tell me, darling.

GEORGE. What it comes to is this. I consider that Dinah is too young to choose a husband for herself, and that Strange isn't the husband I should choose for her.

OLIVIA. You were calling him Brian yesterday.

GEORGE. Yesterday I regarded him as a boy, now he wants me to look upon him as a man.

OLIVIA. He's twenty-four.

GEORGE. And Dinah's nineteen. Ridiculous!

OLIVIA. If he'd been a Conservative, and thought that clouds were round, I suppose he'd have seemed older, somehow.

GEORGE. That's a different point altogether. That has nothing to do with his age.

OLIVIA (*innocently*). Oh, I thought it had.

GEORGE. What I am objecting to is these ridiculously early marriages before either party knows its own mind, much less the mind of the other party. Such marriages invariably lead to unhappiness.

OLIVIA. Of course, *my* marriage wasn't a happy one.

GEORGE. As you know, Olivia, I dislike speaking about your first marriage at all, and I had no intention of bringing it up now, but since you mention it—well, that is a case in point.

OLIVIA (*looking back at it*). When I was eighteen, I was in love. Or perhaps I only thought I was, and I don't know if I should have been happy or not if I had married him. But my father made me marry a man called Jacob Telworthy; and when things were too hot for him in England—"too hot for him"—I think that was the expression we used in those days—then we went to Australia, and I left him there, and the only happy moment I had in all my married life was on the morning when I saw in the papers that he was dead.

GEORGE (*very uncomfortable*). Yes, yes, my dear, I know. You must have had a terrible time. I can hardly bear to think about it. My only hope is that I have made up to you for it in some degree. But I don't see what bearing it has upon Dinah's case.

OLIVIA. Oh, none, except that *my* father *liked* Jacob's political opinions and his views on art. I expect that that was why he chose him for me.

GEORGE. You seem to think that I wish to choose a husband for Dinah. I don't at all. Let her choose whom she likes as long as he can support her and there's a chance of their being happy together. Now, with regard to this fellow——

OLIVIA. You mean Brian?

GEORGE. He's got no money, and he's been brought up in quite a different way from Dinah. Dinah may be prepared to believe that—er—all cows are blue, and that—er—waves are square, but she won't go on believing it for ever.

OLIVIA. Neither will Brian.

GEORGE. Well, that's what I keep telling him, only he won't see it. Just as I keep telling you about those ridiculous curtains. It seems to me that I am the only person in the house with any eyesight left.

OLIVIA. Perhaps you are, darling; but you must let us find out our own mistakes for ourselves. At any rate, Brian is a gentleman; he loves Dinah, Dinah loves him; he's earning enough to support himself, and you are earning enough to support Dinah. I think it's worth risking, George.

GEORGE (*stiffly*). I can only say the whole question demands much more anxious thought than you seem to have given it. You say that he is a gentleman. He knows how to behave, I admit; but if his morals are as topsy-turvy as his tastes and—er—politics, as I've no doubt they are, then—er—— In short, I do *not* approve of Brian Strange as a husband for my niece and ward.

OLIVIA (*looking at him thoughtfully*). You *are* a curious mixture, George. You were so very unconventional when you married me, and you're so very conventional when Brian wants to marry Dinah. . . . George Marden to marry the widow of a convict!

GEORGE. Convict! What do you mean?

OLIVIA. Jacob Telworthy, convict—I forget his number—surely I told you all this, dear, when we got engaged?

GEORGE. Never!

OLIVIA. I told you how he carelessly put the wrong signature to a cheque for a thousand pounds in England; how he made a little mistake about two or three companies he'd promoted in Australia; and how——

GEORGE. Yes, yes, but you never told me he was *convicted*!

OLIVIA. What difference does it make?

GEORGE. My dear Olivia, if you can't see that—a convict!

OLIVIA. So, you see, we needn't be too particular about our niece, need we?

GEORGE. I think we had better leave your first husband out of the conversation altogether. I never wished to refer to him; I never wish to hear about him again. I certainly had not realised that he was actually—er—*convicted* for his—er——

OLIVIA. Mistakes.

GEORGE. Well, we needn't go into that. As for this other matter, I don't for a moment take it seriously. Dinah is an exceptionally pretty girl, and young Strange is a good-looking boy. If they are attracted to each other, it is a mere outward attraction which I am convinced will not lead to any lasting happiness. That must be regarded as my last word in the matter, Olivia. If this Mr.—er—what was his name, comes, I shall be down at the farm.

[*He goes out by the door.*

(*Left alone,* OLIVIA *brings out her curtains again, and gets calmly to work upon them.*)

(DINAH *and* BRIAN *come in by the windows.*)

DINAH. Finished?

OLIVIA. Oh no, I've got all these rings to put on.

DINAH. I meant talking to George.

BRIAN. We walked about outside——

DINAH. Until we heard him *not* talking to you any more——

BRIAN. And we didn't kiss each other once.

DINAH. Brian was very George-like. He wouldn't even let me tickle the back of his neck. (*She goes up suddenly to* OLIVIA *and kneels by her and kisses her*) Darling, being George-like is a very nice thing to be—I mean a nice thing for other people to be—I mean—oh, you know what I mean. But say that he's going to be decent about it.

OLIVIA. Of course he is, Dinah.

BRIAN. You mean he'll let me come here as—as——

DINAH. As my young man?

OLIVIA. Oh, I think so.

DINAH. Olivia, you're a wonder. Have you really talked him round?

OLIVIA. I haven't said anything yet. But I daresay I shall think of something.

DINAH (*disappointedly*). Oh!

BRIAN (*making the best of it*). After all, Dinah, I'm going back to London to-morrow——

OLIVIA. You can be good for one more day, Dinah, and then when Brian isn't here, we'll see what we can do.

DINAH. Yes, but I didn't want him to go back to-morrow.

BRIAN (*sternly*). Must. Hard work before me. Earn thousands a year. Paint the Mayor and Corporation of Pudsey, life-size, including chains of office; paint slice of haddock on plate. Copy Landseer for old gentleman in Bayswater. Design antimacassar for middle-aged sofa in Streatham. Earn a living for you, Dinah.

DINAH (*giggling*). Oh, Brian, you're heavenly. What fun we shall have when we're married.

BRIAN (*stiffly*). Sir Brian Strange, R.A., if you please, Miss Marden. Sir Brian Strange, R.A., writes: "Your Sanogene has proved a most excellent tonic. After completing the third acre of my Academy picture 'The Mayor and Corporation of Pudsey' I was completely exhausted, but one bottle of Sanogene revived me, and I finished the remaining seven acres at a single sitting."

OLIVIA (*looking about her*). Brian, find my scissors for me.

BRIAN. Scissors. (*Looking for them*) Sir Brian Strange, R.A., looks for scissors. (*Finding them*) Aha! Once more we must record an unqualified success for the eminent Academician. Your scissors.

OLIVIA. Thank you so much.

DINAH. Come on, Brian, let's go out. I feel open-airy.

OLIVIA. Don't be late for lunch, there's good people. Lady Marden is coming.

DINAH. Aunt Juli-ah! Help! (*She faints in* BRIAN's *arms*) That means a clean pinafore. Brian, you'll jolly well have to brush your hair.

BRIAN (*feeling it*). I suppose there's no time now to go up to London and get it cut?

Enter ANNE, *followed by* PIM.

ANNE. Mr. Pim!

DINAH (*delighted*). Hullo, Mr. Pim! Here we are again! You can't get rid of us so easily, you see.

PIM. I—er—dear Miss Marden——

OLIVIA. How do you do, Mr. Pim? I can't get up, but

do come and sit down. My husband will be here in a minute. Anne, send somebody down to the farm——

ANNE. I think I heard the Master in the library, madam.

OLIVIA. Oh, will you tell him then?

ANNE. Yes, madam.

[ANNE *goes out.*

OLIVIA. You'll stay to lunch, of course, Mr. Pim?

DINAH. Oh, do!

PIM. It's very kind of you, Mrs. Marden, but——

DINAH. Oh, you simply must, Mr. Pim. You haven't told us half enough about yourself yet. I want to hear all about your early life.

OLIVIA. Dinah!

PIM. Oh, we are almost, I might say, old friends, Mrs. Marden.

DINAH. Of course we are. He knows Brian, too. There's more in Mr. Pim than you think. You *will* stay to lunch, won't you?

PIM. It's very kind of you to ask me, Mrs. Marden, but I am lunching with the Trevors.

OLIVIA. Oh, well, you must come to lunch another day.

DINAH. The reason why we like Mr. Pim so much is that he was the first person to congratulate us. We feel that he is going to have a great influence on our lives.

PIM (*to* OLIVIA). I, so to speak, stumbled on the engagement this morning and—er——

OLIVIA. I see. Children, you must go and tidy yourselves up. Run along.

BRIAN. Sir Brian and Lady Strange never run; they walk. (*Offering his arm*) Madam!

DINAH (*taking it*). Au revoir, Mr. Pim. (*Dramatically*) We —— shall —— meet —— *again*!

PIM (*chuckling*). Good morning, Miss Dinah.

ACT I] MR. PIM PASSES BY 95

BRIAN. Good morning.

[*He and* DINAH *go out.*

OLIVIA. You must forgive them, Mr. Pim. They're such children. And naturally they're rather excited just now.

PIM. Oh, not at all, Mrs. Marden.

OLIVIA. Of course you won't say anything about their engagement. We only heard about it five minutes ago, and nothing has been settled yet.

PIM. Of course, of course!

Enter GEORGE.

GEORGE. Ah, Mr. Pim, we meet at last. Sorry to have kept you waiting before.

PIM. The apology should come from me, Mr. Marden, for having—er——

GEORGE. Not at all. Very glad to meet you now. Any friend of Brymer's. You want a letter to this man Fanshawe?

OLIVIA. Shall I be in your way at all?

PIM. Oh, no, no, please don't.

GEORGE. It's only just a question of a letter. (*Going to his desk*) Fanshawe will put you in the way of seeing all that you want to see. He's a very old friend of mine. (*Taking a sheet of notepaper*) You'll stay to lunch, of course?

PIM. I'm afraid I am lunching with the Trevors——

GEORGE. Oh, well, they'll look after you all right. Good chap, Trevor.

PIM (*to* OLIVIA). You see, Mrs. Marden, I have only recently arrived from Australia after travelling about the world for some years, and I'm rather out of touch with my—er—fellow-workers in London.

OLIVIA. Oh yes. You've been in Australia, Mr. Pim?

GEORGE (*disliking Australia*). I shan't be a moment, Mr. Pim. (*He frowns at* OLIVIA.)

PIM. Oh, that's all right, thank you. (*To* OLIVIA) Oh yes, I have been in Australia more than once in the last few years.

OLIVIA. Really? I used to live at Sydney many years ago. Do you know Sydney at all?

GEORGE (*detesting Sydney*). H'r'm! Perhaps I'd better mention that you are a friend of the Trevors?

PIM. Thank you, thank you. (*To* OLIVIA) Indeed yes, I spent several months in Sydney.

OLIVIA. How curious. I wonder if we have any friends in common there.

GEORGE (*hastily*). Extremely unlikely, I should think. Sydney is a very big place.

PIM. True, but the world is a very small place, Mr. Marden. I had a remarkable instance of that, coming over on the boat this last time.

GEORGE. Ah! (*Feeling that the conversation is now safe, he resumes his letter.*)

PIM. Yes. There was a man I used to employ in Sydney some years ago, a bad fellow, I'm afraid, Mrs. Marden, who had been in prison for some kind of fraudulent company-promoting and had taken to drink and—and so on.

OLIVIA. Yes, yes, I understand.

PIM. Drinking himself to death I should have said. I gave him at the most another year to live. Yet to my amazement the first person I saw as I stepped on board the boat that brought me to England last week was this fellow. There was no mistaking him. I spoke to him, in fact; we recognised each other.

OLIVIA. Really?

PIM. He was travelling steerage; we didn't meet again on board, and as it happened at Marseilles, this poor fellow—er—now what *was* his name? A very unusual one. Began with a—a T, I think.

OLIVIA (*with suppressed feeling*). Yes, Mr. Pim, yes? (*She puts out a hand to* GEORGE.)

GEORGE (*in an undertone*). Nonsense, dear!

PIM (*triumphantly*). I've got it! Telworthy!

OLIVIA. Telworthy!

GEORGE. Good God!

PIM (*a little surprised at the success of his story*). An unusual name, is it not? Not a name you could forget when once you had heard it.

OLIVIA (*with feeling*). No, it is not a name you could forget when once you had heard it.

GEORGE (*hastily coming over to* PIM). Quite so, Mr. Pim, a most remarkable name, a most odd story altogether. Well, well, here's your letter, and if you're sure you won't stay to lunch——

PIM. I'm afraid not, thank you. You see, I——

GEORGE. The Trevors, yes. I'll just see you on your way—— (*To* OLIVIA) Er—my dear——

OLIVIA (*holding out her hand, but not looking at him*). Good-bye, Mr. Pim.

PIM. Good-bye, good-bye!

GEORGE (*leading the way through the windows*). This way, this way. Quicker for you.

PIM. Thank you, thank you.

[GEORGE *hurries* MR. PIM *out*.
(OLIVIA *sits there and looks into the past. Now and then she shudders.*)

[GEORGE *comes back*.

GEORGE. Good God! Telworthy! Is it possible?

(*Before* OLIVIA *can answer*, LADY MARDEN *is announced. They pull themselves together and greet her.*)

ACT II

Lunch is over and coffee has been served on the terrace. Conversation drags on, to the satisfaction of LADY MARDEN, *but of nobody else.* GEORGE *and* OLIVIA *want to be alone; so do* BRIAN *and* DINAH. *At last* BRIAN *murmurs something about a cigarette-case; and, catching* DINAH'S *eye, comes into the house. He leans against the sofa and waits for* DINAH.

DINAH (*loudly as she comes in*). Have you found it?

BRIAN. Found what?

DINAH (*in her ordinary voice*). That was just for *their* benefit. I said I'd help you find it. It *is* your cigarette-case we're looking for, isn't it?

BRIAN (*taking it out*). Yes. Have one?

DINAH. No, thank you, darling. Aunt Juli-ah still thinks it's unladylike. . . . Have you ever seen her beagling?

BRIAN. No. Is that very ladylike?

DINAH. Very. . . . I say, what has happened, do you think?

BRIAN. Everything. I love you, and you love me.

DINAH. Silly! I meant between George and Olivia. Didn't you notice them at lunch?

BRIAN. I noticed that you seemed to be doing most of the talking. But then I've noticed that before sometimes. Do you think Olivia and your uncle have quarrelled because of *us*?

ACT II] MR. PIM PASSES BY 99

DINAH. Of course not. George may *think* he has quarrelled, but I'm quite sure Olivia hasn't. No, I believe Mr. Pim's at the bottom of it. He's brought some terribly sad news about George's investments. The old home will have to be sold up.

BRIAN. Good. Then your uncle won't mind your marrying me.

DINAH. Yes, darling, but you must be more dramatic about it than that. "George," you must say, with tears in your eyes, "I cannot pay off the whole of the mortgage for you. I have only two and ninepence; but at least let me take your niece off your hands." Then George will thump you on the back and say gruffly, "You're a good fellow, Brian, a damn good fellow," and he'll blow his nose very loudly, and say, "Confound this cigar, it won't draw properly." (*She gives us a rough impression of* GEORGE *doing it.*)

BRIAN. Dinah, you're a heavenly idiot. And you've simply got to marry me, uncles or no uncles.

DINAH. It will have to be "uncles," I'm afraid, because, you see, I'm his ward, and I can get sent to Chancery or Coventry or somewhere beastly, if I marry without his consent. Haven't *you* got anybody who objects to your marrying *me*?

BRIAN. Nobody, thank Heaven.

DINAH. Well, that's rather disappointing of you. I saw myself fascinating your aged father at the same time that you were fascinating George. I should have done it much better than you. As a George-fascinator you aren't very successful, sweetheart.

BRIAN. What am I like as a Dinah-fascinator?

DINAH. Plus six, darling.

BRIAN. Then I'll stick to that and leave George to Olivia.

DINAH. I expect she'll manage him all right. I have

great faith in Olivia. But you'll marry me, anyhow, won't you, Brian?

BRIAN. I will.

DINAH. Even if we have to wait till I'm twenty-one?

BRIAN. Even if we have to wait till you're fifty-one.

DINAH (*holding out her hands to him*). Darling!

BRIAN (*uneasily*). I say, don't do that.

DINAH. Why not?

BRIAN. Well, I promised I wouldn't kiss you.

DINAH. Oh! . . . Well, you might just *send* me a kiss. You can look the other way as if you didn't know I was here.

BRIAN. Like this?

> (*He looks the other way, kisses the tips of his fingers, and flicks it carelessly in her direction.*)

DINAH. That was a lovely one. Now here's one coming for you.

> (*He catches it gracefully and conveys it to his mouth.*)

BRIAN (*with a low bow*). Madam, I thank you.

DINAH (*curtseying*). Your servant, Mr. Strange.

OLIVIA (*from outside*). Dinah!

DINAH (*jumping up*). Hullo!

> (OLIVIA *comes in through the windows, followed by* GEORGE *and* LADY MARDEN, *the latter a vigorous young woman of sixty odd, who always looks as if she were beagling.*)

OLIVIA. Aunt Julia wants to see the pigs, dear. I wish you'd take her down. I'm rather tired, and your uncle has some business to attend to.

LADY MARDEN. I've always said that you don't take enough exercise, Olivia. Look at me—sixty-five and proud of it.

OLIVIA. Yes, Aunt Julia, you're wonderful.

ACT II] **MR. PIM PASSES BY** 101

DINAH. How old would Olivia be if she took exercise?

GEORGE. Don't stand about asking silly questions, Dinah. Your aunt hasn't much time.

BRIAN. May I come, too, Lady Marden?

LADY MARDEN. Well, a little exercise wouldn't do *you* any harm, Mr. Strange. You're an artist, ain't you?

BRIAN. Well, I try to paint.

DINAH. He sold a picture last March for——

GEORGE. Yes, yes, never mind that now.

LADY MARDEN. Unhealthy life. Well, come along.

[*She strides out, followed by* DINAH *and* BRIAN.
(GEORGE *sits down at his desk with his head in his hand, and stabs the blotting-paper with a pen.* OLIVIA *takes the curtains with her to the sofa and begins to work on them.*)

GEORGE (*looking up and seeing them*). Really, Olivia, we've got something more important, more vital to us than curtains, to discuss, now that we *are* alone at last.

OLIVIA. I wasn't going to discuss them, dear.

GEORGE. I'm always glad to see Aunt Julia in my house, but I wish she hadn't chosen this day of all days to come to lunch.

OLIVIA. It wasn't Aunt Julia's fault. It was really Mr. Pim who chose the wrong day.

GEORGE (*fiercely*). Good Heavens, is it true?

OLIVIA. About Jacob Telworthy?

GEORGE. You told me he was dead. You always said that he was dead. You—you——

OLIVIA. Well, I always thought that he was dead. He was as dead as anybody could be. All the papers said he was dead.

GEORGE (*scornfully*). The papers!

OLIVIA (*as if this would settle it for* GEORGE). The *Times* said he was dead. There was a paragraph about him. Apparently even his death was fraudulent.

GEORGE. Yes, yes, I'm not blaming you, Olivia, but what are we going to do, that's the question, what are we going to do? My God, it's horrible! You've never been married to me at all! You don't seem to understand.

OLIVIA. It is a little difficult to realise. You see, it doesn't seem to have made any difference to our happiness.

GEORGE. No, that's what's so terrible. I mean—well, of course, we were quite innocent in the matter. But, at the same time, nothing can get over the fact that we —we had no right to—to be happy.

OLIVIA. Would you rather we had been miserable?

GEORGE. You're Telworthy's wife, that's what you don't seem to understand. You're Telworthy's wife. You —er—forgive me, Olivia, but it's the horrible truth— you committed bigamy when you married me. (*In horror*) Bigamy!

OLIVIA. It is an ugly word, isn't it?

GEORGE. Yes, but don't you understand—— (*He jumps up and comes over to her*) Look here, Olivia, old girl, the whole thing is nonsense, eh? It isn't your husband, it's some other Telworthy that this fellow met. That's right, isn't it? Some other shady swindler who turned up on the boat, eh? This sort of thing doesn't happen to people like *us*—committing bigamy and all that. Some other fellow.

OLIVIA (*shaking her head*). I knew all the shady swindlers in Sydney, George. . . . They came to dinner. . . . There were no others called Telworthy.

(GEORGE *goes back despondently to his seat.*)

GEORGE. Well, what are we going to do?

OLIVIA. You sent Mr. Pim away so quickly. He might have told us things. Telworthy's plans. Where he is now. You hurried him away so quickly.

GEORGE. I've sent a note round to ask him to come back. My one idea at the moment was to get him out of the house—to hush things up.

OLIVIA. You can't hush up two husbands.

GEORGE (*in despair*). You can't. Everybody will know. Everybody!

OLIVIA. The children, Aunt Julia, they may as well know now as later. Mr. Pim must, of course.

GEORGE. I do not propose to discuss my private affairs with Mr. Pim——

OLIVIA. But he's mixed himself up in them rather, hasn't he, and if you're going to ask him questions——

GEORGE. I only propose to ask him one question. I shall ask him if he is absolutely certain of the man's name. I can do that quite easily without letting him know the reason for my inquiry.

OLIVIA. You couldn't make a mistake about a name like Telworthy. But he might tell us something about Telworthy's plans. Perhaps he's going back to Australia at once. Perhaps he thinks I'm dead, too. Perhaps—oh, there are so many things I want to know.

GEORGE. Yes, yes, dear. It would be interesting to—that is, one naturally wants to know these things, but of course it doesn't make any real difference.

OLIVIA (*surprised*). No difference?

GEORGE. Well, that is to say, you're as much his wife if he's in Australia as you are if he's in England.

OLIVIA. I am not his wife at all.

GEORGE. But, Olivia, surely you understand the position——

OLIVIA (*shaking her head*). Jacob Telworthy may be alive, but I am not his wife. I ceased to be his wife when I became yours.

GEORGE. You never *were* my wife. That is the terrible part of it. Our union—you make me say it, Olivia—

has been unhallowed by the Church. Unhallowed even by the Law. Legally, we have been living in—living in—well, the point is, how does the Law stand? I imagine that Telworthy could get a—a divorce. . . . Oh, it seems impossible that things like this can be happening to *us*.

OLIVIA (*joyfully*). A divorce?

GEORGE. I—I imagine so.

OLIVIA. But then we could *really* get married, and we shouldn't be living in—living in—whatever we were living in before.

GEORGE. I can't understand you, Olivia. You talk about it so calmly, as if there was nothing blameworthy in being divorced, as if there was nothing unusual in my marrying a divorced woman, as if there was nothing wrong in our having lived together for years without having been married.

OLIVIA. What seems wrong to me is that I lived for five years with a bad man whom I hated. What seems right to me is that I lived for five years with a good man whom I love.

GEORGE. Yes, yes, my dear, I know. But right and wrong don't settle themselves as easily as that. We've been living together when you were Telworthy's wife. That's *wrong*.

OLIVIA. Do you mean wicked?

GEORGE. Well, no doubt the Court would consider that we acted in perfect innocence——

OLIVIA. What Court?

GEORGE. These things have to be done legally, of course. I believe the proper method is a nullity suit, declaring our marriage null and—er—void. It would, so to speak, wipe out these years of—er——

OLIVIA. Wickedness?

GEORGE. Of irregular union, and—er—then——

OLIVIA. Then I could go back to Jacob. . . . Do you really mean that, George?

GEORGE (*uneasily*). Well, dear, you see—that's how things are—one can't get away from—er——

OLIVIA. What you feel is that Telworthy has the greater claim? You are prepared to—make way for him?

GEORGE. Both the Church and the Law would say that I had no claim at all, I'm afraid. I—I suppose I haven't.

OLIVIA. I see. (*She looks at him curiously*) Thank you for making it so clear, George.

GEORGE. Of course, whether or not you go back to—er—Telworthy is another matter altogether. That would naturally be for you to decide.

OLIVIA (*cheerfully*). For me and Jacko to decide.

GEORGE. Er—Jacko?

OLIVIA. I used to call my first husband—I mean my only husband—Jacko. I didn't like the name of Jacob, and Jacko seemed to suit him somehow. . . . He had very long arms. Dear Jacko.

GEORGE (*annoyed*). You don't seem to realise that this is not a joke, Olivia.

OLIVIA (*a trifle hysterically*). It may not be a joke, but it *is* funny, isn't it?

GEORGE. I must say I don't see anything funny in a tragedy that has wrecked two lives.

OLIVIA. Two? Oh, but Jacko's life isn't wrecked. It has just been miraculously restored to him. And a wife, too. There's nothing tragic for Jacko in it.

GEORGE (*stiffly*). I was referring to *our* two lives—yours and mine.

OLIVIA. Yours, George? Your life isn't wrecked. The Court will absolve you of all blame; your friends will sympathise with you, and tell you that I was a designing woman who deliberately took you in; your Aunt Julia——

GEORGE (*overwrought*). Stop it! What do you mean? Have you no heart? Do you think I *want* to lose you, Olivia? Do you think I *want* my home broken up like this? Haven't you been happy with me these last five years?

OLIVIA. Very happy.

GEORGE. Well then, how can you talk like that?

OLIVIA (*pathetically*). But you want to send me away.

GEORGE. There you go again. I don't *want* to. I have hardly had time to realise just what it will mean to me when you go. The fact is I simply daren't realise it. I daren't think about it.

OLIVIA (*earnestly*). Try thinking about it, George.

GEORGE. And you talk as if I *wanted* to send you away!

OLIVIA. Try thinking about it, George.

GEORGE. You don't seem to understand that I'm not *sending* you away. You simply aren't mine to keep.

OLIVIA. Whose am I?

GEORGE. Your husband's. Telworthy's.

OLIVIA (*gently*). If I belong to anybody but myself, I think I belong to you.

GEORGE. Not in the eyes of the Law. Not in the eyes of the Church. Not even in the eyes of—er——

OLIVIA. The County?

GEORGE (*annoyed*). I was about to say "Heaven."

OLIVIA (*unimpressed*). Oh!

GEORGE. That this should happen to *us*!

(*He gets up and walks about the room, wondering when he will wake up from this impossible dream.* OLIVIA *works in silence. Then she stands up and shakes out her curtains.*)

OLIVIA (*looking at them*). I do hope Jacko will like these.

GEORGE. What! You—— (*Going up to her*) Olivia, Olivia, have you no heart?

OLIVIA. Ought you to talk like that to another man's wife?

GEORGE. Confound it, is this just a joke to you?

OLIVIA. You must forgive me, George; I am a little over-excited—at the thought of returning to Jacob, I suppose.

GEORGE. Do you *want* to return to him?

OLIVIA. One wants to do what is right. In the eyes of—er—Heaven.

GEORGE. Seeing what sort of man he is, I have no doubt that you could get a separation, supposing that he didn't—er—divorce you. I don't know *what* is best. I must consult my solicitor. The whole position has been sprung on us, and—(*miserably*) I don't know, I don't know. I can't take it all in.

OLIVIA. Wouldn't you like to consult your Aunt Julia too? She could tell you what the County—I mean what Heaven really thought about it.

GEORGE. Yes, yes. Aunt Julia has plenty of common sense. You're quite right, Olivia. This isn't a thing we can keep from the family.

OLIVIA. Do I still call her *Aunt* Julia?

GEORGE (*looking up from his pacings*). What? What? (ANNE *comes in.*) Well, what is it?

ANNE. Mr. Pim says he will come down at once, sir.

GEORGE. Oh, thank you, thank you.

[ANNE *goes out.*

OLIVIA. George, Mr. Pim has got to know.

GEORGE. I don't see the necessity.

OLIVIA. Not even for me? When a woman suddenly hears that her long-lost husband is restored to her, don't you think she wants to ask questions? Where is he living, and how is he looking, and——

GEORGE (*coldly*). Of course, if you are interested in these things——

OLIVIA. How can I help being? Don't be so silly, George. We *must* know what Jacko——

GEORGE (*annoyed*). I wish you wouldn't call him by that ridiculous name.

OLIVIA. My husband——

GEORGE (*wincing*). Yes, well—your husband?

OLIVIA. Well, we must know his plans—where we can communicate with him, and so on.

GEORGE. I have no wish to communicate with him.

OLIVIA. I'm afraid you'll have to, dear.

GEORGE. I don't see the necessity.

OLIVIA. Well, you'll want to—to apologise to him for living with his wife for so long. And as I belong to him, he ought to be told where he can—call for me.

GEORGE (*after a struggle*). You put it in a very peculiar way, but I see your point. (*With a shudder*) Oh, the horrible publicity of it all!

OLIVIA (*going up to him and comforting him*). Poor George. Dear, don't think I don't sympathise with you. I understand so exactly what you are feeling. The publicity! It's terrible.

GEORGE (*miserably*). I want to do what's right, Olivia. You believe that?

OLIVIA. Of course I do. It's only that we don't quite agree as to what is right and what is wrong.

GEORGE. It isn't a question of agreeing. Right is right, and wrong is wrong, all the world over.

OLIVIA (*with a sad little smile*). But more particularly in Buckinghamshire, I think.

GEORGE. If I only considered myself, I should say: "Let us pack this man Telworthy back to Australia.

He would make no claim. He would accept money to go away and say nothing about it." If I consulted simply my own happiness, Olivia, that is what I should say. But when I consult—er——

OLIVIA (*surprised*). Mine?

GEORGE. My conscience——

OLIVIA. Oh!

GEORGE. Then I can't do it. It's wrong. (*He is at the window as he says this.*)

OLIVIA (*making her first and last appeal*). George, aren't I worth a little——

GEORGE (*turning round*). H'sh! Dinah! (*Loudly for* DINAH's *benefit*) Well, then I'll write to him and—— Ah, Dinah, where's Aunt Julia?

DINAH (*coming in*). We've seen the pigs, and now she's discussing the Art of Landseer with Brian. I just came to ask——

OLIVIA. Dinah, dear, bring Aunt Julia here. And Brian too. We have things we want to talk about with you all.

GEORGE (*outraged*). Olivia!

DINAH. Righto. What fun!

[*Exit* DINAH.

GEORGE. Olivia, you don't seriously suggest that we should discuss these things with a child like Dinah and a young man like Strange, a mere acquaintance.

OLIVIA. Dinah will have to know. I'm very fond of her, George. You can't send me away without telling Dinah. And Brian is my friend. You have your solicitor and your aunt and your conscience to consult—mayn't I even have Brian?

GEORGE (*forgetting*). I should have thought that your *husband*——

OLIVIA. Yes, but we don't know where Jacko is.

GEORGE. I was not referring to—er—Telworthy.

OLIVIA. Well then?

GEORGE. Well, naturally I—you mustn't—— Oh, this is horrible!

(*He comes back to his desk as the others come in.*)

OLIVIA (*getting up*). George and I have had some rather bad news, Aunt Julia. We wanted your advice. Where will you sit?

LADY MARDEN. Thank you, Olivia. I can sit down by myself. (*She does so, near* GEORGE. DINAH *sits on the sofa with* OLIVIA, *and* BRIAN *half leans against the back of it. There is a hush of expectation. . . .*) What is it? Money, I suppose. Nobody's safe nowadays.

GEORGE (*signalling for help*). Olivia——

OLIVIA. We've just heard that my first husband is still alive.

DINAH. Telworthy!

BRIAN. Good Lord!

LADY MARDEN. George!

DINAH (*excitedly*). And only this morning I was saying that nothing ever happened in this house! (*Remorsefully to* OLIVIA) Darling, I don't mean that. Darling one!

LADY MARDEN. What does this mean, George? I leave you for ten minutes—barely ten minutes—to go and look at the pigs, and when I come back you tell me that Olivia is a bigamist.

BRIAN (*indignantly*). I say——

OLIVIA (*restraining him*). H'sh!

BRIAN (*to* OLIVIA). If this is a row, I'm on your side.

LADY MARDEN. Well, George?

GEORGE. I'm afraid it's true, Aunt Julia. We heard the news just before lunch—just before you came. We've only this moment had an opportunity of talking about it, of wondering what to do.

LADY MARDEN. What was his name—Tel—something——

OLIVIA. Jacob Telworthy.

LADY MARDEN. So he's alive still?

GEORGE. Apparently. There seems to be no doubt about it.

LADY MARDEN (*to* OLIVIA). Didn't you see him die? I should always want to *see* my husband die before I married again. Not that I approve of second marriages, anyhow. I told you so at the time, George.

OLIVIA. *And* me, Aunt Julia.

LADY MARDEN. Did I? Well, I generally say what I think.

GEORGE. I ought to tell you, Aunt Julia, that no blame attaches to Olivia over this. Of that I am perfectly satisfied. It's nobody's fault, except——

LADY MARDEN. Except Telworthy's. *He* seems to have been rather careless. Well, what are you going to do about it?

GEORGE. That's just it. It's a terrible situation. There's bound to be so much publicity. Not only all this, but—but Telworthy's past and—and everything.

LADY MARDEN. I should have said that it was Telworthy's present which was the trouble. Had he a past as well?

OLIVIA. He was a fraudulent company promoter. He went to prison a good deal.

LADY MARDEN. George, you never told me this!

GEORGE. I—er——

OLIVIA. I don't see why he should want to talk about it.

DINAH (*indignantly*). What's it got to do with Olivia, anyhow? It's not *her* fault.

LADY MARDEN (*sarcastically*). Oh no, I daresay it's mine.

OLIVIA (*to* GEORGE). You wanted to ask Aunt Julia what was the right thing to do.

BRIAN (*bursting out*). Good Heavens, what *is* there to do except the one and only thing? (*They all look at him and he becomes embarrassed*) I'm sorry. You don't want *me* to——

OLIVIA. *I* do, Brian.

LADY MARDEN. Well, go on, Mr. Strange. What would *you* do in George's position?

BRIAN. Do? Say to the woman I loved, "You're *mine*, and let this other damned fellow come and take you from me if he can!" And he couldn't—how could he?—not if the woman chose *me*.

> (LADY MARDEN *gazes at* BRIAN *in amazement,* GEORGE *in anger.* OLIVIA *presses his hand gratefully. He has said what she has been waiting—oh, so eagerly—for* GEORGE *to say.*)

DINAH (*adoringly*). Oh, Brian! (*In a whisper*) It is me, isn't it, and not Olivia?

BRIAN. You baby, of course!

LADY MARDEN. I'm afraid, Mr. Strange, your morals are as peculiar as your views on Art. If you had led a more healthy life——

BRIAN. This is not a question of morals or of art, it's a question of love.

DINAH. Hear, hear!

LADY MARDEN (*to* GEORGE). Isn't it that girl's bedtime yet?

OLIVIA (*to* DINAH). We'll let her sit up a little longer if she's good.

DINAH. I will be good, Olivia, only I thought anybody, however important a debate was, was allowed to say "Hear, hear!"

GEORGE (*coldly*). I really think we could discuss this

better if Mr. Strange took Dinah out for a walk. Strange, if you—er——

OLIVIA. Tell them what you have settled first, George.

LADY MARDEN. Settled? What is there to be settled? It settles itself.

GEORGE (*sadly*). That's just it.

LADY MARDEN. The marriage must be annulled—is that the word, George?

GEORGE. I presume so.

LADY MARDEN. One's solicitor will know all about that of course.

BRIAN. And when the marriage has been annulled, what then?

LADY MARDEN. Presumably Olivia will return to her husband.

BRIAN (*bitterly*). And that's morality! As expounded by Bishop Landseer!

GEORGE (*angered*). I don't know what you mean by Bishop Landseer. Morality is acting in accordance with the Laws of the Land and the Laws of the Church. I am quite prepared to believe that *your* creed embraces neither marriage nor monogamy, but my creed is different.

BRIAN (*fiercely*). My creed includes both marriage *and* monogamy, and monogamy means sticking to the woman you love, as long as she wants you.

LADY MARDEN (*calmly*). You suggest that George and Olivia should go on living together, although they have never been legally married, and wait for this Telworthy man to divorce her, and then—bless the man, what do you think the County would say?

BRIAN (*scornfully*). Does it matter?

DINAH. Well, if you really want to know, the men would say, "Gad, she's a fine woman; I don't wonder he sticks to her," and the women would say, "I can't *think* what he sees in her to stick to her like that," and they'd both say, "After all, he may be a damn fool, but you can't deny he's a sportsman." That's what the County would say.

GEORGE (*indignantly*). Was it for this sort of thing, Olivia, that you insisted on having Dinah and Mr. Strange in here? To insult me in my own house?

LADY MARDEN. I can't think what young people are coming to nowadays.

OLIVIA. I think, dear, you and Brian had better go.

DINAH (*getting up*). We will go. But I'm just going to say one thing, Uncle George. Brian and I *are* going to marry each other, and when we are married we'll stick to each other, how*ever* many of our dead husbands and wives turn up!

[*She goes out indignantly, followed by* BRIAN.

GEORGE. Upon my word, this is a pleasant discussion.

OLIVIA. I think the discussion is over, George. It is only a question of where I shall go, while you are bringing your—what sort of suit did you call it?

LADY MARDEN (*to* GEORGE). Nullity suit. I suppose that *is* the best thing?

GEORGE. It's horrible. The awful publicity. That it should be happening to us, that's what I can't get over.

LADY MARDEN. I don't remember anything of the sort in the Marden Family before, ever.

GEORGE (*absently*). Lady Fanny.

LADY MARDEN (*recollecting*). Yes, of course; but that was two hundred years ago. The standards were different then. Besides, it wasn't quite the same, anyhow.

GEORGE (*absently*). No, it wasn't quite the same.

LADY MARDEN. No. We shall all feel it. Terribly.

GEORGE (*his apology*). If there were any other way! Olivia, what *can* I do? It *is* the only way, isn't it? All that that fellow said—of course, it sounds very well—

ACT II] MR. PIM PASSES BY 115

but as things are. . . . *Is* there anything in marriage, or isn't there? You believe that there is, don't you? You aren't one of these Socialists. Well, then, *can* we go on living together when you're another man's wife? It isn't only what people will say, but it *is* wrong, isn't it? . . . And supposing he doesn't divorce you, are we to go on living together, unmarried, for *ever?* Olivia, you seem to think that I'm just thinking of the publicity —what people will say. I'm not. I'm not. That comes in any way. But I want to do what's right, what's best. I don't mean what's best for *us,* what makes us happiest, I mean what's really best, what's rightest. What anybody else would do in my place. *I* don't know. It's so unfair. You're not my wife at all, but I want to do what's right. . . . Oh, Olivia, Olivia, you do understand, don't you?

(*They have both forgotten* LADY MARDEN. OLIVIA *has never taken her eyes off him as he makes his last attempt to convince himself.*)

OLIVIA (*almost tenderly*). So very very well, George. Oh, I understand just what you are feeling. And oh, I do so wish that you could—(*with a little sigh*)—but then it wouldn't be George, not the George I married—(*with a rueful little laugh*)—or didn't quite marry.

LADY MARDEN. I must say, I think you are both talking a little wildly.

OLIVIA (*repeating it, oh, so tenderly*). Or didn't—quite —marry. (*She looks at him with all her heart in her eyes. She is giving him his last chance to say "Damn Telworthy; you're mine!" He struggles desperately with himself. . . . Will he?—will he? . . . But we shall never know, for at that moment* ANNE *comes in.*)

ANNE. Mr. Pim is here, sir.

GEORGE (*emerging from the struggle with an effort*).

116   MR. PIM PASSES BY   [ACT II

Pim? Pim? Oh, ah, yes, of course. Mr. Pim. (*Looking up*) Where have you put him?

OLIVIA. I want to see Mr. Pim, too, George.

LADY MARDEN. Who on earth is Mr. Pim?

OLIVIA. Show him in here, Anne.

ANNE. Yes, madam.   [*She goes out.*

OLIVIA. It was Mr. Pim who told us about my husband. He came across with him in the boat, and recognised him as the Telworthy he knew in Australia.

LADY MARDEN. Oh! Shall I be in the way?

GEORGE. No, no. It does't matter, does it, Olivia?

OLIVIA. Please stay.

ANNE *enters followed by* MR. PIM.

ANNE. Mr. Pim.

GEORGE (*pulling himself together*). Ah, Mr. Pim! Very good of you to have come. The fact is—er—— (*It is too much for him; he looks despairingly at* OLIVIA.)

OLIVIA. We're so sorry to trouble you, Mr. Pim. By the way, do you know Lady Marden? (MR. PIM *and* LADY MARDEN *bow to each other.*) Do come and sit down, won't you? (*She makes room for him on the sofa next to her*) The fact is, Mr. Pim, you gave us rather a surprise this morning, and before we had time to realise what it all meant, you had gone.

MR. PIM. A surprise, Mrs. Marden? Dear me, not an unpleasant one, I hope?

OLIVIA. Well, rather a—surprising one.

GEORGE. Olivia, allow me a moment. Mr. Pim, you mentioned a man called Telworthy this morning. My wife used to—that is to say, I used to—that is, there are reasons——

OLIVIA. I think we had better be perfectly frank, George.

LADY MARDEN. I am sixty-five years of age, Mr. Pim,

and I can say that I've never had a moment's uneasiness by telling the truth.

MR. PIM (*after a desperate effort to keep up with the conversation*). Oh! . . . I—er—I'm afraid I am rather at sea. Have I—er—left anything unsaid in presenting my credentials to you this morning? This Telworthy whom you mention—I seem to remember the name——

OLIVIA. Mr. Pim, you told us this morning of a man whom you had met on the boat, a man who had come down in the world, whom you had known in Sydney. A man called Telworthy.

MR. PIM (*relieved*). Ah yes, yes, of course. I did say Telworthy, didn't I? Most curious coincidence, Lady Marden. Poor man, poor man! Let me see, it must have been ten years ago——

GEORGE. Just a moment, Mr. Pim. You're quite sure that his name was Telworthy?

MR. PIM. Telworthy—Telworthy—didn't I say Telworthy? Yes, that was it—Telworthy. Poor fellow!

OLIVIA. I'm going to be perfectly frank with you, Mr. Pim. I feel quite sure that I can trust you. This man Telworthy whom you met is my husband.

MR. PIM. Your husband? (*He looks in mild surprise at* GEORGE.) But—er——

OLIVIA. My first husband. His death was announced six years ago. I had left him some years before that, but there seems no doubt from your story that he's still alive. His record—the country he comes from—above all, the very unusual name—Telworthy.

MR. PIM. Telworthy—yes—certainly a most peculiar name. I remember saying so. Your first husband? Dear me! Dear me!

GEORGE. You understand, Mr. Pim, that all this is in absolute confidence.

MR. PIM. Of course, of course.

OLIVIA. Well, since he is my husband, we naturally want to know something about him. Where is he now, for instance?

MR. PIM (*surprised*). Where is he now? But surely I told you? I told you what happened at Marseilles?

GEORGE. At Marseilles?

MR. PIM. Yes, yes, poor fellow, it was most unfortunate. (*Quite happy again*) You must understand, Lady Marden, that although I had met the poor fellow before in Australia, I was never in any way intimate——

GEORGE (*thumping the desk*). Where is he *now*, that's what we want to know?

(MR. PIM *turns to him with a start.*)

OLIVIA. Please, Mr. Pim!

PIM. Where is he now? But—but didn't I tell you of the curious fatality at Marseilles—poor fellow—the fish-bone?

ALL. Fish-bone?

MR. PIM. Yes, yes, a herring, I understand.

OLIVIA (*understanding first*). Do you mean he's dead?

MR. PIM. Dead—of course—didn't I——?

OLIVIA (*laughing hysterically*). Oh, Mr. Pim, you—oh, what a husband to have—oh, I—— (*But that is all she can say for the moment.*)

LADY MARDEN. Pull yourself together, Olivia. This is so unhealthy for you. (*To* PIM) So he really *is* dead this time?

MR. PIM. Oh, undoubtedly, undoubtedly. A fish-bone lodged in his throat.

GEORGE (*trying to realise it*). Dead!

OLIVIA (*struggling with her laughter*). I think you must excuse me, Mr. Pim—I can never thank you enough—a herring—there's something about a herring—morality depends on such little things—George, you—— (*Shaking her head at him in a weak state of laughter, she hurries out of the room.*)

MR. PIM. Dear me! Dear me!

GEORGE. Now, let us have this quite clear, Mr. Pim. You say that the man, Telworthy, Jacob Telworthy, is dead?

MR. PIM. Telworthy, yes—didn't I say Telworthy? This man I was telling you about——

GEORGE. He's dead?

MR. PIM. Yes, yes, he died at Marseilles.

LADY MARDEN. A dispensation of Providence, George. One can look at it in no other light.

GEORGE. Dead! (*Suddenly annoyed*) Really, Mr. Pim, I think you might have told us before.

MR. PIM. But I—I *was* telling you—I——

GEORGE. If you had only told us the whole story at once, instead of in two—two instalments like this, you would have saved us all a good deal of anxiety.

MR. PIM. Really, I——

LADY MARDEN. I am sure Mr. Pim meant well, George, but it seems a pity he couldn't have said so before. If the man was dead, *why* try to hush it up?

MR. PIM (*lost again*). Really, Lady Marden, I——

GEORGE (*getting up*). Well, well, at any rate, I am much obliged to you, Mr. Pim, for having come down to us this afternoon. Dead! *De mortuis,* and so forth, but the situation would have been impossible had he lived. Good-bye! (*Holding out his hand*) Good-bye!

LADY MARDEN. Good-bye, Mr. Pim.

MR. PIM. Good-bye, good-bye! (GEORGE *takes him to the door.*) Of course, if I had—(*to himself*) Telworthy—I *think* that was the name. (*He goes out, still wondering.*)

GEORGE (*with a sigh of thankfulness*). Well! This is wonderful news, Aunt Julia.

LADY MARDEN. Most providential! . . . You understand, of course, that you are not married to Olivia?

GEORGE (*who didn't*). Not married?

LADY MARDEN. If her first husband only died at Marseilles a few days ago——

GEORGE. Good Heavens!

LADY MARDEN. Not that it matters. You can get married quietly again. Nobody need know.

GEORGE (*considering it*). Yes . . . yes. Then all these years we have been—er—— Yes.

LADY MARDEN. Who's going to know?

GEORGE. Yes, yes, that's true. . . . And in perfect innocence, too.

LADY MARDEN. I should suggest a Registry Office in London.

GEORGE. A Registry Office, yes.

LADY MARDEN. Better go up to town this afternoon. Can't do it too quickly.

GEORGE. Yes, yes. We can stay at an hotel——

LADY MARDEN (*surprised*). George!

GEORGE. What?

LADY MARDEN. *You* will stay at your club.

GEORGE. Oh—ah—yes, of course, Aunt Julia.

LADY MARDEN. Better take your solicitor with you to be on the safe side. . . . To the Registry Office, I mean.

GEORGE. Yes.

LADY MARDEN (*getting up*). Well, I must be getting along, George. Say good-bye to Olivia for me. And those children. Of course, you won't allow this absurd love-business between them to come to anything?

GEORGE. Most certainly not. Good-bye, Aunt Julia!

LADY MARDEN (*indicating the windows*). I'll go *this* way. (*As she goes*) And get Olivia out more, George. I don't like these hysterics. You want to be firm with her.

GEORGE (*firmly*). Yes, yes! Good-bye!

(*He waves to her and then goes back to his seat.*)

(OLIVIA *comes in, and stands in the middle of the room looking at him. He comes to her eagerly.*)

GEORGE (*holding out his hands*). Olivia! Olivia!
               (*But it is not so easy as that.*)
OLIVIA (*drawing herself up proudly*). Mrs. Telworthy!

ACT III

OLIVIA *is standing where we left her at the end of the last act.*

GEORGE (*taken aback*). Olivia, I—I don't understand.

OLIVIA (*leaving melodrama with a little laugh and coming down to him*). Poor George! Did I frighten you rather?

GEORGE. You're so strange to-day. I don't understand you. You're not like the Olivia I know.

(*They sit down on the sofa together.*)

OLIVIA. Perhaps you don't know me very well after all.

GEORGE (*affectionately*). Oh, that's nonsense, old girl. You're just my Olivia.

OLIVIA. And yet it seemed as though I wasn't going to be your Olivia half an hour ago.

GEORGE (*with a shudder*). Don't talk about it. It doesn't bear thinking about. Well, thank Heaven that's over. Now we can get married again quietly and nobody will be any the wiser.

OLIVIA. Married again?

GEORGE. Yes, dear. As you—er—(*he laughs uneasily*) said just now, you are Mrs. Telworthy. Just for the moment. But we can soon put that right. My idea was to go up this evening and—er—make arrangements, and if you come up to-morrow morning, if we can manage it by then, we could get quietly married at a Registry Office, and—er—nobody any the wiser.

OLIVIA. Yes, I see. You want me to marry you at a Registry Office to-morrow?

GEORGE. If we can arrange it by then. I don't know how long these things take, but I should imagine there would be no difficulty.

OLIVIA. Oh no, that part ought to be quite easy. But—— (*She hesitates.*)

GEORGE. But what?

OLIVIA. Well, if you want to marry me to-morrow, George, oughtn't you to propose to me first?

GEORGE (*amazed*). Propose?

OLIVIA. Yes. It is usual, isn't it, to propose to a person before you marry her, and—and we want to do the usual thing, don't we?

GEORGE (*upset*). But you—but we . . .

OLIVIA. You see, dear, you're George Marden, and I'm Olivia Telworthy, and you—you're attracted by me, and think I would make you a good wife, and you want to marry me. Well, naturally you propose to me first, and—tell me how much you are attracted by me, and what a good wife you think I shall make, and how badly you want to marry me.

GEORGE (*falling into the humour of it, as he thinks*). The baby! Did she want to be proposed to all over again?

OLIVIA. Well, she did rather.

GEORGE (*rather fancying himself as an actor*). She shall then. (*He adopts what he considers to be an appropriate attitude*) Mrs. Telworthy, I have long admired you in silence, and the time has now come to put my admiration into words. Er—— (*But apparently he finds a difficulty.*)

OLIVIA (*hopefully*). Into words.

GEORGE. Er——

OLIVIA (*with the idea of helping*). Oh, Mr. Marden!

GEORGE. Er—may I call you Olivia?

OLIVIA. Yes, George.

GEORGE (*taking her hand*). Olivia—I—— (*He hesitates.*)

OLIVIA. I don't want to interrupt, but oughtn't you to be on your knees? It is—usual, I believe. If one of the servants came in, you could say you were looking for my scissors.

GEORGE. Really, Olivia, you must allow me to manage my own proposal in my own way.

OLIVIA (*meekly*). I'm sorry. Do go on.

GEORGE. Well, er—confound it, Olivia, I love you. Will you marry me?

OLIVIA. Thank you, George, I will think it over.

GEORGE (*laughing*). Silly girl! Well then, to-morrow morning. No wedding-cake, I'm afraid, Olivia. (*He laughs again*) But we'll go and have a good lunch somewhere.

OLIVIA. I will think it over, George.

GEORGE (*good-humouredly*). Well, give us a kiss while you're thinking.

OLIVIA. I'm afraid you musn't kiss me until we are actually engaged.

GEORGE (*laughing uneasily*). Oh, we needn't take it as seriously as all that.

OLIVIA. But a woman must take a proposal seriously.

GEORGE (*alarmed at last*). What do you mean?

OLIVIA. I mean that the whole question, as I heard somebody say once, demands much more anxious thought than either of us has given it. These hasty marriages——

GEORGE. Hasty!

OLIVIA. Well, you've only just proposed to me, and you want to marry me to-morrow.

GEORGE. Now you're talking perfect nonsense, Olivia.

You know quite well that our case is utterly different from—from any other.

OLIVIA. All the same, one has to ask oneself questions. With a young girl like—well, with a young girl, love may well seem to be all that matters. But with a woman of my age, it is different. I have to ask myself if you can afford to support a wife.

GEORGE (*coldly*). Fortunately that is a question that you can very easily answer for yourself.

OLIVIA. Well, but I have been hearing rather bad reports lately. What with taxes always going up, and rents always going down, some of our landowners are getting into rather straitened circumstances. At least, so I'm told.

GEORGE. I don't know what you're talking about.

OLIVIA (*surprised*). Oh, isn't it true? I heard of a case only this morning—a landowner who always seemed to be very comfortably off, but who couldn't afford an allowance for his only niece when she wanted to get married. It made me think that one oughtn't to judge by appearances.

GEORGE. You know perfectly well that I can afford to support a wife as my wife *should* be supported.

OLIVIA. I'm so glad, dear. Then your income—you aren't getting anxious at all?

GEORGE (*stiffly*). You know perfectly well what my income is. I see no reason for anxiety in the future.

OLIVIA. Ah, well, then we needn't think about that any more. Well, then, there is another thing to be considered.

GEORGE. I can't make out what you're up to. Don't you want to get married; to—er—legalise this extraordinary situation in which we are placed?

OLIVIA. I want to be sure that I am going to be happy, George. I can't just jump at the very first offer I have had since my husband died, without considering the whole question very carefully.

GEORGE. So I'm under consideration, eh?

OLIVIA. Every suitor is.

GEORGE (*sarcastically, as he thinks*). Well, go on.

OLIVIA. Well, then, there's your niece. You have a niece who lives with you. Of course Dinah is a delightful girl, but one doesn't like marrying into a household in which there is another grown-up woman. But perhaps she will be getting married herself soon?

GEORGE. I see no prospect of it.

OLIVIA. I think it would make it much easier if she did.

GEORGE. Is this a threat, Olivia? Are you telling me that if I do not allow young Strange to marry Dinah, you will not marry me?

OLIVIA. A threat? Oh no, George.

GEORGE. Then what does it mean?

OLIVIA. I'm just wondering if you love me as much as Brian loves Dinah. You *do* love me?

GEORGE (*from his heart*). You know I do, old girl. (*He comes to her.*)

OLIVIA. You're not just attracted by my pretty face? . . . *Is* it a pretty face?

GEORGE. It's an adorable one. (*He tries to kiss it, but she turns away.*)

OLIVIA. How can I be sure that it is not *only* my face which makes you think that you care for me? Love which rests upon a mere outward attraction cannot lead to any lasting happiness—as one of our thinkers has observed.

GEORGE. What's come over you, Olivia? I don't understand what you're driving at. Why should you doubt my love?

OLIVIA. Ah!—Why?

GEORGE. You can't pretend that we haven't been happy

together. I've—I've been a good pal to you, eh? We—we suit each other, old girl.

OLIVIA. Do we?

GEORGE. Of course we do.

OLIVIA. I wonder. When two people of our age think of getting married, one wants to be very sure that there is real community of ideas between them. Whether it is a comparatively trivial matter, like the right colour for a curtain, or some very much more serious question of conduct which arises, one wants to feel that there is some chance of agreement betwen husband and wife.

GEORGE. We—we love each other, old girl.

OLIVIA. We do now, yes. But what shall we be like in five years' time? Supposing that after we have been married five years, we found ourselves estranged from each other upon such questions as Dinah's future, or the decorations of the drawing-room, or even the advice to give to a friend who had innocently contracted a bigamous marriage? How bitterly we should regret then our hasty plunge into a matrimony which was no true partnership, whether of tastes, or of ideas, or even of consciences! (*With a sigh*) Ah me!

GEORGE (*nastily*). Unfortunately for your argument, Olivia, I can answer you out of your own mouth. You seem to have forgotten what you said this morning in the case of—er—young Strange.

OLIVIA (*reproachfully*). Is it quite fair, George, to drag up what was said this morning?

GEORGE. You've brought it on yourself.

OLIVIA. I? . . . Well, and what did I say this morning?

GEORGE. You said that it was quite enough that Strange was a gentleman and in love with Dinah for me to let them marry each other.

OLIVIA. Oh! . . . *Is* that enough, George?

GEORGE (*triumphantly*). You said so.

OLIVIA (*meekly*). Well, if you think so, too, I—I don't mind risking it.

GEORGE (*kindly*). Aha, my dear! You see!

OLIVIA. Then you do think it's enough?

GEORGE. I—er—— Yes, yes, I—I think so.

OLIVIA (*going to him*). My darling one! Then we can have a double wedding. How jolly!

GEORGE (*astounded*). A double one!

OLIVIA. Yes. You and me, Brian and Dinah.

GEORGE (*firmly*). Now look here, Olivia, understand once and for all, I am not to be blackmailed into giving my consent to Dinah's engagement. Neither blackmailed nor tricked. Our marriage has nothing whatever to do with Dinah's.

OLIVIA. No, dear. I quite understand. They may take place about the same time, but they have nothing to do with each other.

GEORGE. I see no prospect of Dinah's marriage taking place for many years.

OLIVIA. No, dear, that was what I said.

GEORGE (*not understanding for the moment*). You said . . . ? I see. Now, Olivia, let us have this perfectly clear. You apparently insist on treating my—er—proposal as serious.

OLIVIA (*surprised*). Wasn't it serious? Were you trifling with me?

GEORGE. You know quite well what I mean. You treat it as an ordinary proposal from a man to a woman who have never been more than acquaintances before. Very well then. Will you tell me what you propose to do, if you decide to—ah—refuse me? You do not suggest that we should go on living together—unmarried?

OLIVIA (*shocked*). Of course not, George! What would

the County—I mean Heaven—I mean the Law—I mean, of *course* not! Besides, it's so unnecessary. If I decide to accept you, of *course* I shall marry you.

GEORGE. Quite so. And if you—ah—decide to refuse me? What will you do?

OLIVIA. Nothing.

GEORGE. Meaning by that?

OLIVIA. Just that, George. I shall stay here—just as before. I like this house. It wants a little re-decorating perhaps, but I do like it, George. . . . Yes, I shall be quite happy here.

GEORGE. I see. You will continue to live down here —in spite of what you said just now about the immorality of it.

OLIVIA (*surprised*). But there's nothing immoral in a widow living alone in a big country house, with perhaps the niece of a friend of hers staying with her, just to keep her company.

GEORGE (*sarcastic*). And what shall *I* be doing, when you've so very kindly taken possession of my house for me?

OLIVIA. I don't know, George. Travelling, I expect. You could come down sometimes with a chaperone. I suppose there would be nothing wrong in that.

GEORGE (*indignant*). Thank you! And what if I refuse to be turned out of my house?

OLIVIA. Then, seeing that we can't *both* be in it, it looks as though you'd have to turn *me* out. (*Casually*) I suppose there are legal ways of doing these things. You'd have to consult your solicitor again.

GEORGE (*amazed*). Legal ways?

OLIVIA. Well, you couldn't *throw* me out, could you? You'd have to get an injunction against me—or prosecute me for trespass—or something. It would make an awfully unusual case, wouldn't it? The papers would be full of it.

GEORGE. You must be mad!

OLIVIA (*dreamily*). Widow of well-known ex-convict takes possession of J.P.'s house. Popular country gentleman denied entrance to his own home. Doomed to travel.

GEORGE (*angrily*). I've had enough of this. Do you mean all this nonsense?

OLIVIA. I do mean, George, that I am in no hurry to go up to London and get married. I love the country just now, and (*with a sigh*) after this morning, I'm—rather tired of husbands.

GEORGE (*in a rage*). I've never heard so much—damned nonsense in my life. I will leave you to come to your senses. (*He goes out indignantly.*)

> (OLIVIA, *who has forgiven him already, throws a loving kiss after him, and then turns triumphantly to her dear curtains. She takes them, smiling, to the sofa, and has just got to work again, when* MR. PIM *appears at the open windows.*)

PIM (*in a whisper*). Er, may I come in, Mrs. Marden?

OLIVIA (*turning round in surprise*). Mr. Pim!

PIM (*anxiously*). Mr. Marden is—er—not here?

OLIVIA (*getting up*). Do you want to see him? I will tell him.

PIM. No, no, no! Not for the world! (*He comes in and looks anxiously at the door*) There is no immediate danger of his returning, Mrs. Marden?

OLIVIA (*surprised*). No, I don't think so. What is it? You——

PIM. I took the liberty of returning by the window in the hope of—er—coming upon you alone, Mrs. Marden.

OLIVIA. Yes?

PIM (*still rather nervous*). I—er—Mr. Marden will

ACT III] **MR. PIM PASSES BY** 131

be very angry with me. Quite rightly. I blame myself entirely. I do not know how I can have been so stupid.

OLIVIA. What is it, Mr. Pim? Has my husband come to life again?

PIM. Mrs. Marden, I throw myself on your mercy entirely. The fact is—his name was Polwittle.

OLIVIA (*at a loss*). Whose? My husband's?

PIM. Yes, yes. The name came back to me suddenly, just as I reached the gate. Polwittle, poor fellow.

OLIVIA. But, Mr. Pim, my husband's name was Telworthy.

PIM. No, no, Polwittle.

OLIVIA. But, really I ought to . . .

PIM (*firmly*). Polwittle. It came back to me suddenly just as I reached the gate. For the moment, I had thoughts of conveying the news by letter. I was naturally disinclined to return in person, and—— Polwittle. (*Proudly*) If you remember, I always said it was a curious name.

OLIVIA. But who *is* Polwittle?

PIM (*in surprise at her stupidity*). The man I have been telling you about, who met with the sad fatality at Marseilles. Henry Polwittle—or was it Ernest? No, Henry, I think. Poor fellow.

OLIVIA (*indignantly*). But you said his name was Telworthy! How *could* you?

PIM. Yes, yes, I blame myself entirely.

OLIVIA. But how could you *think* of a name like Telworthy, if it wasn't Telworthy?

PIM (*eagerly*). Ah, that is the really interesting thing about the whole matter.

OLIVIA. Mr. Pim, all your visits here to-day have been interesting.

PIM. Yes, but you see, on my first appearance here this morning, I was received by—er—Miss Diana.

OLIVIA. Dinah.

PIM. Miss Dinah, yes. She was in—er—rather a communicative mood, and she happened to mention, by way of passing the time, that before your marriage to Mr. Marden you had been a Mrs.—er——

OLIVIA. Telworthy.

PIM. Yes, yes, Telworthy, of course. She mentioned also Australia. By some process of the brain—which strikes me as decidedly curious—when I was trying to recollect the name of the poor fellow on the boat, whom you remember I had also met in Australia, the fact that this other name was also stored in my memory, a name equally peculiar—this fact I say . . .

OLIVIA (*seeing that the sentence is rapidly going to pieces*). Yes, I understand.

PIM. I blame myself, I blame myself entirely.

OLIVIA. Oh, you mustn't do that, Mr. Pim. It was really Dinah's fault for inflicting all our family history on you.

PIM. Oh, but a charming young woman. I assure you I was very much interested in all that she told me. (*Getting up*) Well, Mrs.—er—Marden, I can only hope that you will forgive me for the needless distress I have caused you to-day.

OLIVIA. Oh, you mustn't worry about that—please.

PIM. And you will tell your husband—you will break the news to him?

OLIVIA (*smiling to herself*). I will—break the news to him.

PIM. You understand how it is that I thought it better to come to you in the first place?

OLIVIA. I am very glad you did.

PIM (*holding out his hand*). Then I will say good-bye, and—er——

OLIVIA. Just a moment, Mr. Pim. Let us have it quite clear this time. You never knew my husband, Jacob Telworthy, you never met him in Australia, you never saw him on the boat, and nothing whatever happened to him at Marseilles. Is that right?

PIM. Yes, yes, that is so.

OLIVIA. So that, since he was supposed to have died in Australia six years ago, he is presumably still dead?

PIM. Yes, yes, undoubtedly.

OLIVIA (*holding out her hand with a charming smile*). Then good-bye, Mr. Pim, and thank you so much for—for all your trouble.

PIM. Not at all, Mrs. Marden. I can only assure you I——

DINAH (*from the window*). Hullo, here's Mr. Pim! (*She comes in, followed by* BRIAN.)

PIM (*anxiously looking at the door in case* MR. MARDEN *should come in*). Yes, yes, I—er——

DINAH. Oh, Mr. Pim, you mustn't run away without even saying how do you do! Such old friends as we are. Why, it is ages since I saw you! Are you staying to tea?

PIM. I'm afraid I——

OLIVIA. Mr. Pim has to hurry away, Dinah. You mustn't keep him.

DINAH. Well, but you'll come back again?

PIM. I fear that I am only a passer-by, Miss—er—Dinah.

OLIVIA. You can walk with him to the gate, dear.

PIM (*gratefully to* OLIVIA). Thank you. (*He edges towards the window*) If you would be so kind, Miss Dinah——

BRIAN. I'll catch you up.

DINAH. Come along then, Mr. Pim. (*As they go out*)

I want to hear all about your *first* wife. You haven't really told me anything yet.

(OLIVIA *resumes her work, and* BRIAN *sits on the back of the sofa looking at her.*)

BRIAN (*awkwardly*). I just wanted to say, if you don't think it cheek, that I'm—I'm on your side, if I may be, and if I can help you at all I should be very proud of being allowed to.

OLIVIA (*looking up at him*). Brian, you dear. That's sweet of you. . . . But it's quite all right now, you know.

BRIAN. Oh, I'm so glad.

OLIVIA. Yes, that's what Mr. Pim came back to say. He'd made a mistake about the name. (*Smiling*) George is the only husband I have.

BRIAN (*surprised*). What? You mean that the whole thing—that Pim—— (*With conviction*) Silly ass!

OLIVIA (*kindly*). Oh, well, he didn't mean to be. (*After a pause*) Brian, do you know anything about the Law?

BRIAN. I'm afraid not. I hate the Law. Why?

OLIVIA (*casually*). Oh, I just—I was wondering—thinking about all the shocks we've been through to-day. Second marriages, and all that.

BRIAN. Oh! It's a rotten business.

OLIVIA. I suppose there's nothing wrong in getting married to the *same* person twice?

BRIAN. A hundred times if you like, I should think.

OLIVIA. Oh?

BRIAN. After all, in France, they always go through it twice, don't they? Once before the Mayor or somebody, and once in church.

OLIVIA. Of course they do! How silly of me. . . . I think it's rather a nice idea. They ought to do it in England more.

BRIAN. Well, once will be enough for Dinah and me, if you can work it. (*Anxiously*) D'you think there's any chance, Olivia?

OLIVIA (*smiling*). Every chance, dear.

BRIAN (*jumping up*). I say, do you really? Have you squared him? I mean, has he——

OLIVIA. Go and catch them up now. We'll talk about it later on.

BRIAN. Bless you. Righto.

(*As he goes out by the windows,* GEORGE *comes in at the door.* GEORGE *stands looking after him, and then turns to* OLIVIA, *who is absorbed in her curtains. He walks up and down the room, fidgeting with things, waiting for her to speak. As she says nothing, he begins to talk himself, but in an obviously unconcerned way. There is a pause after each answer of hers, before he gets out his next remark.*)

GEORGE (*casually*). Good-looking fellow, Strange.

OLIVIA (*equally casually*). Brian—yes, isn't he? And such a nice boy. . . .

GEORGE. Got fifty pounds for a picture the other day, didn't he? Hey?

OLIVIA. Yes. Of course he has only just begun. . . .

GEORGE. Critics think well of him, what?

OLIVIA. They all say he has genius. Oh, I don't think there's any doubt about it. . . .

GEORGE. Of course, I don't profess to know anything about painting.

OLIVIA. You've never had time to take it up, dear.

GEORGE. I know what I like, of course. Can't say I see much in this new-fangled stuff. If a man can paint, why can't he paint like—like Rubens or—or Reynolds?

OLIVIA. I suppose we all have our own styles. Brian

will find his directly. Of course, he's only just beginning. . . .

GEORGE. But they think a lot of him, what?

OLIVIA. Oh yes!

GEORGE. H'm! . . . Good-looking fellow.

(*There is rather a longer silence this time.* GEORGE *continues to hope that he is appearing casual and unconcerned. He stands looking at* OLIVIA's *work for a moment.*)

GEORGE. Nearly finished 'em?

OLIVIA. Very nearly. Are my scissors there?

GEORGE (*looking round*). Scissors?

OLIVIA. Ah, here they are. . . .

GEORGE. Where are you going to put 'em?

OLIVIA (*as if really wondering*). I don't quite know. . . . I *had* thought of this room, but—I'm not quite sure.

GEORGE. Brighten the room up a bit.

OLIVIA. Yes. . . .

GEORGE (*walking over to the present curtains*). H'm. They *are* a bit faded.

OLIVIA (*shaking out hers, and looking at them critically*). Sometimes I think I love them, and sometimes I'm not quite sure.

GEORGE. Best way is to hang 'em up and see how you like 'em then. Always take 'em down again.

OLIVIA. That's rather a good idea, George!

GEORGE. Best way.

OLIVIA. Yes. . . . I think we might do that. . . . The only thing is—— (*she hesitates*).

GEORGE. What?

OLIVIA. Well, the carpet and the chairs, and the cushions and things——

GEORGE. What about 'em?

OLIVIA. Well, if we had new curtains——

ACT III]   MR. PIM PASSES BY   137

GEORGE. You'd want a new carpet, eh?

OLIVIA (*doubtfully*). Y—yes. Well, new chair-covers anyhow.

GEORGE. H'm. . . . Well, why not?

OLIVIA. Oh, but——

GEORGE (*with an awkward laugh*). We're not so hard up as all that, you know.

OLIVIA. No, I suppose not. (*Thoughtfully*) I suppose it would mean that I should have to go up to London for them. That's rather a nuisance.

GEORGE (*extremely casual*). Oh, I don't know. We might go up together one day.

OLIVIA. Well, of course if we *were* up—for anything else—we could just look about us, and see if we could find what we want.

GEORGE. That's what I meant.

> (*There is another silence.* GEORGE *is wondering whether to come to closer quarters with the great question.*)

OLIVIA. Oh, by the way, George——

GEORGE. Yes?

OLIVIA (*innocently*). I told Brian, and I expect he'll tell Dinah, that Mr. Pim had made a mistake about the name.

GEORGE (*astonished*). You told Brian that Mr. Pim——

OLIVIA. Yes—I told him that the whole thing was a mistake. It seemed the simplest way.

GEORGE. Olivia! Then you mean that Brian and Dinah think that—that we have been married all the time?

OLIVIA. Yes. . . . They both think so now.

GEORGE (*coming close to her*). Olivia, does that mean that you *are* thinking of marrying me?

OLIVIA. At your old Registry Office?

GEORGE (*eagerly*). Yes!

OLIVIA. To-morrow?

GEORGE. Yes!

OLIVIA. Do you want me to *very* much?

GEORGE. My darling, you know I do!

OLIVIA (*a little apprehensive*). We should have to do it very quietly.

GEORGE. Of course, darling. Nobody need know at all. We don't *want* anybody to know. And now that you've put Brian and Dinah off the scent, by telling them that Mr. Pim made a mistake—— (*He breaks off, and says admiringly*) That was very clever of you, Olivia. I should never have thought of that.

OLIVIA (*innocently*). No, darling. . . . You don't think it was wrong, George?

GEORGE (*his verdict*). An innocent deception . . . perfectly harmless.

OLIVIA. Yes, dear, that was what I thought about— about what I was doing.

GEORGE. Then you will come to-morrow? (*She nods.*) And if we happen to see the carpet, or anything that you want——

OLIVIA. Oh, what fun!

GEORGE (*beaming*). And a wedding lunch at the Carlton, what? (*She nods eagerly.*) And—and a bit of a honeymoon in Paris?

OLIVIA. Oh, George!

GEORGE (*hungrily*). Give us a kiss, old girl.

OLIVIA (*lovingly*). George!

(*She holds up her cheek to him. He kisses it, and then suddenly takes her in his arms.*)

GEORGE. Don't ever leave me, old girl.

OLIVIA (*affectionately*). Don't ever send me away, old boy.

GEORGE (*fervently*). I won't. . . . (*Awkwardly*) I—I don't think I would have, you know. I—I——

(DINAH *and* BRIAN *appear at the windows, having seen* MR. PIM *safely off.*)

DINAH (*surprised*). Oo, I say!

(GEORGE *hastily moves away.*)

GEORGE. Hallo!

DINAH (*going up impetuously to him*). Give *me* one, too, George; Brian won't mind.

BRIAN. Really, Dinah, you are the limit.

GEORGE (*formally, but enjoying it*). Do you mind, Mr. Strange?

BRIAN (*a little uncomfortably*). Oh, I say, sir——

GEORGE. We'll risk it, Dinah. (*He kisses her.*)

DINAH (*triumphantly to* BRIAN). Did you notice that one? That wasn't just an ordinary affectionate kiss. It was a special bless-you-my-children one. (*To* GEORGE) Wasn't it?

OLIVIA. You do talk nonsense, darling.

DINAH. Well, I'm so happy, now that Mr. Pim has relented about your first husband——

(GEORGE *catches* OLIVIA'S *eye and smiles; she smiles back; but they are different smiles.*)

GEORGE (*the actor*). Yes, yes, stupid fellow Pim, what?

BRIAN. Absolute idiot.

DINAH. —And now that George has relented about *my* first husband.

GEORGE. You get on much too quickly, young woman. (*To* BRIAN) So you want to marry my Dinah, eh?

BRIAN (*with a smile*). Well, I do rather, sir.

DINAH (*hastily*). Not at once, of course, George. We want to be engaged for a long time first, and write letters to each other, and tell each other how much we love each other, and sit next to each other when we go out to dinner.

GEORGE (*to* OLIVIA). Well, *that* sounds fairly harmless, I think.

OLIVIA (*smiling*). I think so. . . .

GEORGE (*to* BRIAN). Then you'd better have a talk with me—er—Brian.

BRIAN. Thank you very much, sir.

GEORGE. Well, come along then. (*Looking at his watch*) I am going up to town after tea, so we'd better——

DINAH. I say! Are you going to London?

GEORGE (*with the smile of the conspirator*). A little business. Never you mind, young lady.

DINAH (*calmly*). All right. Only, bring me back something nice.

GEORGE (*to* BRIAN). Shall we walk down and look at the pigs?

BRIAN. Righto!

OLIVIA. Don't go far, dear. I may want you in a moment.

GEORGE. All right, darling, we'll be on the terrace.

[*They go out together.*

DINAH. Brian and George always try to discuss me in front of the pigs. So tactless of them. Are you going to London, too, darling?

OLIVIA. To-morrow morning.

DINAH. What are you going to do in London?

OLIVIA. Oh, shopping, and—one or two little things.

DINAH. With George?

OLIVIA. Yes. . . .

DINAH. I say, wasn't it lovely about Pim?

OLIVIA. Lovely?

DINAH. Yes; he told me all about it. Making such a hash of things, I mean.

OLIVIA (*innocently*). Did he make a hash of things?

DINAH. Well, I mean keeping on coming like that. And if you look at it all round—well, for all he had to say, he needn't really have come at all.

OLIVIA (*smiling to herself*). I shouldn't quite say that, Dinah. (*She stands up and shakes out the curtains.*)

DINAH. I say, aren't they jolly?

OLIVIA (*demurely*). I'm so glad everybody likes them. Tell George I'm ready, will you?

DINAH. I say, is *he* going to hang them up for you?

OLIVIA. Well, I thought he could reach best.

DINAH. Righto! What fun! (*At the windows*) George! George! (*To* OLIVIA) Brian is just telling George about the five shillings he's got in the Post Office. . . . George!

GEORGE (*from the terrace*). Coming!

(*He hurries in, the model husband.* BRIAN *follows.*)

OLIVIA. Oh, George, just hang these up for me, will you?

GEORGE. Of course, darling. I'll get the steps from the library.

[*He hurries out.*

(BRIAN *takes out his sketching block. It is obvious that his five shillings has turned the scale. He bows to* DINAH. *He kisses* OLIVIA's *hand with an air. He motions to* DINAH *to be seated.*)

DINAH (*impressed*). What is it?

BRIAN (*beginning to draw*). Portrait of Lady Strange.

(GEORGE *hurries in with the steps, and gets to work. There is a great deal of curtain, and for the moment he becomes slightly involved in it. However, by draping it over his head and shoulders, he manages to get successfully up the steps. There we may leave him. But we have not quite finished with* MR. PIM. *It is a matter of honour with him now that he should get his little story quite accurate before passing out of the* MARDENS' *life for ever. So he comes back for the last time; for the last time we see his head at the window. He whispers to* OLIVIA.)

MR. PIM. Mrs. Marden! I've just remembered. His name was *Ernest* Polwittle—*not* Henry.

(*He goes off happily. A curious family the* MARDENS. *Perhaps somebody else would have committed bigamy if he had not remembered in time that it was Ernest. . . . Ernest. . . . Yes. . . . Now he can go back with an easy conscience to the Trevors.*)

THE CAMBERLEY TRIANGLE

A COMEDY IN ONE ACT

CHARACTERS

KATE CAMBERLEY.
CYRIL NORWOOD (*her lover*).
DENNIS CAMBERLEY (*her husband*).

THIS play was first produced by Mr. Godfrey Tearle at the Coliseum on September 8, 1919, with the following cast:

Dennis Camberley	- -	GODFREY TEARLE.
Kate Camberley	- -	MARY MALONE.
Cyril Norwood	- -	EWAN BROOK.

THE CAMBERLEY TRIANGLE

It is an evening of 1919 in KATE's *drawing-room. She is expecting him, and the Curtain goes up as he is announced.*

MAID. Mr. Cyril Norwood.

> (*He comes in.*)

NORWOOD (*for the* MAID's *benefit, but you may be sure she knows*). Ah, good evening, Mrs. Camberley!

KATE. Good evening!

> (*They shake hands.* NORWOOD *is sleek and prosperous, in a morning coat with a white slip to his waistcoat. He is good-looking in rather an obvious way with rather an obvious moustache. Most women like him—at least, so he will tell you.*)

NORWOOD (*as soon as they are alone*). My darling!

KATE. Cyril!

> (*He takes her hands and kisses them. He would kiss her face, but she is not quite ready for this.*)

NORWOOD. You let me yesterday. Why mayn't I kiss you to-day?

KATE. Not just yet, dear. I want to talk to you. Come and sit down.

> (*They sit on the sofa together.*)

NORWOOD. You aren't sorry for what you said yesterday?

KATE (*looking at him thoughtfully, and then shaking her head*). No.

NORWOOD. Then what's happened?

KATE. I've just had a letter from Dennis.

NORWOOD (*anxiously*). Dennis—your husband?

KATE. Yes.

NORWOOD. Where does he write from?

KATE. India.

NORWOOD. Oh, well!

KATE. He says I may expect him home almost as soon as I get the letter.

NORWOOD. Good Heavens!

KATE. Yes. . . .

NORWOOD (*always hopeful*). Perhaps he didn't catch the boat that he expected to. Wouldn't he have cabled from somewhere on the way?

KATE. You can't depend on cables nowadays. *I* don't know—— What are we to do, Cyril?

NORWOOD. You know what I always wanted you to do. (*He takes her hands*) Come away with me.

KATE (*doubtfully*). And let Dennis come home and find—an empty house?

NORWOOD (*eagerly*). You are nothing to him, and he is nothing to you. A war-wedding!—after you'd been engaged to each other for a week! And forty-eight hours afterwards he is sent out to India—and you haven't seen him since.

KATE. Yes. I keep telling myself that.

NORWOOD. The world may say that you're his wife and he's your husband, but—what do you know of him? He won't even be the boy you married. He'll be a stranger whom you'll hardly recognize. And you aren't the girl *he* married. You're a woman now, and you're just beginning to learn what love is. Come with *me*.

THE CAMBERLEY TRIANGLE

KATE. It's true, it's true. But he *has* been fighting for us. And to come home again after those four years of exile, and find——

NORWOOD. Exile—that's making much too much of it. He's come through the war safely, and he's probably had what he'd call a topping good time. Like enough he's been in love half-a-dozen times himself since—on leave in India and that sort of thing. India! Well, you should read Kipling.

KATE. I wonder. Of course, as you say, I don't know him. But I feel that we should be happier afterwards if we were quite straight about it and told him just what had happened. If he had been doing what you say, he would understand—and perhaps be glad of it.

NORWOOD (*uneasily*). Really, darling, it's hardly a thing you can talk over calmly with a husband, even if he—— We don't want any unpleasantness, and—er—— (*Taking her hands again*) Besides, I want you, Kate. It may be weeks before he comes back. We can't go on like this . . . Kate!

KATE. Do you love me so very much?

NORWOOD. My darling!

KATE. Well, let us wait till the end of the week—in case he comes. I don't want to seem to be afraid of him.

NORWOOD (*eagerly*). And then?

KATE. Then I'll come with you.

NORWOOD (*taking her in his arms*). My darling! . . . There! And now what are you going to do? Ask me to stay to dinner or what?

KATE. Certainly not, sir. I'm going *out* to dinner to-night.

NORWOOD (*jealously*). Who with?

KATE. You.

NORWOOD (*eagerly*). At our little restaurant? (*She

nods) Good girl! Then go and put on a hat, while I ring 'em up and see if they've got a table.

KATE. What fun! I won't be a moment. (*She goes to the door*) Cyril, you will *always* love me?

NORWOOD. Of course I will, darling. (*She nods at him and goes out. He is very well pleased with himself when he is left alone. He goes to the telephone with a smile*) Gerrard 11,001. Yes . . . I want a table for two. To-night . . . Mr. Cyril Norwood. . . . Oh, in about half an hour. . . . Yes, for two. Is that all right? . . . Thank you.

> (*He puts the receiver back and turns round to see* DENNIS CAMBERLEY, *who has just come in.* DENNIS *is certainly a man now; very easily and pleasantly master of himself and of anybody else who gets in his way.*)

NORWOOD (*surprised*). Hallo!

DENNIS (*nodding pleasantly*). Hallo!

NORWOOD (*wondering who he is*). You—er——?

DENNIS. I just came in, Mr. Norwood.

NORWOOD. You know my name?

DENNIS. Oh yes, I've heard a good deal about you, Mr. Cyril Norwood.

NORWOOD (*stiffly*). I don't think I've had the pleasure of—er——

DENNIS (*winningly*). Oh, but I'm sure you must have heard a good deal about *me*.

NORWOOD. Good God, you don't mean——

DENNIS. I do, indeed. (*With a bow*) Dennis Camberley, the missing husband. (*Pleadingly*) You *have* heard about me, *haven't* you?

NORWOOD. I—er—Mr. Camberley, yes, of course. So you're back?

DENNIS. Yes, I'm back. Sometimes they don't come back, Mr. Norwood, and sometimes—they do. . . . Even

THE CAMBERLEY TRIANGLE 149

after four years. . . . But you *did* talk about me sometimes?

NORWOOD. How did you know my name?

DENNIS. A little bird told me about you.

NORWOOD (*turning away in anger*). Pooh!

DENNIS. One of those little Eastern birds, which sit on the backs of crocodiles, searching for—well, let us say, breakfast. He said to me one morning: "Talking of parasites," he said, "do you know Mr. Cyril Norwood?" he said, "because I could tell you an interesting story about him," he said, "if you care to——"

NORWOOD (*wheeling round furiously*). Look here, sir, we'd better have it out quite plainly. I don't want any veiled insults and sneers from you. I admit that an unfortunate situation has arisen, but we must look facts in the face. You may be Mrs. Camberley's husband, but she has not seen you for four years, and—well, she and I love each other. There you have it. What are you going to do?

DENNIS (*anxiously*). You don't feel that I have neglected her, Mr. Norwood? You see, I couldn't come home for week-ends very well, and——

NORWOOD. What are you going to do?

DENNIS (*pleasantly*). Well, what do you suggest?

NORWOOD (*taken aback*). Really, sir, I—er——

DENNIS. You see, I feel so out of it all. I've been leading such a nasty, uncivilised life for the last four years, I really hardly know what is—what is being done. Now *you* have been mixing in Society . . . making munitions . . .

NORWOOD (*stiffly*). I have been engaged on important work for the Government of a confidential nature——

DENNIS. You, as I was saying, have been mixing in

Society, engaged on important work for the Government of a confidential nature——

NORWOOD. It was my great regret that I had no opportunity of enlisting——

DENNIS. With no opportunity, as I was about to say, of enlisting, but with many opportunities, fortunately, of making love to my wife.

NORWOOD. Now look here, Mr. Camberley, I've already told you——

DENNIS (*soothing him*). But, my dear Mr. Norwood, I'm only doing what you said. I'm looking facts in the face. (*Surprised*) You aren't ashamed of having made love to my wife, are you?

NORWOOD (*impatiently*). What are you going to do? That's all that matters between you and me. What are you going to do?

DENNIS. Well, that was what I was going to ask you. You're so much more in the swim than I am. (*Earnestly*) What *is* being done in Society just now? You must have heard a good deal of gossip about it. All your friends, who were also engaged on important work of a confidential nature, with no opportunity of enlisting—don't they tell you their own experiences? What *have* the husbands been doing lately when they came back from the front?

NORWOOD (*advancing on him angrily*). Now, once and for all, sir——

(KATE *comes in, with a hat in each hand, calling to* NORWOOD *as she comes.*)

KATE. Oh, Cyril—which of these two hats—(*she sees her husband*)—Dennis!

DENNIS (*looking at her steadfastly*). How are *you*, Kate?

KATE (*stammering*). You've—you've come back? (*She puts the hats down.*)

THE CAMBERLEY TRIANGLE 151

DENNIS. I've come back. As I was telling Mr. Norwood.

KATE (*looking from one to the other*). You——?

DENNIS (*smiling*). Oh, we're quite old friends.

NORWOOD (*going to her*). I've told him, Kate.

> (*He takes her hands, and tries to look defiantly at* DENNIS, *though he is not feeling like that at all.*)

KATE (*looking anxiously at* DENNIS). What are you going to do?

> (*She can hardly make him out. He is different from the husband who left her four years ago.*)

DENNIS. Well, that's what Cyril keeps asking me. (*To* NORWOOD) You don't mind my calling you Cyril?—such an old friend of my wife's——

KATE (*unable to make him out*). Dennis! (*She is frightened.*)

NORWOOD (*soothingly*). It's all right, dear.

DENNIS. Do let's sit down and talk it over in a friendly way.

KATE (*going to him*). Dennis, can you ever forgive me? We never ought to have got married—we knew each other so little—you had to go away so soon—I—I was going to write and tell you—oh, I wish——

DENNIS. That's all right, Kate. (*He will not let her come too close to him. He steps back and looks at her from head to feet*) You've altered.

KATE. That's just it, Dennis. I'm not the girl who——

DENNIS. You've grown four years younger and four years prettier.

KATE (*dropping her eyes*). Have I?

DENNIS. Yes. . . . You do your hair a new way.

KATE (*surprised*). Do you like it?

DENNIS. I love it.

NORWOOD (*coughing*). Yes, well, perhaps we'd better——

DENNIS (*with a start*). I beg your pardon, Cyril. I was forgetting you for the moment. Well, now do sit down. (NORWOOD *and* KATE *sit down together on the sofa, but* DENNIS *remains standing*) That's right.

KATE. Well?

DENNIS (*to* KATE). You want to marry him, eh?

NORWOOD. We have already told you the circumstances, Mr. Camberley. I need hardly say how regrettable it is that—er—but at the same time these —er—things will happen, and since it—er—has happened——

KATE. I feel I hardly know you, Dennis. Did I love you when I married you? I don't know. It was so sudden. We had no time to find out anything about each other. And now you come back—a stranger——

DENNIS (*jerking his head at* NORWOOD). And he's not a stranger, eh?

KATE (*dropping her eyes*). N-no.

DENNIS. You feel you know all about *him*?

KATE. I—we—— (*She is unhappy.*)

NORWOOD. We have discovered that we love each other. (*Taking her hands*) My darling one, this is distressing for you. Let *me*——

DENNIS (*sharply*). It wouldn't be distressing for her, if you didn't keep messing her about. Why the devil can't you sit on a chair by yourself?

NORWOOD (*indignantly*). Really!

KATE (*freeing herself from him, and moving to the extreme end of the sofa*). What are you going to do, Dennis?

DENNIS (*looking at them thoughtfully, his chin on his hand*). I don't know. . . . It's difficult. I don't want to do anything melodramatic. I mean (*to* KATE) it

THE CAMBERLEY TRIANGLE

wouldn't really help matters if I did shoot him, would it?

> (KATE *looks at him without saying anything, trying to understand this new man who has come into her life.* NORWOOD *swallows, and tries very hard to say something.*)

NORWOOD. I—I——

DENNIS (*turning to him*). *You* don't think so, do you?

NORWOOD. I—I——

DENNIS. No, I'm quite sure you're right. It wouldn't really help. It is difficult, isn't it? You see (*to* KATE) *you* love *him*—(*he waits a moment for her to say it if she will, but she only looks at him*)—and *he* says *he* loves *you*, but at the same time I *am* your husband. . . . (*He walks up and down thoughtfully, and then says suddenly to* NORWOOD) I'll tell you what—I'll fight you for her.

NORWOOD (*trying to be firm*). I think we'd better leave this eighteenth-century nonsense out of it.

DENNIS (*pleasantly*). They fight in the twentieth century, too, Mr. Norwood. Perhaps you hadn't heard what we've been doing these last four years? Oh, quite a lot of it. . . . Well?

NORWOOD. You don't wish me to believe that you're serious?

DENNIS. Perfectly. Swords, pistols, fists, catch-as-catch-can—what would you like?

NORWOOD. I do not propose to indulge in an undignified scuffle for the—er—lady of my heart.

DENNIS (*cheerfully*). Nothing doing in scuffles, eh? All right, then, I'll toss you for her.

NORWOOD. Now you're merely being vulgar. (*To* KATE) My dear——

> (*She motions him back with her hand, but does not take her eyes off* DENNIS.)

DENNIS. Really, Mr. Norwood, you're a little hard to please. If you don't like my suggestions, perhaps you will make one of your own.

NORWOOD. This is obviously a matter in which it is for the—er—lady to choose.

DENNIS. You think Mrs. Camberley should choose between us?

NORWOOD. Certainly.

DENNIS. What do you say, Kate?

KATE. You are very generous, Dennis.

DENNIS (*after a pause*). Very well, you shall choose.

NORWOOD (*complacently*). Ah!

DENNIS. Wait a moment, Mr. Norwood. (*To* KATE) When did you first meet him?

KATE. A year ago.

DENNIS. And he's been making love to you for a year? (KATE *bends her head*) He's been making love to you for a year?

NORWOOD. I think, sir, that the sooner the lady makes her choice, and brings this distressing scene to a close —— After all, is it fair to her to——?

DENNIS. Are you fair to *me*? You've been making love to her for a year. *I* made love to her for a fortnight—four years ago. And now you want her to choose between us. Is *that* fair?

NORWOOD. You hardly expect us to wait a year before she is allowed to make up her mind?

DENNIS. I waited four years for her out there. . . . However, I won't ask you to wait a year. I'll ask you to wait for five minutes.

KATE. What is it you want us to do, Dennis?

DENNIS. I want you to listen to both of us, for five minutes each; that's all. After all, we're your suitors, aren't we? You're going to choose between us. Very well, then, you must hear what we have to say. Mr.

THE CAMBERLEY TRIANGLE

Norwood shall have five minutes alone with you in which to present his case; five minutes in which to tell you how beautiful you are . . . and how rich he is . . . and how happy you'll be together. And I shall have *my* five minutes.

NORWOOD (*sneering*). Five minutes in which to tell her lies about *me*, eh?

DENNIS. Damn it, you've had a whole year in which to tell her lies about yourself; you oughtn't to grudge me five minutes. (*To* KATE) Well?

KATE. I agree, Dennis.

DENNIS. Good. (*He spins a coin, puts it on the back of his hand, and says to* NORWOOD) Call!

NORWOOD. What on earth——

DENNIS. Choice of innings.

NORWOOD. I never heard of anything so—Tails.

DENNIS (*uncovering it*). Heads. You shall have first knock.

NORWOOD (*bewildered*). What do you—I don't——

DENNIS. You have five minutes in which to lay your case before Mrs. Camberley. (*He looks at his watch*) Five minutes—and then I shall come back. . . . Is there a fire in the dining-room, Kate?

KATE (*smiling in spite of herself*). A gas-fire; it isn't lit.

DENNIS. Then I shall light it. (*To* NORWOOD) That will make the room nice and warm for you by the time you've finished. (*He goes to the door and says again*) Five minutes.

> (*There is an awkward silence after he is gone.* KATE *waits for* NORWOOD *to say something, but* NORWOOD *doesn't know in the least what is expected of him.*)

NORWOOD (*looking anxiously at the door*). What's the fellow's game, eh?

KATE. Game?

NORWOOD. Yes. What's he up to?

KATE. Is he up to anything?

NORWOOD. I don't like it. Why the devil did he choose to-day to come back? If he'd waited another week, we'd have been safely away together. What's his game, I wonder?

(*He walks up and down, worrying it out.*)

KATE. I don't think he's playing a game. He's just giving me my chance.

NORWOOD. What chance?

KATE. A chance to decide between you.

NORWOOD. You've decided that, Kate. You've had a year to think about it in, and you've decided. We love each other; you're coming away with me; that's all settled. Only . . . what the deuce is he up to?

KATE (*sitting down and talking to herself*). You're quite right about my not knowing him. . . . How one rushed into marriage in those early days of the war— knowing nothing about each other. And then they come back, and even the little one thought one did know is different. . . . I suppose he feels the same about me.

NORWOOD (*to himself*). Damn him!

KATE (*after a pause*). Well, Cyril?

NORWOOD (*looking sharply round at her*). Well?

KATE. We haven't got very long.

NORWOOD (*looking at his watch*). He really means to come back—in five minutes?

KATE. You heard him say so.

NORWOOD (*going up to her and speaking eagerly*). What's the matter with slipping out now? You've got a hat here. We can slip out quietly. He won't hear us. He'll come back and find us gone—well, what can he do? Probably he'll hang about for a bit and then go to his club. We'll have a bit of dinner; ring up your

THE CAMBERLEY TRIANGLE

maid; get her to meet you with some things, and go off by the night mail. Scotland—anywhere you like. Let the whole business simmer down a bit. We don't want any melodramatic eighteenth-century nonsense.

KATE. Go out now, and not wait for him to have *his* five minutes?

NORWOOD (*impatiently*). What does he *want* with five minutes? What's the *good* of it to him? Just to take a pathetic farewell of you, and pretend that you've ruined his life, when all the time he's chuckling in his sleeve at having got rid of you so easily. *I* know these young fellows. Some Major's wife in India is what *he's* got his eye on. . . . Or else he'll try fooling around with the hands-up business. You don't want to be mixed up with any scandal of *that* sort. No, the best thing we can do—I'm speaking for *your* sake, Kate—is to slip off quietly, while we've got the chance. We can *write* and explain all that we want to explain.

KATE (*looking wonderingly at him—another man whom she doesn't know*). Is that playing quite fair to Dennis?

NORWOOD. Good Lord, this isn't a game! Camberley may think so with his tossing-up and all the rest of it, but you and I aren't children. Everything's fair in a case like this. Put your hat on—quickly—(*he gets it for her*)—here you are——

KATE (*standing up*). I'm not sure, Cyril.

NORWOOD. What d'you mean?

KATE. He expects me to wait for him.

NORWOOD. If it comes to that, he expected you to wait for him four years ago.

KATE. Yes. . . . (*Quietly*) Thank you for reminding me.

NORWOOD. Kate, don't be stupid. What's happened to you? Of course, I know it's been beastly upsetting for you, all this—but then, why do you want to go on with it? Why do you want *more* upsetting scenes? You've got a chance now of getting out of it all, and—— (*He looks at his watch*) Good Lord!

KATE. Is the five minutes over?

NORWOOD. Quick, quick! (*He puts his fingers to his lips*) Quietly. (*He walks on tiptoe to the door.*)

KATE. Cyril!

NORWOOD. H'sh!

KATE (*sitting down again*). It's no good, Cyril, I must wait for him.

> (*The door opens, and* NORWOOD *starts back quickly as* DENNIS *comes in.*)

DENNIS (*looking at his watch*). Innings declared closed. (*To* NORWOOD) The dining-room is nicely warmed now, and I've left you an evening paper.

NORWOOD (*going to* KATE). Look here, Mr. Camberley, Kate and I——

DENNIS. Mrs. Camberley, no doubt, will tell me.

> (*He holds the door open and waits politely for* NORWOOD *to go.*)

NORWOOD. I don't know what your game is——

DENNIS. You've never been in Mesopotamia, Mr. Norwood?

NORWOOD. Never.

DENNIS. It's a very trying place for the temper. . . . I'm waiting for you.

NORWOOD (*irresolute*). Well, I—— (*He comes sulkily to the door*) Well, I shall come back for Kate in five minutes.

DENNIS. Mrs. Camberley and I will be ready for you. You know your way?

> [NORWOOD *goes out.*
> (DENNIS *shuts the door. He comes into the room and stands looking at* KATE.)

THE CAMBERLEY TRIANGLE

KATE (*uncomfortably*). Well?

DENNIS. No, don't move. I just want to look at you . . . I've seen you like that for four years. Don't move. . . . I've been in some dreary places, but you've been with me most of the time. Just let's have a last look.

KATE. A last look?

DENNIS. Yes.

KATE. You're saying good-bye to me?

DENNIS. I don't know whether it's to you, Kate. To the girl who has been with me these last four years. Was that you?

KATE (*dropping her eyes*). I don't know, Dennis.

DENNIS. I wish to God I wasn't your husband.

KATE. What would you do if you weren't my husband?

DENNIS. Make love to you.

KATE. Can't you do that now?

DENNIS. Being your husband rather handicaps me, you know. I never really stood a chance against the other fellow.

KATE. I was to choose between you, you said. You think that I have already made up my mind?

DENNIS (*smiling*). I think so.

KATE. And chosen him?

DENNIS (*shaking his head*). Oh, no!

KATE (*surprised*). You think I have chosen *you*?

DENNIS (*nodding*). M'm.

KATE (*indignantly*). Really, Dennis! Considering that I had practically arranged to run away with him twenty minutes ago! You must think me very fickle.

DENNIS. Not fickle. Imaginative.

KATE. What do you mean? And why are you so certain that I am going to choose you? And why in that case did you talk about taking a last look at me? And what——?

DENNIS. Of course, we've only got five minutes, but I think that if you asked your questions one at a time——

KATE (*smiling*). Well, you needn't *answer* them all together.

DENNIS. All right then, one at a time. Why am I certain that you will choose me? Because for the first time in your life you have just been alone with Mr. Cyril Norwood. That's what I meant by saying you were imaginative. The Norwood you've been thinking yourself in love with doesn't exist. I'm certain that you've seen him for the first time in these last few minutes. Why, the Archangel Gabriel would have made a hash of a five minutes like that; it would have been impossible for him to have said the right thing to you. Norwood? Good Lord, he didn't stand a chance. You were judging him all the time, weren't you?

KATE (*thoughtfully*). You're very clever, Dennis.

DENNIS (*cheerfully*). Four years' study of the Turkish character.

KATE. But how do you know I'm not judging *you* all the time?

DENNIS. Of course you are. But there's all the difference in the world between judging a stranger like me, and judging the man you thought you were in love with.

KATE. You *are* a stranger to me.

DENNIS. I know. That's why I said good-bye to the girl who had been with me these last four years, the girl I had married. Well, I've said good-bye to her. You're not my wife any longer, Kate; but if you don't mind pretending that I'm not your husband, and just give me a chance of making love to you—well, that's all I want.

KATE. You're very generous, Dennis.

DENNIS. No, I'm not. I'm very much in love; and

THE CAMBERLEY TRIANGLE

for a man very much in love I'm being rather less of a silly ass than usual. Why should you love me? You fell in love with my uniform at the beginning of the war. I was ordered out, and you fell in love with the departing hero. After that? Well, I had four years —alone—in which to think about *you*, and you had four years—with other men—in which to forget *me*. Is it any wonder that——?

[NORWOOD *comes in.*

NORWOOD (*roughly*). Well?

DENNIS. You arrive just in time, Mr. Norwood. I was talking too much. (*To* KATE) Mrs. Camberley, we are both at your disposal. Will you choose between us, which one is to have the happiness of—serving you?

NORWOOD (*holding out his hand to her, and speaking in the voice of the proprietor*). Kate!

(KATE *goes slowly up to him with her hand held out.*)

KATE (*shaking* NORWOOD's *hand*). Good-bye, Mr. Norwood.

NORWOOD (*astounded*). Kate! (*To* DENNIS) You devil!

DENNIS. And only a moment ago I was comparing you to the Archangel Gabriel.

NORWOOD (*sneeringly to* KATE). So you're going to be a loving wife to him after all?

DENNIS (*tapping him kindly on the shoulder*). You'll remember what I said about Mesopotamia?

NORWOOD (*pulling himself together hastily*). Goodbye, Mrs. Camberley. I can only hope that you will be happy.

[*He goes out with dignity.*

DENNIS (*closing the door*). Well, there we agree.

(*He comes back to her.*)

KATE. What a stupid little fool I have been. (*She holds out her arms to him*) Dennis!

DENNIS (*retreating in mock alarm*). Oh no, you don't!

(*He shakes a finger at her*) We're not going to rush it *this* time.

KATE (*reproachfully*). Dennis!

DENNIS. I think you should call me Mr. Camberley.

KATE (*with a smile*). Mr. Camberley.

DENNIS. That's better. Now our courtship begins. (*Bowing low*) Madam, will you do me the great honour of dining with me this evening?

KATE (*curtseying*). I shall be charmed.

DENNIS. Then let us hasten. The carriage waits.

KATE (*holding up the two hats*). Which of these two chapeaux do you prefer, Mr. Camberley?

DENNIS. Might I express a preference for the black one with the pink roses?

KATE. It is very elegant, is it not? (*She puts it on.*)

DENNIS. Vastly becoming, upon my life. . . . I might mention that I am staying at the club. Is your ladyship doing anything to-morrow?

KATE. Nothing of any great importance.

(*He offers his arm and she takes it.*)

DENNIS (*as they go to the door*). Then perhaps I may be permitted to call round to-morrow morning about eleven, and make inquiries as to your ladyship's health.

KATE. It would be very obliging of you, sir.

[*They go out together.*

THE ROMANTIC AGE

A COMEDY IN THREE ACTS

CHARACTERS

HENRY KNOWLE.
MARY KNOWLE (*his wife*).
MELISANDE (*his daughter*).
JANE BAGOT (*his niece*).
BOBBY COOTE.
GERVASE MALLORY.
ERN.
GENTLEMAN SUSAN.
ALICE.

ACT I
The hall of MR. KNOWLE'S *house. Evening.*

ACT II
A glade in the wood. Morning.

ACT III
The hall again. Afternoon.

THIS play was first produced by Mr. Arthur Wontner at the Comedy Theatre on October 18, 1920, with the following cast:

Henry Knowle	A. BROMLEY-DAVENPORT.
Mary Knowle	LOTTIE VENNE.
Melisande	BARBARA HOFFE.
Jane	DOROTHY TETLEY.
Bobby	JOHN WILLIAMS.
Gervase Mallory	ARTHUR WONTNER.
Ern	ROY LENNOL.
Gentleman Susan	H. O. NICHOLSON.
Alice	IRENE RATHBONE.

THE ROMANTIC AGE

ACT I

We are looking at the inner hall of MR. HENRY KNOWLE'S *country house, at about 9.15 of a June evening. There are doors R. and L.—on the right leading to the drawing-room, on the left to the entrance hall, the dining-room and the library. At the back are windows—French windows on the right, then an interval of wall, then casement windows.*

MRS. HENRY KNOWLE, *her daughter,* MELISANDE, *and her niece,* JANE BAGOT, *are waiting for their coffee.* MRS. KNOWLE, *short and stoutish, is reclining on the sofa;* JANE, *pleasant-looking and rather obviously pretty, is sitting in a chair near her, glancing at a book;* MELISANDE, *the beautiful, the romantic, is standing by the open French windows, gazing into the night.*

ALICE, *the parlourmaid, comes in with the coffee. She stands in front of* MRS. KNOWLE, *a little embarrassed because* MRS. KNOWLE'S *eyes are closed. She waits there until* JANE *looks up from her book.*

JANE. Aunt Mary, dear, are you having coffee?

MRS. KNOWLE (*opening her eyes with a start*). Coffee. Oh, yes, coffee. Jane, put the milk in for me. And no sugar. Dr. Anderson is very firm about that. "No sugar, Mrs. Knowle," he said. "Oh, Dr. Anderson!" I said.

(ALICE *has taken the tray to* JANE, *who pours out her own and her aunt's coffee, and takes her cup off the tray.*)

JANE. Thank you.

(ALICE *takes the tray to* MRS. KNOWLE.)

MRS. KNOWLE. Thank you.

(ALICE *goes over to* MELISANDE, *who says nothing, but waves her away.*)

MRS. KNOWLE (*as soon as* ALICE *is gone*). Jane!

JANE. Yes, Aunt Mary?

MRS. KNOWLE. Was my mouth open?

JANE. Oh, *no,* Aunt Mary.

MRS. KNOWLE. Ah, I'm glad of that. It's so bad for the servants. (*She finishes her coffee.*)

JANE (*getting up*). Shall I put it down for you?

MRS. KNOWLE. Thank you, dear.

(JANE *puts the two cups down and goes back to her book.* MRS. KNOWLE *fidgets a little on her sofa.*)

MRS. KNOWLE. Sandy! (*There is no answer*) Sandy!

JANE. Melisande!

(MELISANDE *turns round and comes slowly towards her mother.*)

MELISANDE. Did you call me, Mother?

MRS. KNOWLE. Three times, darling. Didn't you hear me?

MELISANDE. I am sorry, Mother, I was thinking of other things.

MRS. KNOWLE. You think too much, dear. You remember what the great poet tells us. "Do noble things, not dream them all day long." Tennyson, wasn't it? I know I wrote it in your album for you when you were a little girl. It's so true.

MELISANDE. Kingsley, Mother, not Tennyson.

JANE (*nodding*). Kingsley, that's right.

MRS. KNOWLE. Well, it's the same thing. I know when *my* mother used to call me I used to come running up, saying, "What is it, Mummy, darling?" And even if it was anything upstairs, like a handkerchief or a pair of socks to be mended, I used to trot off happily, saying to myself, "Do noble things, not dream them all day long."

MELISANDE. I am sorry, Mother. What is the noble thing you want doing?

MRS. KNOWLE. Well now, you see, I've forgotten. If only you'd come at once, dear——

MELISANDE. I was looking out into the night. It's a wonderful night. Midsummer Night.

MRS. KNOWLE. Midsummer Night. And now I suppose the days will start drawing in, and we shall have winter upon us before we know where we are. All these changes of the seasons are very inconsiderate to an invalid. Ah, now I remember what I wanted, dear. Can you find me another cushion? Dr. Anderson considers it most important that the small of the back should be well supported after a meal. (*Indicating the place*) Just here, dear.

JANE (*jumping up with the cushion from her chair*). Let me, Aunt Mary.

MRS. KNOWLE. Thank you, Jane. Just here, please.

(JANE *arranges it.*)

JANE. Is that right?

MRS. KNOWLE. Thank you, dear. I only do it for Dr. Anderson's sake.

(JANE *goes back to her book and* MELISANDE *goes back to her Midsummer Night. There is silence for a little.*)

MRS. KNOWLE. Oh, Sandy . . . Sandy!

JANE. Melisande!

MELISANDE (*coming patiently down to them*). Yes, Mother?

MRS. KNOWLE. Oh, Sandy, I've just remembered—— (MELISANDE *shudders*.) What is it, darling child? Are you cold? That comes of standing by the open window in a treacherous climate like this. Close the window and come and sit down properly.

MELISANDE. It's a wonderful night, Mother. Midsummer Night. I'm not cold.

MRS. KNOWLE. But you shuddered. I distinctly saw you shudder. Didn't you see her, Jane?

JANE. I'm afraid I wasn't looking, Aunt Mary.

MELISANDE. I didn't shudder because I was cold. I shuddered because you will keep calling me by that horrible name. I shudder every time I hear it.

MRS. KNOWLE (*surprised*). What name, Sandy?

MELISANDE. There it is again. Oh, why did you christen me by such a wonderful, beautiful, magical name as Melisande, if you were going to call me Sandy?

MRS. KNOWLE. Well, dear, as I think I've told you, that was a mistake of your father's. I suppose he got it out of some book. I should certainly never have agreed to it, if I had heard him distinctly. I thought he said Millicent—after your Aunt Milly. And not being very well at the time, and leaving it all to him, I never really knew about it until it was too late to do anything. I did say to your father, "Can't we christen her again?" But there was nothing in the prayer book about it except "riper years," and nobody seemed to know when riper years began. Besides, we were all calling you Sandy then. I think Sandy is a very pretty name, don't you, Jane?

JANE. Oh, but don't you think Melisande is beautiful, Aunt Mary? I mean really beautiful.

MRS. KNOWLE. Well, it never seems to me quite respectable, not for a nicely-brought-up young girl in a Christian house. It makes me think of the sort of person who meets a strange young man to whom she has never been introduced, and talks to him in a forest with her hair coming down. They find her afterwards floating in a pool. Not at all the thing one wants for one's daughter.

JANE. Oh, but how thrilling it sounds!

MRS. KNOWLE. Well, I think you are safer with "Jane," dear. Your mother knew what she was about. And if I can save my only child from floating in a pool by calling her Sandy, I certainly think it is my duty to do so.

MELISANDE (*to herself ecstatically*). Melisande!

MRS. KNOWLE (*to* MELISANDE). Oh, and talking about floating in a pool reminds me about the bread-sauce at dinner to-night. You heard what your father said? You must give cook a good talking to in the morning. She has been getting very careless lately. I don't know what's come over her.

MELISANDE. *I've* come over her. When *you* were over her, everything was all right. You know all about housekeeping; you take an interest in it. I don't. I hate it. How can you expect the house to be run properly when they all know I hate it? Why did you ever give it up and make me do it when you know how I hate it?

MRS. KNOWLE. Well, you must learn not to hate it. I'm sure Jane here doesn't hate it, and her mother is always telling me what a great help she is.

MELISANDE (*warningly*). It's no good your saying you like it, Jane, after what you told me yesterday.

JANE. I don't like it, but it doesn't make me miserable doing it. But then I'm different. I'm not romantic like Melisande.

MELISANDE. One doesn't need to be very romantic not to want to talk about bread-sauce. Bread-sauce on a night like this!

MRS. KNOWLE. Well, I'm only thinking of you, Sandy,

not of myself. If I thought about myself I should disregard all the warnings that Dr. Anderson keeps giving me, and I should insist on doing the housekeeping just as I always used to. But I have to think of you. I want to see you married to some nice, steady young man before I die—my handkerchief, Jane—(JANE *gets up and gives her her handkerchief from the other end of the sofa*)—before I die (*she touches her eyes with her handkerchief*), and no nice young man will want to marry you, if you haven't learnt how to look after his house for him.

MELISANDE (*contemptuously*). If that's marriage, I shall never get married.

JANE (*shocked*). Melisande, darling!

MRS. KNOWLE. Dr. Anderson was saying, only yesterday, trying to make me more cheerful, "Why, Mrs. Knowle," he said, "you'll live another hundred years yet." "Dr. Anderson," I said, "I don't *want* to live another hundred years. I only want to live until my dear daughter, Melisande"—I didn't say Sandy to him because it seemed rather familiar—"I only want to live until my daughter Melisande is happily married to some nice, steady young man. Do this for me, Dr. Anderson," I said, "and I shall be your lifelong debtor." He promised to do his best. It was then that he mentioned about the cushion in the small of the back after meals. And so don't forget to tell cook about the bread-sauce, will you, dear?

MELISANDE. I will tell her, Mother.

MRS. KNOWLE. That's right. I like a man to be interested in his food. I hope both your husbands, Sandy and Jane, will take a proper interest in what they eat. You will find that, after you have been married some years, and told each other everything you did and saw before you met, there isn't really anything to talk about at meals except food. And you must talk; I hope you will both remember that. Nothing breaks up the home so quickly as silent meals. Of course, breakfast doesn't matter, because he has his paper then; and after you have said, "Is there anything in the paper, dear?" and he has said, "No," then he doesn't expect anything more. I wonder sometimes why they go on printing the newspapers. I've been married twenty years, and there has never been anything in the paper yet.

MELISANDE. Oh, Mother, I hate to hear you talking about marriage like that. Wasn't there ever *any* kind of romance between you and Father? Not even when he was wooing you? Wasn't there ever one magic Midsummer morning when you saw suddenly "a livelier emerald twinkle in the grass, a purer sapphire melt into the sea"? Wasn't there ever one passionate ecstatic moment when "once he drew with one long kiss my whole soul through my lips, as sunlight drinketh dew"? Or did you talk about bread-sauce *all* the time?

JANE (*eagerly*). Tell us about it, Aunt Mary.

MRS. KNOWLE. Well, dear, there isn't very much to tell. I am quite sure that we never drank dew together, or anything like that, as Sandy suggests, and it wasn't by the sea at all, it was at Surbiton. He used to come down from London with his racquet and play tennis with us. And then he would stay on to supper sometimes, and then after supper we would go into the garden together—it was quite dark then, but everything smelt so beautifully, I shall always remember it—and we talked, oh, I don't know what about, but I knew somehow that I should marry him one day. I don't think *he* knew—he wasn't sure—and then he came to a subscription dance one evening—I think Mother, your grandmother, guessed that that was to be my great evening, because she was very particular about my dress, and I remember she sent me upstairs again before we started, because I hadn't got the right pair of shoes on—rather a tight pair—however, I put them on. And there was a hansom outside the hall, and it was our last dance together, and he said, "Shall we sit it out, Miss Bagot?" Well, of course, I was only too glad to, and we sat it out in the hansom, driving all round Surbiton, and what your grandmother would have said I don't know, but, of course, I never told her. And when we got home after the dance, I went up to her room—as soon as I'd got my shoes off—and said, "Mother, I have some wonderful news for you," and she said, "*Not* Mr. Knowle—Henry?" and I said, "'M," rather bright-eyed you know, and wanting to cry. And she said, "Oh, my darling child!" and—Jane, where's my handkerchief? (*It has dropped off the sofa and* JANE *picks it up*) Thank you, dear. (*She dabs her eyes*) Well, that's really all, you know, except that—(*she dabs her eyes again*)—I'm afraid I'm feeling rather overcome. I'm sure Dr. Anderson would say it was very bad for me to feel overcome. Your poor dear grandmother. Jane, dear, why did you ask me to tell you all this? I must go away and compose myself before your uncle and Mr. Coote come in. I don't know what I should do if Mr. Coote saw me like this. (*She begins to get up*) And after calling me a Spartan Mother only yesterday, because I said that if any nice, steady young man came along and took my own dear little girl away from me, I should bear the terrible wrench in silence rather than cause either of them a moment's remorse. (*She is up now*) There!

JANE. Shall I come with you?

MRS. KNOWLE. No, dear, not just now. Let me be by myself for a little. (*She turns back suddenly at the door*) Oh! Perhaps later on, when the men come from

ACT I]   THE ROMANTIC AGE   173

the dining-room, dear Jane, you might join me, with your Uncle Henry—if the opportunity occurs. . . . But only if it occurs, of course.

[*She goes.*

JANE (*coming back to the sofa*). Poor Aunt Mary! It always seems so queer that one's mother and aunts and people should have had their romances too.

MELISANDE. Do you call that romance, Jane? Tennis and subscription dances and wearing tight shoes?

JANE (*awkwardly*). Well, no, darling, not romance of course, but you know what I mean.

MELISANDE. Just think of the commonplace little story which mother has just told us, and compare it with any of the love-stories of history. Isn't it pitiful, Jane, that people should be satisfied now with so little?

JANE. Yes, darling, very, very sad, but I don't think Aunt Mary——

MELISANDE. I am not blaming Mother. It is the same almost everywhere nowadays. There is no romance left.

JANE. No, darling. Of course, I am not romantic like you, but I do agree with you. It is very sad. Somehow there is no—(*she searches for the right word*)—no *romance* left.

MELISANDE. Just think of the average marriage. It makes one shudder.

JANE (*doing her best*). Positively shudder!

MELISANDE. He meets Her at—(*she shudders*)—a subscription dance, or a tennis party—(*she shudders again*) or—at *golf*. He calls upon her mother—perhaps in a top hat—perhaps (*tragically*) even in a bowler hat.

JANE. A bowler hat! One shudders.

MELISANDE. Her mother makes tactful inquiries about his income—discovers that he is a nice, steady young man—and decides that he shall marry her daughter. He is asked to come again, he is invited to parties; it is understood that he is falling in love with the daughter. The rest of the family are encouraged to leave them alone together—if the opportunity occurs, Jane. (*Contemptuously*) But, of course, only if it occurs.

JANE (*awkwardly*). Yes, dear.

MELISANDE. One day he proposes to her.

JANE (*to herself ecstatically*). Oh!

MELISANDE. He stutters out a few unbeautiful words which she takes to be a proposal. She goes and tells Mother. He goes and tells Father. They are engaged. They talk about each other as "my fiancé." Perhaps they are engaged for months and months——

JANE. Years and years sometimes, Melisande.

MELISANDE. For years and years—and wherever they go, people make silly little jokes about them, and cough very loudly if they go into a room where the two of them are. And then they get married at last, and everybody comes and watches them get married, and makes more silly jokes, and they go away for what they call a honeymoon, and they tell everybody—they shout it out in the newspapers—*where* they are going for their honeymoon; and then they come back and start talking about bread-sauce. Oh, Jane, it's horrible.

JANE. Horrible, darling. (*With a French air*) But what would you?

MELISANDE (*in a now thrilling voice*). What would I? Ah, what would I, Jane?

JANE. Because you see, Sandy—I mean Melisande—you see, darling, this *is* the twentieth century, and——

MELISANDE. Sometimes I see him clothed in mail, riding beneath my lattice window.

> All in the blue unclouded weather
> Thick-jewelled shone the saddle leather,
> The helmet and the helmet feather

> Burned like one burning flame together,
> As he rode down to Camelot.
>
> And from his blazoned baldric slung
> A mighty silver bugle hung,
> And as he rode his armour rung
> As he rode down to Camelot.

JANE. I know, dear. But of course they *don't* nowadays.

MELISANDE. And as he rides beneath my room, singing to himself, I wave one lily hand to him from my lattice, and toss him down a gage, a gage for him to wear in his helm, a rose—perhaps just a rose.

JANE (*awed*). No, Melisande, would you really? Wave a lily hand to him? (*She waves one*) I mean, wouldn't it be rather—*you* know. Rather forward.

MELISANDE. Forward!

JANE (*upset*). Well, I mean—— Well, of course, I suppose it was different in those days.

MELISANDE. How else could he know that I loved him? How else could he wear my gage in his helm when he rode to battle?

JANE. Well, of course, there *is* that.

MELISANDE. And then when he has slain his enemies in battle, he comes back to me. I knot my sheets together so as to form a rope—for I have been immured in my room—and I let myself down to him. He places me on the saddle in front of him, and we ride forth together into the world—together for always!

JANE (*a little uncomfortably*). You do get *married*, I suppose, darling, or do you—er——

MELISANDE. We stop at a little hermitage on the way, and a good priest marries us.

JANE (*relieved*). Ah, yes.

MELISANDE. And sometimes he is not in armour. He is a prince from Fairyland. My father is king of a neighbouring country, a country which is sorely troubled by a dragon.

JANE. By a what, dear?

MELISANDE. A dragon.

JANE. Oh, yes, of course.

MELISANDE. The king, my father, offers my hand and half his kingdom to anybody who will slay the monster. A prince who happens to be passing through the country essays the adventure. Alas, the dragon devours him.

JANE. Oh, Melisande, that isn't *the* one?

MELISANDE. My eyes have barely rested upon him. He has aroused no emotion in my heart.

JANE. Oh, I'm so glad.

MELISANDE. Another prince steps forward. Impetuously he rushes upon the fiery monster. Alas, he likewise is consumed.

JANE (*sympathetically*). Poor fellow.

MELISANDE. And then one evening a beautiful and modest youth in blue and gold appears at my father's court, and begs that he too be allowed to try his fortune with the dragon. Passing through the great hall on my way to my bed-chamber, I see him suddenly. Our eyes meet. . . . Oh, Jane!

JANE. Darling! . . . You ought to have lived in those days, Melisande. They would have suited you so well.

MELISANDE. Will they never come back again?

JANE. Well, I don't quite see how they can. People don't dress in blue and gold nowadays. I mean men.

MELISANDE. No. (*She sighs*) Well, I suppose I shall never marry.

JANE. Of course, I'm not romantic like you, darling, and I don't have time to read all the wonderful books you read, and though I quite agree with everything

ACT I] THE ROMANTIC AGE 177

you say, and of course it must have been thrilling to have lived in those wonderful old days, still here we are, and (*with a wave of the hand*)—and what I mean is—here we are.

MELISANDE. You are content to put romance out of your life, and to make the ordinary commonplace marriage?

JANE. What I mean is, that it wouldn't be commonplace if it was the right man. Some nice, clean-looking Englishman—I don't say beautiful—pleasant, and good at games, dependable, not very clever perhaps, but making enough money——

MELISANDE (*carelessly*). It sounds rather like Bobby.

JANE (*confused*). It isn't like Bobby, or any one else particularly. It's just anybody. It wasn't any particular person. I was just describing the sort of man without thinking of any one in——

MELISANDE. All right, dear, all right.

JANE. Besides, we all know Bobby's devoted to *you*.

MELISANDE (*firmly*). Now, look here, Jane, I warn you solemnly that if you think you are going to leave me and Bobby alone together this evening—— (*Voices are heard outside.*) Well, I warn you.

JANE (*in a whisper*). Of course not, darling. (*With perfect tact*) And, as I was saying, Melisande, it was quite the most—— Ah, here you are at last! We wondered what had happened to you!

Enter BOBBY *and* MR. KNOWLE. JANE *has already described* BOBBY *for us.* MR. KNOWLE *is a pleasant, middle-aged man with a sense of humour, which he cultivates for his own amusement entirely.*

BOBBY. Were you very miserable without us? (*He goes towards them.*)

JANE (*laughing*). Very.

(MELISANDE *gets up as* BOBBY *comes, and moves away.*)

MR. KNOWLE. Where's your Mother, Sandy?

MELISANDE. In the dining-room, I think, Father.

MR. KNOWLE. Ah! Resting, no doubt. By the way, you won't forget what I said about the bread-sauce, will you?

MELISANDE. You don't want it remembered, Father, do you? What you said?

MR. KNOWLE. Not the actual words. All I want, my dear, is that you should endeavour to explain to the cook the difference between bread-sauce and a bread-poultice. Make it clear to her that there is no need to provide a bread-poultice with an obviously healthy chicken, such as we had to-night, but that a properly made bread-sauce is a necessity, if the full flavour of the bird is to be obtained.

MELISANDE. "Full flavour of the bird is to be obtained." Yes, Father.

MR. KNOWLE. That's right, my dear. Bring it home to her. A little quiet talk will do wonders. Well, and so it's Midsummer Night. Why aren't you two out in the garden looking for fairies?

BOBBY. I say, it's a topping night, you know. We ought to be out. D'you feel like a stroll, Sandy?

MELISANDE. No, thank you, Bobby, I don't think I'll go out.

BOBBY. Oh, I say, it's awfully warm.

MR. KNOWLE. Well, Jane, I shall take *you* out. If we meet any of Sandy's fairy friends, you can introduce me.

MELISANDE (*looking across warningly at her*). Jane——

JANE (*awkwardly*). I'm afraid, Uncle Henry, that Melisande and I—I promised Sandy—we——

MR. KNOWLE (*putting her arm firmly through his*). Nonsense. I'm not going to have my niece taken away from me, when she is only staying with us for such a short time. Besides I insist upon being introduced to Titania. I want to complain about the rings on the tennis-lawn. They must dance somewhere else.

JANE (*looking anxiously at* MELISANDE). You see, Uncle Henry, I'm not feeling very——

MELISANDE (*resigned*). All right, Jane.

JANE (*brightly*). All right, Uncle Henry.

MR. KNOWLE (*very brightly*). It's all right, Bobby.

JANE. Come along! (*They go to the open windows together.*)

MR. KNOWLE (*as they go*). Any message for Oberon, if we meet him?

MELISANDE (*gravely*). No, thank you, Father.

MR. KNOWLE. It's his turn to write, I suppose.

(JANE *laughs as they go out together.*)
(*Left alone,* MELISANDE *takes up a book and goes to the sofa with it, while* BOBBY *walks about the room unhappily, whistling to himself. He keeps looking across at her, and at last their eyes meet.*)

MELISANDE (*putting down her book*). Well, Bobby?

BOBBY (*awkwardly*). Well, Sandy?

MELISANDE (*angrily*). Don't call me that; you know how I hate it.

BOBBY. Sorry, Melisande. But it's such a dashed mouthful. And your father was calling you Sandy just now, and you didn't say anything.

MELISANDE. One cannot always control one's parents. There comes a time when it is almost useless to say things to them.

BOBBY (*eagerly*). I never mind your saying things to *me*, Sandy—I mean, Melisande. I never shall mind, really I shan't. Of course, I know I'm not worthy of you, and all that, but—I say, Melisande, isn't there *any* hope?

MELISANDE. Bobby, I asked you not to talk to me like that again.

BOBBY (*coming to her*). I know you did, but I must. I can't believe that you——

MELISANDE. I told you that, if you promised not to talk like that again, then I wouldn't tell anybody anything about it, so that it shouldn't be awkward for you. And I haven't told anybody, not even Jane, to whom I tell all my secrets. Most men, when they propose to a girl, and she refuses them, have to go right out of the country and shoot lions; it's the only thing left for them to do. But I did try and make it easy for *you*, Bobby. (*Sadly*) And now you're beginning all over again.

BOBBY (*awkwardly*). I thought perhaps you might have changed your mind. Lots of girls do.

MELISANDE (*contemptuously*). Lots of girls! Is that how you think of me?

BOBBY. Well, your mother said—— (*He breaks off hurriedly.*)

MELISANDE (*coldly*). Have you been discussing me with my mother?

BOBBY. I say, Sandy, don't be angry. Sorry; I mean Melisande.

MELISANDE. Don't apologise. Go on.

BOBBY. Well, I didn't *discuss* you with your mother. She just happened to say that girls never knew their own minds, and that they always said "No" the first time, and that I needn't be downhearted, because——

MELISANDE. That *you* needn't? You mean you *told* her?

BOBBY. Well, it sort of came out.

MELISANDE. After I had promised that I wouldn't say anything, you went and *told* her! And then I suppose you went and told the cook, and *she* said that her brother's young woman was just the same, and then you told the butcher, and *he* said, "You stick to it, sir. All women are alike. My missis said 'No' to me the first time." And then you went and told the gardeners—I suppose you had all the gardeners together in the potting-shed, and gave them a lecture about it—and when you had told them, you said, "Excuse me a moment, I must now go and tell the postman," and then——

BOBBY. I say, steady; you know that isn't fair.

MELISANDE. Oh, what a world!

BOBBY. I say, you know that isn't fair.

MELISANDE (*picking up her book*). Father and Jane are outside, Bobby, if you have anything you wish to tell them. But I suppose they know already. (*She pretends to read.*)

BOBBY. I say, you know—— (*He doesn't quite know what to say. There is an awkward silence. Then he says humbly*) I'm awfully sorry, Melisande. Please forgive me.

MELISANDE (*looking at him gravely*). That's nice of you, Bobby. Please forgive *me*. I wasn't fair.

BOBBY. I swear I never said anything to anybody else, only your mother. And it sort of came out with *her*. She began talking about you——

MELISANDE. *I* know.

BOBBY. But I never told anybody else.

MELISANDE. It wouldn't be necessary if you told Mother.

BOBBY. I'm awfully sorry, but I really don't see why you should mind so much. I mean, I know I'm not anybody very much, but I can't help falling in love with you, and—well, it *is* a sort of a compliment to you, isn't it?—even if it's only me.

MELISANDE. Of course it is, Bobby, and I do thank you for the compliment. But mixing Mother up in it makes it all so—so unromantic. (*After a pause*) Sometimes I think I shall never marry.

BOBBY. Oh, rot! . . . I say, you do *like* me, don't you?

MELISANDE. Oh yes. You are a nice, clean-looking Englishman—I don't say beautiful——

BOBBY. I should hope not!

MELISANDE. Pleasant, good at games, dependable—not very clever, perhaps, but making enough money——

BOBBY. Well, I mean, that's not so bad.

MELISANDE. Oh, but I want so much more!

BOBBY. What sort of things?

MELISANDE. Oh, Bobby, you're so—so ordinary!

BOBBY. Well, dash it all, you didn't want me to be a freak, did you?

MELISANDE. So—commonplace. So—unromantic.

BOBBY. I say, steady on! I don't say I'm always reading poetry and all that, if that's what you mean by romantic, but—commonplace! I'm blessed if I see how you make out that.

MELISANDE. Bobby, I don't want to hurt your feelings——

BOBBY. Go on, never mind my feelings.

MELISANDE. Well then, look at yourself in the glass!

(BOBBY *goes anxiously to the glass, and then pulls at his clothes.*)

BOBBY (*looking back at her*). Well?

MELISANDE. Well!

BOBBY. I don't see what's wrong.

MELISANDE. Oh, Bobby, everything's wrong. The man to whom I give myself must be not only my lover, but my true knight, my hero, my prince. He must perform deeds of derring-do to win my love. Oh, how can you perform deeds of derring-do in a stupid little suit like that!

BOBBY (*looking at it*). What's the matter with it? It's what every other fellow wears.

MELISANDE (*contemptuously*). What every other fellow wears! And you think what every other fellow thinks, and talk what every other fellow talks, and eat what every other—— I suppose *you* didn't like the bread-sauce this evening?

BOBBY (*guardedly*). Well, not as bread-sauce.

MELISANDE (*nodding her head*). I thought so, I thought so.

BOBBY (*struck by an idea*). I say, you didn't make it, did you?

MELISANDE. Do I look as if I made it?

BOBBY. I thought perhaps—— You know, I really don't know what you *do* want, Sandy. Sorry; I mean——

MELISANDE. Go on calling me Sandy, I'd rather you did.

BOBBY. Well, when you marry this prince of yours, is *he* going to do the cooking? I don't understand you, Sandy, really I don't.

MELISANDE (*shaking her head gently at him*). No, I'm sure you don't, Bobby.

BOBBY (*still trying, however*). I suppose it's because he's doing the cooking that he won't be able to dress for dinner. He sounds a funny sort of chap; I should like to see him.

MELISANDE. You wouldn't understand him if you did see him.

BOBBY (*jealously*). Have you seen him?

MELISANDE. Only in my dreams.

BOBBY (*relieved*). Oh, well.

MELISANDE (*dreamily to herself*). Perhaps I shall never see him in this world—and then I shall never marry. But if he ever comes for me, he will come not like other men; and because he is so different from everybody else, then I shall know him when he comes for me. He won't talk about bread-sauce—billiards—and the money market. He won't wear a little black suit, with a little black tie—all sideways. (BOBBY *hastily pulls his tie straight.*) I don't know how he will be dressed, but I know this, that when I see him, that when my eyes have looked into his, when his eyes have looked into mine——

BOBBY. I say, steady!

MELISANDE (*waking from her dream*). Yes? (*She gives a little laugh*) Poor Bobby!

BOBBY (*appealingly*). I say, Sandy! (*He goes up to her.*)

> (MRS. KNOWLE *has seized this moment to come back for her handkerchief. She sees them together, and begins to walk out on tiptoe.*)
>
> (*They hear her and turn round suddenly.*)

MRS. KNOWLE (*in a whisper*). Don't take any notice of me. I only just came for my handkerchief. (*She continues to walk on tiptoe towards the opposite door.*)

MELISANDE (*getting up*). We were just wondering where you were, Mother. Here's your handkerchief. (*She picks it up from the sofa.*)

MRS. KNOWLE (*still in the voice in which you speak to an invalid*). Thank you, dear. Don't let me interrupt you —I was just going——

MELISANDE. But I am just going into the garden. Stay and talk to Bobby, won't you?

MRS. KNOWLE (*with a happy smile, hoping for the best*). Yes, my darling.

MELISANDE (*going to the windows*). That's right. (*She stops at the windows and holds out her hands to the night*)—

> The moon shines bright: In such a night as this
> When the sweet wind did gently kiss the trees
> And they did make no noise, in such a night
> Troilus methinks mounted the Troyan walls,
> And sighed his soul towards the Grecian tents,
> Where Cressid lay that night. In such a night
> Stood Dido with a willow in her hand,
> Upon the wild sea banks, and waft her love
> To come again to Carthage.

(*She stays there a moment, and then says in a thrilling voice*) In such a night! Ah!

[*She goes to it.*

MRS. KNOWLE (*in a different voice*). Ah! . . . Well, Mr. Coote?

BOBBY (*turning back to her with a start*). Oh—er—yes?

MRS. KNOWLE. No, I think I must call you Bobby. I may call you Bobby, mayn't I?

BOBBY. Oh, please do, Mrs. Knowle.

MRS. KNOWLE (*archly*). Not Mrs. Knowle! Can't you think of a better name?

BOBBY (*wondering if he ought to call her* MARY). Er—I'm—I'm afraid I don't quite——

MRS. KNOWLE. Mother.

BOBBY. Oh, but I say——

MRS. KNOWLE (*giving him her hand*). And now come and sit on the sofa with me, and tell me all about it.

(*They go to the sofa together.*)

BOBBY. But I say, Mrs. Knowle——

MRS. KNOWLE (*shaking a finger playfully at him.*) Not Mrs. Knowle, Bobby.

BOBBY. But I say, you mustn't think—I mean Sandy and I—we aren't——

MRS. KNOWLE. You don't mean to tell me, Mr. Coote, that she has refused you again.

BOBBY. Yes. I say, I'd much rather not talk about it.

MRS. KNOWLE. Well, it just shows you that what I said the other day was true. Girls don't know their own minds.

BOBBY (*ruefully*). I think Sandy knows hers—about me, anyhow.

MRS. KNOWLE. Mr. Coote, you are forgetting what the poet said—Shakespeare, or was it the other man?— "Faint heart never won fair lady." If Mr. Knowle had had a faint heart, he would never have won me. Seven times I refused him, and seven times he came again—like Jacob. The eighth time he drew out a revolver, and threatened to shoot himself. I was shaking like an aspen leaf. Suddenly I realised that I loved him. "Henry," I said, "I am yours." He took me in his arms —putting down the revolver first, of course. I have never regretted my surrender, Mr. Coote. (*With a sigh*) Ah, me! We women are strange creatures.

BOBBY. I don't believe Sandy would mind if I did shoot myself.

MRS. KNOWLE. Oh, don't say that, Mr. Coote. She is very warm-hearted. I'm sure it would upset her a good deal. Oh no, you are taking too gloomy a view of the situation, I am sure of it.

BOBBY. Well, I shan't shoot myself, but I shan't propose to her again. I know when I'm not wanted.

MRS. KNOWLE. But we do want you, Mr. Coote. Both my husband and I——

BOBBY. I say, I'd much rather not talk about it, if you don't mind. I practically promised her that I wouldn't say anything to you this time.

MRS. KNOWLE. What, not say anything to her only mother? But how should I know if I were to call you "Bobby," or not?

BOBBY. Well, of course—I mean I haven't really said anything, have I? Nothing she'd really mind. She's so funny about things.

MRS. KNOWLE. She is indeed, Mr. Coote. I don't know where she gets it from. Neither Henry nor I are in the least funny. It was all the result of being christened in that irreligious way—I quite thought he said Millicent—and reading all those books, instead of visiting the sick as I used to do. I was quite a little Red Riding Hood until Henry sprang at me so fiercely. (MR. KNOWLE *and* JANE *come in by the window, and she turns round towards them.*) Ah, there you both are. I was wondering where you had got to. Mr. Coote has been telling me all about his prospects in the city. So comforting. Jane, you didn't get your feet wet, I hope.

JANE. It's quite dry, Aunt Mary.

MR. KNOWLE. It's a most beautiful night, my dear. We've been talking to the fairies—haven't we, Jane?

MRS. KNOWLE. Well, as long as you didn't get cold. Did you see Sandy?

MR. KNOWLE. We didn't see any one but Titania—and Peters. He had an appointment, apparently—but not with Titania.

JANE. He is walking out with Alice, I think.

MRS. KNOWLE. Well, Melisande will have to talk to Alice in the morning. I always warned you, Henry, about the danger of having an unmarried chauffeur on the premises. I always felt it was a mistake.

MR. KNOWLE. Apparently, my dear, Peters feels as strongly about it as you. He is doing his best to remedy the error.

MRS. KNOWLE (*getting up*). Well, I must be going to

bed. I have been through a good deal to-night; more than any of you know about.

MR. KNOWLE (*cheerfully*). What's the matter, my love? Indigestion?

MRS. KNOWLE. Beyond saying that it is not indigestion, Henry, my lips are sealed. I shall suffer my cross—my mental cross—in silence.

JANE. Shall I come with you, Aunt Mary?

MRS. KNOWLE. In five minutes, dear. (*To Heaven*) My only daughter has left me, and gone into the night. Fortunately my niece has offered to help me out of my—to help me. (*Holding out her hand*) Good-night, Mr. Coote.

BOBBY. Good-night, Mrs. Knowle.

MRS. KNOWLE. Good-night! And remember (*in a loud whisper*) what Shakespeare said. (*She presses his hand and holds it*) Good-night! Good-night! . . . Good-night!

MR. KNOWLE. Shakespeare said so many things. Among others, he said, "Good-night, good-night, parting is such sweet sorrow, that I could say good-night till it be morrow." (MRS. KNOWLE *looks at him severely, and then, without saying anything, goes over to him and holds up her cheek.*) Good-night, my dear. Sleep well.

MRS. KNOWLE. In five minutes, Jane.

JANE. Yes, Aunt Mary.

(MRS. KNOWLE *goes to the door,* BOBBY *hurrying in front to open it for her.*)

MRS. KNOWLE (*at the door*). I shall *not* sleep well. I shall lie awake all night. Dr. Anderson will be very much distressed. "Dr. Anderson," I shall say, "it is not your fault. I lay awake all night, thinking of my loved ones." In five minutes, Jane.

[*She goes out.*

MR. KNOWLE. An exacting programme. Well, I shall

be in the library, if anybody wants to think of me—or say good-night to me—or anything like that.

JANE. Then I'd better say good-night to you now, Uncle Henry. (*She goes up to him.*)

MR. KNOWLE (*kissing her*). Good-night, dear.

JANE. Good-night.

MR. KNOWLE. If there's anybody else who wants to kiss me—what about you, Bobby? Or will you come into the library and have a smoke first?

BOBBY. Oh, I shall be going to bed directly, I think. Rather tired to-day, somehow.

MR. KNOWLE. Then good-night to you also. Dear me, what a business this is. Sandy has left us for ever, I understand. If she should come back, Jane, and wishes to kiss the top of my head, she will find it in the library —just above the back of the armchair nearest the door.

[*He goes out.*

JANE. Did Sandy go out into the garden?

BOBBY (*gloomily*). Yes—about five minutes ago.

JANE (*timidly*). I'm so sorry, Bobby.

BOBBY. Thanks, it's awfully decent of you. (*After a pause*) Don't let's talk about it.

JANE. Of course I won't if it hurts you, Bobby. But I felt I *had* to say something, I felt so sorry. You didn't mind, did you?

BOBBY. It's awfully decent of you to mind.

JANE (*gently*). I mind very much when my friends are unhappy.

BOBBY. Thanks awfully. (*He stands up, buttons his coat, and looks at himself*) I say, do *you* see anything wrong with it?

JANE. Wrong with what?

BOBBY. My clothes. (*He revolves slowly.*)

JANE. Of course not. They fit beautifully.

BOBBY. Sandy's so funny about things. I don't know what she means half the time.

JANE. Of course, I'm very fond of Melisande, but I do see what you mean. She's so (*searching for the right word*)—so *romantic*.

BOBBY (*eagerly*). Yes, that's just it. It takes a bit of living up to. I say, have a cigarette, won't you?

JANE. No, thank you. Of course, I'm very fond of Melisande, but I do feel sometimes that I don't altogether envy the man who marries her.

BOBBY. I say, do you really feel that?

JANE. Yes. She's too (*getting the right word at last*) —too *romantic*.

BOBBY. You're about right, you know. I mean she talks about doing deeds of derring-do. Well, I mean that's all very well, but when one marries and settles down— you know what I mean?

JANE. Exactly. That's just how I feel about it. As I said to Melisande only this evening, this is the twentieth century. Well, I happen to like the twentieth century. That's all.

BOBBY. I see what you mean.

JANE. It may be very unromantic of me, but I like men to be keen on games, and to wear the clothes that everybody else wears—as long as they fit well, of course —and to talk about the ordinary things that everybody talks about. Of course, Melisande would say that that was very stupid and unromantic of me——

BOBBY. I don't think it is at all.

JANE. How awfully nice of you to say that, Bobby. You do understand so wonderfully.

BOBBY (*with a laugh*). I say, that's rather funny. I was just thinking the same about you.

JANE. I say, were you really? I'm so glad. I like to feel that we are really friends, and that we understand each other. I don't know whether I'm different from other girls, but I don't make friends very easily.

BOBBY. Do you mean men or women friends?

JANE. Both. In fact, but for Melisande and you, I can hardly think of any—not what you call real friends.

BOBBY. Melisande is a great friend, isn't she? You tell each other all your secrets, and that sort of thing, don't you?

JANE. Yes, we're great friends, but there are some things that I could never tell even her. (*Impressively*) I could never show her my inmost heart.

BOBBY. I don't believe about your not having any men friends. I bet there are hundreds of them, as keen on you as anything.

JANE. I wonder. It would be rather nice to think there were. That sounds horrid, doesn't it, but a girl can't help wanting to be liked.

BOBBY. Of course she can't; nobody can. I don't think it's a bit horrid.

JANE. How nice of you. (*She gets up*) Well, I must be going, I suppose.

BOBBY. What's the hurry?

JANE. Aunt Mary. She said five minutes.

BOBBY. And how long will you be with her? You'll come down again, won't you?

JANE. No, I don't think so. I'm rather tired this evening. (*Holding out her hand*) Good-night, Bobby.

BOBBY (*taking it*). Oh, but look here, I'll come and light your candle for you.

JANE. How nice of you!

(*She manages to get her hand back, and they walk to the door together.*)

BOBBY. I suppose I may as well go to bed myself.

JANE (*at the door*). Well, if you are, we'd better put the lights out.

BOBBY. Righto. (*He puts them out.*) I say, what a night! (*The moonlight streams through the windows on them.*) You'll hardly want a candle.

> [*They go out together.*
> (*The hall is empty. Suddenly the front door bell is heard to ring. After a little interval,* ALICE *comes in, turns on the light, and looks round the hall. She is walking across the hall to the drawing-room when* MR. KNOWLE *comes in from behind her, and she turns round.*)

MR. KNOWLE. Were you looking for me, Alice?

ALICE. Yes, sir. There's a gentleman at the front door, sir.

MR. KNOWLE. Rather late for a call, isn't it?

ALICE. He's in a motor car, sir, and it's broken down, and he wondered if you'd lend him a little petrol. He told me to say how very sorry he was to trouble you——

MR. KNOWLE. But he's not troubling me at all—particularly if Peters is about. I daresay you could find Peters, Alice, and if it's not troubling Peters too much, perhaps he would see to it. And ask the gentleman to come in. We can't keep him standing on the door-mat.

ALICE. Yes, sir. I did ask him before, sir.

MR. KNOWLE. Well, ask him this time in the voice of one who is about to bring in the whiskey.

ALICE. Yes, sir.

MR. KNOWLE. And then—bring in the whiskey.

ALICE. Yes, sir. (*She goes out, and returns a moment later*) He says, thank you very much, sir, but he really won't come in, and he's very sorry indeed to trouble you about the petrol.

MR. KNOWLE. Ah! I'm afraid we were too allusive for him.

ALICE (*hopefully*). Yes, sir.

MR. KNOWLE. Well, we won't be quite so subtle this

time. Present Mr. Knowle's compliments, and say that I shall be very much honoured if he will drink a glass of whiskey with me before proceeding on his journey.

ALICE. Yes, sir.

MR. KNOWLE. And then—bring in the whiskey.

ALICE. Yes, sir. (*She goes out. In a little while she comes back followed by the stranger, who is dressed from head to foot in a long cloak.*) Mr. Gervase Mallory.
[*She goes out.*

MR. KNOWLE. How do you do, Mr. Mallory? I'm very glad to see you. (*They shake hands.*)

GERVASE. It's very kind of you. I really must apologise for bothering you like this. I'm afraid I'm being an awful nuisance.

MR. KNOWLE. Not at all. Are you going far?

GERVASE. Collingham. I live at Little Malling, about twenty miles away. Do you know it?

MR. KNOWLE. Yes. I've been through it. I didn't know it was as far away as that.

GERVASE (*with a laugh*). Well, perhaps only by the way I came. The fact is I've lost myself rather.

MR. KNOWLE. I'm afraid you have. Collingham. You oughtn't to have come within five miles of us.

GERVASE. I suppose I oughtn't.

MR. KNOWLE. Well, all the more reason for having a drink now that you *are* here.

GERVASE. It's awfully kind of you.

ALICE *comes in.*

MR. KNOWLE. Ah, here we are. (ALICE *puts down the whiskey.*) You've told Peters?

ALICE. Yes, sir. He's looking after it now.

MR. KNOWLE. That's right. (ALICE *goes out.*) You'll have some whiskey, won't you?

GERVASE. Thanks very much.

(*He comes to the table.*)

MR. KNOWLE. And do take your coat off, won't you, and make yourself comfortable?

GERVASE. Er—thanks. I don't think——

(*He smiles to himself and keeps his cloak on.*)

MR. KNOWLE (*busy with the drinks*). Say when.

GERVASE. Thank you.

MR. KNOWLE. And soda?

GERVASE. Please. . . . Thanks!

(*He takes the glass.*)

MR. KNOWLE (*giving himself one*). I'm so glad you came, because I have a horror of drinking alone. Even when my wife gives me cough-mixture, I insist on somebody else in the house having cough-mixture too. A glass of cough-mixture with an old friend just before going to bed—— (*He looks up*) But do take your coat off, won't you, and sit down and be comfortable?

GERVASE. Er—thanks very much, but I don't think—— (*With a shrug and a smile*) Oh, well! (*He puts down his glass and begins to take it off. He is in fancy dress—the wonderful young Prince in blue and gold of* MELISANDE'S *dream.*)

(MR. KNOWLE *turns round to him again just as he has put his cloak down. He looks at* GERVASE *in amazement.*)

MR. KNOWLE (*pointing to his whiskey glass*). But I haven't even begun it yet. . . . Perhaps it's the port.

GERVASE (*laughing*). I'm awfully sorry. You must wonder what on earth I'm doing.

MR. KNOWLE. No, no; I wondered what on earth *I'd* been doing.

GERVASE. You see, I'm going to a fancy dress dance at Collingham.

MR. KNOWLE. You relieve my mind considerably.

GERVASE. That's why I didn't want to come in—or take my cloak off.

MR. KNOWLE (*inspecting him*). It becomes you extraordinarily well, if I may say so.

GERVASE. Oh, thanks very much. But one feels rather absurd in it when other people are in ordinary clothes.

MR. KNOWLE. On the contrary, you make other people feel absurd. I don't know that that particular style would have suited me, but (*looking at himself*) I am sure that I could have found something more expressive of my emotions than this.

GERVASE. You're quite right. "Dress does make a difference, Davy."

MR. KNOWLE. It does indeed.

GERVASE. I feel it's almost wicked of me to be drinking a whiskey and soda.

MR. KNOWLE. Very wicked. (*Taking out his case*) Have a cigarette, too?

GERVASE. May I have one of my own?

MR. KNOWLE. Do.

GERVASE (*feeling for it*). If I can find it. They were very careless about pockets in the old days. I had a special one put in somewhere, only it's rather difficult to get at. . . . Ah, here it is. (*He takes a cigarette from his case, and after trying to put the case back in his pocket again, places it on the table.*)

MR. KNOWLE. Match?

GERVASE. Thanks. (*Picking up his whiskey*) Well, here's luck, and—my most grateful thanks.

MR. KNOWLE (*raising his glass*). May you slay all your dragons.

GERVASE. Thank you. (*They drink.*)

MR. KNOWLE. Well, now about Collingham. I don't know if you saw a map outside in the hall.

GERVASE. I saw it, but I am afraid I didn't look at it. I was too much interested in your prints.

MR. KNOWLE (*eagerly*). You don't say that you are interested in prints?

GERVASE. Very much—as an entire amateur.

MR. KNOWLE. Most of the young men who come here think that the art began and ended with Kirchner. If you are really interested, I have something in the library —but of course I mustn't take up your time now. If you could bear to come over another day—after all, we are neighbors——

GERVASE. It's awfully nice of you; I should love it.

MR. KNOWLE. Hedgling is the name of the village. I mention it because you seem to have lost your way so completely——

GERVASE. Oh, by Jove, now I know where I am. It's so different in the moonlight. I'm lunching this way to-morrow. Might I come on afterwards? And then I can return your petrol, thank you for your hospitality, and expose my complete ignorance of old prints, all in one afternoon.

MR. KNOWLE. Well, but you must come anyhow. Come to tea.

GERVASE. That will be ripping. (*Getting up*) Well, I suppose I ought to be getting on. (*He picks up his cloak.*)

MR. KNOWLE. We might just have a look at that map on the way.

GERVASE. Oh yes, do let's.

(*They go to the door together, and stand for a moment looking at the casement windows.*)

MR. KNOWLE. It really is a wonderful night. (*He switches off the lights, and the moon streams through the windows*) Just look.

GERVASE (*with a deep sigh*). Wonderful!

> [*They go out together.*
>
> (*The hall is empty for a moment. Then* GERVASE *reappears. He has forgotten his cigarette-case. He finds it, and on his way out again stops for a moment in the moonlight, looking through the casement windows.*)
>
> (MELISANDE *comes in by the French windows. He hears her, and at the same moment she sees him. She gives a little wondering cry. It is He! The knight of her dreams. They stand gazing at each other. . . . Silently he makes obeisance to her; silently she acknowledges it. . . . Then he is gone.*)

ACT II

It is seven o'clock on a beautiful midsummer morning. The scene is a glade in a wood a little way above the village of Hedgling.

GERVASE MALLORY, *still in his fancy dress, but with his cloak on, comes in. He looks round him and says, "By Jove, how jolly!" He takes off his cloak, throws it down, stretches himself, turns round, and, seeing the view behind him, goes to look at it. While he is looking he hears an unmelodious whistling. He turns round with a start; the whistling goes on; he says "Good Lord!" and tries to get to his cloak. It is too late.* ERN, *a very small boy, comes through the trees into the glade.* GERVASE *gives a sigh of resignation and stands there.* ERN *stops in the middle of his tune and gazes at him.*

ERN. Oo—er! Oo! (*He circles slowly round* GERVASE.)

GERVASE. I quite agree with you.

ERN. Oo! Look!

GERVASE. Yes, it is a bit dressy, isn't it? Come round to the back—take a good look at it while you can. That's right. . . . Been all round? Good!

ERN. Oo!

GERVASE. You keep saying "Oo." It makes conversation very difficult. Do you mind if I sit down?

ERN. Oo!

GERVASE (*sitting down on a log*). I gather that I have your consent. I thank you.

ERN. Oo! Look! (*He points at* GERVASE's *legs.*)

GERVASE. What is it now? My legs? Oh, but surely you've noticed those before?

ERN (*sitting down in front of* GERVASE). Oo!

GERVASE. Really, I don't understand you. I came up here for a walk in a perfectly ordinary blue suit, and you do nothing but say "Oo." What does your father wear when he's ploughing? I suppose you don't walk all round *him* and say "Oo!" What does your Uncle George wear when he's reaping? I suppose you don't—— By the way, I wish you'd tell me your name. (ERN *gazes at him dumbly.*) Oh, come! They must have told you your name when you got up this morning.

ERN (*smiling sheepishly*). Ern.

GERVASE (*bowing*). How do you do? I am very glad to meet you, Mr. Hearne. My name is Mallory. (ERN *grins*) Thank you.

ERN (*tapping himself*). I'm Ern.

GERVASE. Yes, I'm Mallory.

ERN. Ern.

GERVASE. Mallory. We can't keep on saying this to each other, you know, because then we never get any farther. Once an introduction is over, Mr. Hearne, we are——

ERN. Ern.

GERVASE. Yes, I know. I was very glad to hear it. But now—— Oh, I see what you mean. Ern—short for Ernest?

ERN (*nodding*). They calls me Ern.

GERVASE. That's very friendly of them. Being more of a stranger I shall call you Ernest. Well, Ernest— (*getting up*) Just excuse me a moment, will you? Very penetrating bark this tree has. It must be a Pomeranian. (*He folds his cloak upon it and sits down again*) That's better. Now we can talk comfortably together. I don't know if there's anything you particularly want to discuss—nothing?—well, then, I will suggest the subject of breakfast.

ERN (*grinning*). 'Ad my breakfast.

GERVASE. You've *had* yours? You selfish brute! . . . Of course, you're wondering why I haven't had mine.

ERN. Bacon fat. (*He makes reminiscent noises.*)

GERVASE. Don't keep on going through all the courses. Well, what happened was this. My car broke down. I suppose you never had a motor car of your own.

ERN. Don't like moty cars.

GERVASE. Well, really, after last night I'm inclined to agree with you. Well, no, I oughtn't to say that, because, if I hadn't broken down, I should never have seen Her. Ernest, I don't know if you're married or anything of that sort, but I think even your rough stern heart would have been moved by that vision of loveliness which I saw last night. (*He is silent for a little, thinking of her.*) Well, then, I lost my way. There I was—ten miles from anywhere—in the middle of what was supposed to be a short cut—late at night—Midsummer Night—what would *you* have done, Ernest?

ERN. Gone 'ome.

GERVASE. Don't be silly. How could I go home when I didn't know where home was, and it was a hundred miles away, and I'd just seen the Princess? No, I did what your father or your Uncle George or any wise man would have done, I sat in the car and thought of Her.

ERN. Oo!

GERVASE. You are surprised? Ah, but if you'd seen her. . . . Have you ever been alone in the moonlight on Midsummer Night—I don't mean just for a minute or two, but all through the night until the dawn came? You aren't really alone, you know. All round you there are little whisperings going on, little breathings, little rustlings. Somebody is out hunting; somebody stirs in his sleep as he dreams again the hunt of yesterday; somebody up in the tree-tops pipes suddenly to the dawn, and then, finding that the dawn has not come, puts his silly little head back under his wing and goes to sleep again. . . . And the fairies are out. Do you believe in fairies, Ernest? You would have believed in them last night. I heard them whispering.

ERN. Oo!

GERVASE (*coming out of his thoughts with a laugh*). Well, of course, I can't expect you to believe me. But don't go about thinking that there's nothing in the world but bacon fat and bull's-eyes. Well, then, I suppose I went to sleep, for I woke up suddenly and it was morning, the most wonderful sparkling magical morning—but, of course, *you* were just settling down to business then.

ERN. Oo! (*He makes more reminiscent noises.*)

GERVASE. Yes, that's just what I said. I said to myself, breakfast.

ERN. 'Ad my breakfast.

GERVASE. Yes, but I 'adn't. I said to myself, "Surely my old friend, Ernest, whom I used to shoot bison with in the Himalayas, has got an estate somewhere in these parts. I will go and share his simple meal with him." So I got out of the car, and I did what you didn't do, young man, I had a bathe in the river, and then a dry on a pocket-handkerchief—one of my sister's, unfortunately—and then I came out to look for breakfast. And suddenly, whom should I meet but my old friend, Ernest, the same hearty fellow, the same inveterate talker as when we shot dragon-flies together in the swamps of Malay. (*Shaking his hand*) Ernest, old boy, pleased to meet you. What about it?

ERN. 'Ad my——

GERVASE. S'sh. (*He gets up*) Now then—to business. Do you mind looking the other way while I try to find my purse. (*Feeling for it*) Every morning when you get up, you should say, "Thank God, I'm getting a big boy now and I've got pockets in my trousers." And you should feel very sorry for the poor people who lived in fairy books and had no trousers to put pockets in. Ah, here we are. Now then, Ernest, attend very carefully. Where do you live?

ERN. 'Ome.

GERVASE. You mean, you haven't got a flat of your own yet? Well, how far away is your home? (ERN *grins and says nothing*) A mile? (ERN *continues to grin*) Half a mile? (ERN *grins*) Six inches?

ERN (*pointing*). Down there.

GERVASE. Good. Now then, I want you to take this—(*giving him half-a-crown*)——

ERN. Oo!

GERVASE. Yes, I thought that would move you—and I want you to ask your mother if you can bring me some breakfast up here. Now, listen very carefully, because we are coming to the important part. Hard-boiled eggs, bread, butter, and a bottle of milk—and anything else she likes. Tell her that it's most important, because your old friend Mallory whom you shot white mice with in Egypt is starving by the roadside. And if you come back here with a basket quickly, I'll give you as many bull's-eyes as you can eat in a week. (*Very earnestly*) Now, Ernest, with all the passion and emotion of which I am capable before breakfast, I ask you: have you got that?

ERN (*nodding*). Going 'ome. (*He looks at the half-crown again.*)

GERVASE. Going 'ome. Yes. But—returning with breakfast. Starving man—lost in forest—return with basket—

save life. (*To himself*) I believe I could explain it better to a Chinaman. (*To* ERN) Now then, off you go.

ERN (*as he goes off*). 'Ad my breakfast.

GERVASE. Yes, and I wonder if I shall get mine.

> (GERVASE *walks slowly after him and stands looking at him as he goes down the hill. Then, turning round, he sees another stranger in the distance.*)

GERVASE. Hullo, here's another of them. (*He walks towards the log*) Horribly crowded the country's getting nowadays. (*He puts on his coat.*)

> (*A moment later a travelling Peddler, name of* SUSAN, *comes in singing. He sees* GERVASE *sitting on the log.*)

SUSAN (*with a bow*). Good morning, sir.

GERVASE (*looking round*). Good morning.

SUSAN. I had thought to be alone. I trust my singing did not discommode you.

GERVASE. Not at all. I like it. Do go on.

SUSAN. Alas, the song ends there.

GERVASE. Oh, well, couldn't we have it again?

SUSAN. Perhaps later, sir, if you insist. (*Taking off his hat*) Would it inconvenience you if I rested here for a few minutes?

GERVASE. Not a bit. It's a jolly place to rest at, isn't it? Have you come far this morning?

SUSAN. Three or four miles—a mere nothing on a morning like this. Besides, what does the great William say?

GERVASE. I don't think I know him. What does he say?

SUSAN. A merry heart goes all the way.

GERVASE. Oh, Shakespeare, yes.

SUSAN. And why, you ask, am I merry?

GERVASE. Well, I didn't, but I was just going to. Why are you merry?

SUSAN. Can you not guess? What does the great Ralph say?

GERVASE (*trying hard*). The great Ralph. . . . No, you've got me there. I'm sure I don't know him. Well, what does he say?

SUSAN. Give me health and a day, and I will make the pomp of Empires ridiculous.

GERVASE. Emerson, of *course*. Silly of me.

SUSAN. So you see, sir—I am well, the day is well, all is well.

GERVASE. Sir, I congratulate you. In the words of the great Percy—(*to himself*) that's got him.

SUSAN (*at a loss*). The—er—great Percy?

GERVASE. Hail to thee, blithe spirit!

SUSAN (*eagerly*). I take you, I take you! Shelley! Ah, there's a poet, Mr.—er—I don't think I quite caught your name.

GERVASE. Oh! My name's Gervase Mallory—to be referred to by posterity, I hope, as the great Gervase.

SUSAN. Not a poet, too?

GERVASE. Well, no, not professionally.

SUSAN. But one with the poets in spirit—like myself. I am very glad to meet you, Mr. Mallory. It is most good-natured of you to converse with me. My name is Susan. (GERVASE *bows*.) Generally called Master Susan in these parts, or sometimes Gentleman Susan. I am a travelling Peddler by profession.

GERVASE. A delightful profession, I am sure.

SUSAN. The most delightful of all professions. (*He begins to undo his pack.*) Speaking professionally for the moment, if I may so far venture, you are not in any need of boot-laces, buttons, or collar-studs?

GERVASE (*smiling*). Well, no, not at this actual moment. On almost any other day perhaps—but no, not this morning.

SUSAN. I only just mentioned it in passing—*en passant,* as the French say. (*He brings out a paper bag from his pack.*) Would the fact of my eating my breakfast in this pleasant resting place detract at all from your appreciation of the beautiful day which Heaven has sent us?

GERVASE. Eating your *what?*

SUSAN. My simple breakfast.

GERVASE (*shaking his head*). I'm very sorry, but I really don't think I could bear it. Only five minutes ago Ernest—I don't know if you know Ernest?

SUSAN. The great Ernest?

GERVASE (*indicating with his hand*). No, the very small one—— Well, *he* was telling me all about the breakfast he'd just had, and now *you're* showing me the breakfast you're just going to have—no, I can't bear it.

SUSAN. My dear sir, you don't mean to tell me that you would do me the honour of joining me at my simple repast?

GERVASE (*jumping up excitedly*). The honour of joining you!—the *honour!* My dear Mr. Susan! Now I know why they call you Gentleman Susan. (*Shaking his head sadly*) But no. It wouldn't be fair to you. I should eat too much. Besides, Ernest may come back. No, I will wait. It wouldn't be fair.

SUSAN (*unpacking his breakfast*). Bacon or cheese?

GERVASE. Cheese—I mean bacon—I mean—I say, you aren't serious?

SUSAN (*handing him bread and cheese*). I trust you will find it up to your expectations.

GERVASE (*taking it*). I say, you really—— (*Solemnly*) Master Susan, with all the passion and emotion of which

I am capable before breakfast, I say "Thank you." (*He takes a bite*) Thank you.

SUSAN (*eating also*). Please do not mention it. I am more than repaid by your company.

GERVASE. It is charming of you to say so, and I am very proud to be your guest, but I beg you to allow me to pay for this delightful cheese.

SUSAN. No, no. I couldn't hear of it.

GERVASE. I warn you that if you will not allow me to pay for this delightful cheese, I shall insist on buying all your boot-laces. Nay, more, I shall buy all your studs, and all your buttons. Your profession would then be gone.

SUSAN. Well, well, shall we say tuppence?

GERVASE. Tuppence for a banquet like this? My dear friend, nothing less than half-a-crown will satisfy me.

SUSAN. Sixpence. Not a penny more.

GERVASE (*with a sigh*). Very well, then. (*He begins to feel in his pocket, and in so doing reveals part of his dress.* SUSAN *opens his eyes at it, and then goes on eating.* GERVASE *finds his purse and produces sixpence, which he gives to* SUSAN.) Sir, I thank you. (*He resumes his breakfast.*)

SUSAN. You are too generous. . . . Forgive me for asking, but you are not by chance a fellow-traveller upon the road?

GERVASE. Do you mean professionally?

SUSAN. Yes. There is a young fellow, a contortionist and sword-swallower, known locally in these parts as Humphrey the Human Hiatus, who travels from village to village. Just for a moment I wondered——

        (*He glances at* GERVASE's *legs, which are uncovered.* GERVASE *hastily wraps his coat round them.*)

GERVASE. I am not Humphrey. No. Gervase the Cheese Swallower. . . . Er—my costume——

SUSAN. Please say nothing more. It was ill-mannered of me to have inquired. Let a man wear what he likes. It is a free world.

GERVASE. Well, the fact is, I have been having a bathe.

SUSAN (*with a bow*). I congratulate you on your bathing costume.

GERVASE. Not at all.

SUSAN. You live near here then?

GERVASE. Little Malling. I came over in a car.

SUSAN. Little Malling? That's about twenty miles away.

GERVASE. Oh, much more than that surely.

SUSAN. No. There's Hedgling down there.

GERVASE (*surprised*). Hedgling? Heavens, how I must have lost my way. . . . Then I have been within a mile of her all night. And I never knew!

SUSAN. You are married, Mr. Mallory?

GERVASE. No. Not yet.

SUSAN. Get married.

GERVASE. What?

SUSAN. Take my advice and get married.

GERVASE. You recommend it?

SUSAN. I do. . . . There is no companion like a wife, if you marry the right woman.

GERVASE. Oh?

SUSAN. I have been married thirty years. Thirty years of happiness.

GERVASE. But in your profession you must go away from your wife a good deal.

SUSAN (*smiling*). But then I come back to her a good deal.

GERVASE (*thoughtfully*). Yes, that must be rather jolly.

SUSAN. Why do you think I welcomed your company so much when I came upon you here this morning?

GERVASE (*modestly*). Oh, well——

SUSAN. It was something to tell my wife when I got back to her. When you are married, every adventure becomes two adventures. You have your adventure, and then you go back to your wife and have your adventure again. Perhaps it is a better adventure that second time. You can say the things which you didn't quite say the first time, and do the things which you didn't quite do. When my week's travels are over, and I go back to my wife, I shall have a whole week's happenings to tell her. They won't lose in the telling, Mr. Mallory. Our little breakfast here this morning—she will love to hear about that. I can see her happy excited face as I tell her all that I said to you, and—if I can remember it—all that you said to me.

GERVASE (*eagerly*). I say, how jolly! (*Thoughtfully*) You won't forget what I said about the Great Percy? I thought that was rather good.

SUSAN. I hope it wasn't too good, Mr. Mallory. If it was, I shall find myself telling it to her as one of my own remarks. That's why I say "Get married." Then you can make things fair for yourself. You can tell her all the good things of mine which *you* said.

GERVASE. But there must be more in marriage than that.

SUSAN. There are a million things in marriage, but companionship is at the bottom of it all. . . . Do you know what companionship means?

GERVASE. How do you mean? Literally?

SUSAN. The derivation of it in the dictionary. It means the art of having meals with a person. Cynics talk of the impossibility of sitting opposite the same woman every day at breakfast. Impossible to *them*, perhaps, poor shallow-hearted creatures, but not impossible to two people who have found what love is.

GERVASE. It doesn't sound very romantic.

SUSAN (*solemnly*). It is the most romantic thing in the whole world. . . . Some more cheese?

GERVASE (*taking it*). Thank you. . . . (*Thoughtfully*) Do you believe in love at first sight, Master Susan?

SUSAN. Why not? If it's the woman you love at first sight, not only the face.

GERVASE. I see. (*After a pause*) It's rather hard to tell, you know. I suppose the proper thing to do is to ask her to have breakfast with you, and see how you get on.

SUSAN. Well, you might do worse.

GERVASE (*laughing*). And propose to her after breakfast?

SUSAN. If you will. It is better than proposing to her at a ball as some young people do, carried away suddenly by a snatched kiss in the moonlight.

GERVASE (*shaking his head*). Nothing like that happened last night.

SUSAN. What does the Great Alfred say of the kiss?

GERVASE. I never read the *Daily Mail*.

SUSAN. Tennyson, Mr. Mallory, Tennyson.

GERVASE. Oh, I beg your pardon.

SUSAN. "The kiss," says the Great Alfred, "the woven arms, seem but to be weak symbols of the settled bliss, the comfort, I have found in thee." The same idea, Mr. Mallory. Companionship, or the art of having breakfast with a person. (*Getting up*) Well, I must be moving on. *We* have been companions for a short time; I thank you for it. I wish you well.

GERVASE (*getting up*). I say, I've been awfully glad

to meet you. And I shall never forget the breakfast you gave me.

SUSAN. It is friendly of you to say so.

GERVASE (*hesitatingly*). You won't mind my having another one when Ernest comes back—I mean, if Ernest comes back? You won't think I'm slighting yours in any way? But after an outdoor bathe, you know, one does——

SUSAN. Please! I am happy to think you have such an appetite.

GERVASE (*holding out his hand*). Well, good-bye, Mr. Susan. (SUSAN *looks at his hand doubtfully, and* GERVASE *says with a laugh*) Oh, come on!

SUSAN (*shaking it*). Good-bye, Mr. Mallory.

GERVASE. And I shan't forget what you said.

SUSAN (*smiling*). I expect you will, Mr. Mallory. Good-bye.

[*He goes off.*

GERVASE (*calling after him*). Because it wasn't the moonlight, it wasn't really. It was just *Her*. (*To himself*) It was just *Her*. . . . I suppose the great whatsisname would say, "It was just *She*," but then, that isn't what I mean.

> (GERVASE *watches him going down the hill. Then he turns to the other side, says, "Hallo!" suddenly in great astonishment, and withdraws a few steps.*)

GERVASE. It can't be! (*He goes cautiously forward and looks again*) It is!

> (*He comes back, and walks gently off through the trees.*)
>
> (MELISANDE *comes in. She has no hat; her hair is in two plaits to her waist; she is wearing a dress which might belong to any century. She stands in the middle of the glade, looks*

ACT II] THE ROMANTIC AGE 215

when you are cutting wood, they always put you where the sawdust gets into your mouth. Because, you see, they have never read history, and so they don't know that the third and youngest son is always the nicest of the family.

MELISANDE. And the tallest and the bravest and the most handsome.

GERVASE. *And* all the other things you mention.

MELISANDE. So you ran away?

GERVASE. So I ran away—to seek my fortune.

MELISANDE. But your uncle the wizard, or your godmother or somebody, gave you a magic ring to take with you on your travels? (*Nodding*) They always do, you know.

GERVASE (*showing the ring on his finger*). Yes, my fairy godmother gave me a magic ring. Here it is.

MELISANDE (*looking at it*). What does it do?

GERVASE. You turn it round once and think very hard of anybody you want, and suddenly the person you are thinking of appears before you.

MELISANDE. How wonderful! Have you tried it yet?

GERVASE. Once. . . . That's why you are here.

MELISANDE. Oh! (*Softly*) Have you been thinking of me?

GERVASE. All night.

MELISANDE. I dreamed of you all night.

GERVASE (*happily*). Did you, Melisande? How dear of you to dream of me! (*Anxiously*) Was I—was I all right?

MELISANDE. Oh, yes!

GERVASE (*pleased*). Ah! (*He spreads himself a little and removes a speck of dust from his sleeve.*)

MELISANDE (*thinking of it still*). You were so brave.

GERVASE. Yes, I expect I'm pretty brave in other

people's dreams—I'm so cowardly in my own. Did I kill anybody?

MELISANDE. You were engaged in a terrible fight with a dragon when I woke up.

GERVASE. Leaving me and the dragon still asleep— I mean, still fighting? Oh, Melisande, how could you leave us until you knew who had won?

MELISANDE. I tried so hard to get back to you.

GERVASE. I expect I was winning, you know. I wish you could have got back for the finish. . . . Melisande, let me come into your dreams again to-night.

MELISANDE. You never asked me last night. You just came.

GERVASE. Thank you for letting me come.

MELISANDE. And then when I woke up early this morning, the world was so young, so beautiful, so fresh that I had to be with it. It called to me so clearly— to come out and find its secret. So I came up here, to this enchanted place, and all the way it whispered to me—wonderful things.

GERVASE. What did it whisper, Melisande?

MELISANDE. The secret of happiness.

GERVASE. Ah, what is it, Melisande? (*She smiles and shakes her head.*) . . . I met a magician in the woods this morning.

MELISANDE. Did he speak to you?

GERVASE. *He* told *me* the secret of happiness.

MELISANDE. What did he tell you?

GERVASE. He said it was marriage.

MELISANDE. Ah, but he didn't mean by marriage what so many people mean.

GERVASE. He seemed a very potent magician.

MELISANDE. Marriage to many people means just food. Housekeeping. *He* didn't mean that.

GERVASE. A very wise and reverend magician.

MELISANDE. Love is romance. Is there anything romantic in breakfast—or lunch?

GERVASE. Well, not so much in lunch, of course, but——

MELISANDE. How well you understand! Why do the others not understand?

GERVASE (*smiling at her*). Perhaps because they have not seen Melisande.

MELISANDE. Oh no, no, that isn't it. All the others——

GERVASE. Do you mean your suitors?

MELISANDE. Yes. They are so unromantic, so material. The clothes they wear; the things they talk about. But you are so different. Why is it?

GERVASE. I don't know. Perhaps because I am the third son of a woodcutter. Perhaps because they don't know that you are the Princess. Perhaps because they have never been in the enchanted forest.

MELISANDE. What would the forest tell them?

GERVASE. All the birds in the forest are singing "Melisande"; the little brook runs through the forest murmuring "Melisande"; the tall trees bend their heads and whisper to each other "Melisande." All the flowers have put on their gay dresses for her. Oh, Melisande!

MELISANDE (*awed*). Is it true? (*They are silent for a little, happy to be together. . . . He looks back at her and gives a sudden little laugh.*) What is it?

GERVASE. Just you and I—together—on the top of the world like this.

MELISANDE. Yes, that's what I feel, too. (*After a pause*) Go on pretending.

GERVASE. Pretending?

MELISANDE. That the world is very young.

GERVASE. *We* are very young, Melisande.

MELISANDE (*timidly*). It is only a dream, isn't it?

GERVASE. Who knows what a dream is? Perhaps we

fell asleep in Fairyland a thousand years ago, and all that we thought real was a dream, until now at last we are awake again.

MELISANDE. How wonderful that would be.

GERVASE. Perhaps we are dreaming now. But is it your dream or my dream, Melisande?

MELISANDE (*after thinking it out*). I think I would rather it were your dream, Gervase. For then I should be in it, and that would mean that you had been thinking of me.

GERVASE. Then it shall be *my* dream, Melisande.

MELISANDE. Let it be a long one, my dear.

GERVASE. For ever and for ever.

MELISANDE (*dreamily*). Oh, I know that it is only a dream, and that presently we shall wake up; or else that you will go away and I will go away, too, and we shall never meet again; for in the real world, what could I be to you, or you to me? So go on pretending.

(*He stands up and faces her.*)

GERVASE. Melisande, if this were Fairyland, or if we were knights and ladies in some old romance, would you trust yourself to me?

MELISANDE. So very proudly.

GERVASE. You would let me come to your father's court and claim you over all your other suitors, and fight for you, and take you away with me?

MELISANDE. If this were Fairyland, yes.

GERVASE. You would trust me?

MELISANDE. I would trust my lord.

GERVASE (*smiling at her*). Then I will come for the Princess this afternoon. (*With sudden feeling*) Ah, how can I keep away now that I have seen the Princess?

MELISANDE (*shyly—happily*). When you saw me last night, did you know that you would see me again?

GERVASE. I have been waiting for you here.

ACT II]   THE ROMANTIC AGE   219

MELISANDE. How did you know that I would come?

GERVASE. On such a morning—in such a place—how could the loved one not be here?

MELISANDE (*looking away*). The loved one?

GERVASE. I saw you last night.

MELISANDE (*softly*). Was that enough?

GERVASE. Enough, yes. Enough? Oh no, no, no!

MELISANDE (*nodding*). I will wait for you this afternoon.

GERVASE. And you will come away with me? Out into the world with me? Over the hills and far away with me?

MELISANDE (*softly*). Over the hills and far away.

GERVASE (*going to her*). Princess!

MELISANDE. Not Princess.

GERVASE. Melisande!

MELISANDE (*holding out her hand to him*). Ah!

GERVASE. May I kiss your hands, Melisande?

MELISANDE. They are my lord's to kiss.

GERVASE (*kissing them*). Dear hands.

MELISANDE. Now I shall love them, too.

GERVASE. May I kiss your lips, Melisande?

MELISANDE (*proudly*). Who shall, if not my lord?

GERVASE. Melisande! (*He touches her lips with his.*)

MELISANDE (*breaking away from him*). Oh!

GERVASE (*triumphantly*). I love you, Melisande! I love you!

MELISANDE (*wonderingly*). Why didn't I wake up when you kissed me? We are still here. The dream goes on.

GERVASE. It is no dream, Melisande. Or if it is a dream, then in my dream I love you, and if we are awake, then awake I love you. I love you if this is Fairyland, and if there is no Fairyland, then my love will make a faery land of the world for you. For I love you, Melisande.

MELISANDE (*timidly*). Are we pretending still?

GERVASE. No, no, no!

(*She looks at him gravely for a moment and then nods her head.*)

MELISANDE (*pointing*). I live down there. You will come for me?

GERVASE. I will come.

MELISANDE. I am my lord's servant. I will wait for him. (*She moves away from him. Then she curtsies and says*) This afternoon, my lord.

(*She goes down the hill.*)

(*He stands looking after her. While he is standing there,* ERN *comes through the trees with breakfast.*)

ACT III

It is about four o'clock in the afternoon of the same day. JANE *is sitting on the sofa in the hall, glancing at a paper, but evidently rather bored with it, and hoping that somebody*—BOBBY, *did you say?—will appear presently. However, it is* MR. KNOWLE *who comes in.*

MR. KNOWLE. Ah, Jane!

JANE (*looking up*). Hallo, Uncle Henry. Did you have a good day?

MR. KNOWLE. Well, Peters and I had a very enjoyable drive.

JANE. But you found nothing at the sale? What a pity!

MR. KNOWLE (*taking a catalogue from his pocket*). Nothing which I wanted myself, but there were several very interesting lots. Peters was strongly tempted by Lot 29—"Two hip-baths and a stuffed crocodile." Very useful things to have by you if you think of getting married, Jane, and setting up house for yourself. I don't know if you have any thoughts in that direction?

JANE (*a little embarrassed*). Well, I suppose I shall some day.

MR. KNOWLE. Ah! . . . Where's Bobby?

JANE (*carelessly*). Bobby? Oh, he's about somewhere.

MR. KNOWLE. I think Bobby would like to hear about Lot 29. (*Returning to his catalogue*) Or perhaps Lot 42. "Lot 42—Twelve aspidistras, towel-horse, and 'The

Maiden's Prayer.'" All for seven and sixpence. I ought to have had Bobby with me. He could have made a firm offer of eight shillings. . . . By the way, I have a daughter, haven't I? How was Sandy this morning?

JANE. I didn't see her. Aunt Mary is rather anxious about her.

MR. KNOWLE. Has she left us for ever?

JANE. There's nothing to be frightened about really.

MR. KNOWLE. I'm not frightened.

JANE. She had breakfast before any of us were up, and went out with some sandwiches afterwards, and she hasn't come back yet.

MR. KNOWLE. A very healthy way of spending the day. (MRS. KNOWLE *comes in*) Well, Mary, I hear that we have no daughter now.

MRS. KNOWLE. Ah, there you are, Henry. Thank Heaven that *you* are back safely.

MR. KNOWLE. My dear, I always meant to come back safely. Didn't you expect me?

MRS. KNOWLE. I had given up hope. Jane here will tell you what a terrible morning I have had; prostrate on the sofa, mourning for my loved ones. My only child torn from me, my husband—dead.

MR. KNOWLE (*surprised*). Oh, I was dead?

MRS. KNOWLE. I pictured the car smashed to atoms, and you lying in the road, dead, with Peters by your side.

MR. KNOWLE. Ah! How was Peters?

MRS. KNOWLE (*with a shrug*). I didn't look. What is a chauffeur to one who has lost her husband and her only child in the same morning?

MR. KNOWLE. Still, I think you might have looked.

JANE. Sandy's all right, Aunt Mary. You know she often goes out alone all day like this.

ACT III] THE ROMANTIC AGE 223

MRS. KNOWLE. Ah, *is* she alone? Jane, did you count the gardeners as I asked you?

MR. KNOWLE. Count the gardeners?

MRS. KNOWLE. To make sure that none of them is missing too.

JANE. It's quite all right, Aunt Mary. Sandy will be back by tea-time.

MRS. KNOWLE (*resigned*). It all comes of christening her Melisande. You know, Henry, I quite thought you said Millicent.

MR. KNOWLE. Well, talking about tea, my dear—at which happy meal our long-lost daughter will be restored to us—we have a visitor coming, a nice young fellow who takes an interest in prints.

MRS. KNOWLE. I've heard nothing of this, Henry.

MR. KNOWLE. No, my dear, that's why I'm telling you now.

MRS. KNOWLE. A young man?

MR. KNOWLE. Yes.

MRS. KNOWLE. Nice-looking?

MR. KNOWLE. Yes.

MRS. KNOWLE. Rich?

MR. KNOWLE. I forgot to ask him, Mary. However, we can remedy that omission as soon as he arrives.

MRS. KNOWLE. It's a very unfortunate day for him to have chosen. Here's Sandy lost, and I'm not fit to be seen, and—Jane, your hair wants tidying——

MR. KNOWLE. He is not coming to see you or Sandy or Jane, my dear; he is coming to see me. Fortunately, I am looking very beautiful this afternoon.

MRS. KNOWLE. Jane, you had better be in the garden, dear, and see if you can stop Sandy before she comes in, and just give her a warning. I don't know *what* she'll look like after roaming the fields all day, and falling into pools——

MR. KNOWLE. A sweet disorder in the dress kindles in clothes a wantonness.

MRS. KNOWLE. I will go and tidy myself. Jane, I think your mother would like you to—but, after all, one must think of one's own child first. You will tell Sandy, won't you? We had better have tea in here. . . . Henry, your trousers—(*she looks to see that* JANE *is not listening, and then says in a loud whisper*) your trousers——

MR. KNOWLE. I'm afraid I didn't make myself clear, Mary. It's a young fellow who is coming to see my prints; not the Prince of Wales who is coming to see my trousers.

MRS. KNOWLE (*turning to* JANE). You'll remember, Jane?

JANE (*smiling*). Yes, Aunt Mary.

MRS. KNOWLE. That's a good girl.

[*She goes out.*

MR. KNOWLE. Ah! . . . Your aunt wasn't very lucid, Jane. Which one of you is it who is going to marry the gentleman?

JANE. Don't be so absurd, Uncle Henry.

MR. KNOWLE (*taking out his catalogue again*). Perhaps *he* would be interested in Lot 29. (BOBBY *comes in through the windows.*) Ah, here's Bobby. Bobby, they tell me that you think of setting up house.

BOBBY (*looking quickly at* JANE). Who told you that?

MR. KNOWLE. Now, starting with two hip-baths and a stuffed crocodile for nine shillings and sixpence, and working up to twelve aspidistras, a towel-horse and "The Maiden's Prayer" for eight shillings, you practically have the spare room furnished for seventeen and six. But perhaps I had better leave the catalogue with you. (*He presses it into the bewildered* BOBBY'S *hands*) I must go and tidy myself up. Somebody is coming to propose to me this afternoon.

[*He hurries out.*

(BOBBY *looks after him blankly, and then turns to* JANE.)

BOBBY. I say, what's happened?

JANE. Happened?

BOBBY. Yes, why did he say that about my setting up house?

JANE. I think he was just being funny. He is sometimes, you know.

BOBBY. You don't think he guessed——

JANE. Guessed what? About you and Melisande?

BOBBY. I say, shut up, Jane. I thought we agreed not to say anything more about that.

JANE. But what else could he have guessed?

BOBBY. *You* know well enough.

JANE (*shaking her head*). No, I don't.

BOBBY. I told you this morning.

JANE. What did you tell me?

BOBBY. *You* know.

JANE. No, I don't.

BOBBY. Yes, you do.

JANE. No, I don't.

BOBBY (*coming closer*). All right, shall I tell you again?

JANE (*edging away*). I don't want to hear it.

BOBBY. How do you know you don't want to hear it, if you don't know what it is?

JANE. I can guess what it is.

BOBBY. There you are!

JANE. It's what you say to everybody, isn't it?

BOBBY (*loftily*). If you want to know, Miss Bagot, I have only said it to one other person in my life, and that was in mistake for you.

JANE (*coldly*). Melisande and I are not very much alike, Mr. Coote.

BOBBY. No. You're much prettier.

JANE (*turning her head away*). You don't really think so. Anyhow, it isn't true.

BOBBY. It is true, Jane. I swear it.

JANE. Well, you didn't think so yesterday.

BOBBY. Why do you keep talking about yesterday? I'm talking about to-day.

JANE. A girl has her pride, Bobby.

BOBBY. So has a man. I'm awfully proud of being in love with *you*.

JANE. That isn't what I mean.

BOBBY. What do you mean?

JANE (*awkwardly*). Well—well—well, what it comes to is that you get refused by Sandy, and then you immediately come to me and expect me to jump at you.

BOBBY. Suppose I had waited a year and then come to you, would that have been better?

JANE. Of course it would.

BOBBY. Well, really I can't follow you, darling.

JANE (*indignantly*). You mustn't call me darling.

BOBBY. Mustn't call you what?

JANE (*awkwardly*). Darling.

BOBBY. Did I call you darling?

JANE (*shortly*). Yes.

BOBBY (*to himself*). "Darling." No, I suppose I mustn't. But it suits you so awfully well—darling. (*She stamps her foot*) I'm sorry, darl—— I mean Jane, but really I can't follow you. Because you're so frightfully fascinating, that after twenty-four hours of it, I simply have to tell you how much I love you, then your pride is hurt. But if you had been so frightfully unattractive that it took me a whole year to see anything in you at all, then apparently you'd have been awfully proud.

JANE. You *have* known me a whole year, Bobby.

BOBBY. Not really, you know. Directly I saw you and Sandy together I knew I was in love with one of you, but—well, love is a dashed rummy thing, and I thought it was Sandy. And so I didn't really see you till last night, when you were so awfully decent to me.

JANE (*wistfully*). It sounds very well, but the trouble is that it will sound just as well to the next girl.

BOBBY. What next girl?

JANE. The one you propose to to-morrow.

BOBBY. You know, Jane, when you talk like that I feel that you don't deserve to be proposed to at all.

JANE (*loftily*). I'm sure I don't want to be.

BOBBY (*coming closer*). Are you?

JANE. Am I what?

BOBBY. Quite sure.

JANE. I should have thought it was pretty obvious seeing that I've just refused you.

BOBBY. Have you?

JANE. Have I what?

BOBBY. Refused me.

JANE. I thought I had.

BOBBY. And would you be glad if I went away and never saw you again? (*She hesitates*) Honest, Jane. Would you?

JANE (*awkwardly*). Well, of course, I *like* you, Bobby. I always have.

BOBBY. But you feel that you would like me better if I were somebody else's husband?

JANE (*indignantly*). Oh, I *never* said that.

BOBBY. Dash it, you've been saying it all this afternoon.

JANE (*weakly*). Bobby, don't; I can't argue with you.

But really, dear, I can't say now that I will marry you. Oh, you *must* understand. Oh, *think* what Sandy——

BOBBY. We won't tell Sandy.

JANE (*surprised*). But she's bound to know.

BOBBY. We won't tell anybody.

JANE (*eagerly*). Bobby!

BOBBY (*nodding*). Just you and me. Nobody else for a long time. A little private secret.

JANE. Bobby!

BOBBY (*coming to her*). Is it a bargain, Jane? Because if it's a bargain——

JANE (*going away from him*). No, no, Bobby. Not now. I must go upstairs and tidy myself—no, I mustn't, I must wait for Melisande—no, Bobby, don't. Not yet. I mean it, really. Do go, dear, anybody might come in.

> (BOBBY, *who has been following her round the hall, as she retreats nervously, stops and nods to her.*)

BOBBY. All right, darling, I'll go.

JANE. You mustn't say "darling." You might say it accidentally in front of them all.

BOBBY (*grinning*). All right, Miss Bagot . . . I am going now, Miss Bagot. (*At the windows*) Good-bye, Miss Bagot. (JANE *blows him a kiss. He bows*) Your favour to hand, Miss Bagot. (*He turns and sees* MELISANDE *coming through the garden*) Hallo, here's Sandy! (*He hurries off in the opposite direction.*)

MELISANDE. Oh, Jane, Jane! (*She sinks into a chair.*)

JANE. What, dear?

MELISANDE. Everything.

JANE. Yes, but that's so vague, darling. Do you mean that——

MELISANDE (*dreamily*). I have seen him; I have talked to him; he has kissed me.

JANE (*amazed*). *Kissed* you? Do you mean that he has—kissed you?

MELISANDE. I have looked into his eyes, and he has looked into mine.

JANE. Yes, but who?

MELISANDE. The true knight, the prince, for whom I have been waiting so long.

JANE. But *who* is he?

MELISANDE. They call him Gervase.

JANE. Gervase *who?*

MELISANDE (*scornfully*). Did Elaine say, "Lancelot who" when they told her his name was Lancelot?

JANE. Yes, dear, but this is the twentieth century. He must have a name.

MELISANDE (*dreamily*). Through the forest he came to me, dressed in blue and gold.

JANE (*sharply*). Sandy! (*Struck with an idea*) Have you been out all day without your hat, darling?

MELISANDE (*vaguely*). Have I?

JANE. I mean—blue and gold. They don't do it nowadays.

MELISANDE (*nodding to her*). *He* did, Jane.

JANE. But how?—Why? Who can he be?

MELISANDE. He said he was a humble woodcutter's son. That means he was a prince in disguise. He called me his princess.

JANE. Darling, how could he be a prince?

MELISANDE. I have read stories sometimes of men who went to sleep and woke up thousands of years afterwards and found themselves in a different world. Perhaps, Jane, *he* lived in those old days, and——

JANE. Did he *talk* like an ordinary person?

MELISANDE. Oh no, no!

JANE. Well, it's really extraordinary. . . . Was he a gentleman?

MELISANDE (*smiling at her*). I didn't ask him, Jane.

JANE (*crossly*). You know what I mean.

MELISANDE. He is coming this afternoon to take me away.

JANE (*amazed*). To take you away? But what about Aunt Mary?

MELISANDE (*vaguely*). Aunt Mary? What has *she* got to do with it?

JANE (*impatiently*). Oh, but—— (*With a shrug of resignation*) I don't understand. Do you mean he's coming *here*? (MELISANDE *nods gravely*.) Melisande, you'll let me see him?

MELISANDE. Yes. I've thought it all out. I wanted you here, Jane. He will come in; I will present you; and then you must leave us alone. But I should like you to see him. Just to see how different, how utterly different he is from every other man. . . . But you will promise to go when you have seen him, won't you?

JANE (*nodding*). I'll say, "I'm afraid I must leave you now, and——" Sandy, how *can* he be a prince?

MELISANDE. When you see him, Jane, you will say, "How can he not be a prince?"

JANE. But one has to leave princes backward. I mean —he won't expect—*you* know——

MELISANDE. I don't think so. Besides, after all, you are my cousin.

JANE. Yes. I think I shall get that in; just to be on the safe side. "Well, cousin, I must leave you now, as I have to attend my aunt." And then a sort of— not exactly a curtsey, but—(*she practises, murmuring the words to herself*). I suppose you didn't happen to mention *me* to him this morning?

MELISANDE (*half smiling*). Oh no!

JANE (*hurt*). I don't see why you shouldn't have. What did you talk about?

MELISANDE. I don't know. (*She grips* JANE's *arm suddenly*) Jane, I didn't dream it all this morning, did I? It did happen? I saw him—he kissed me—he is coming for me—he——

Enter ALICE

ALICE. Mr. Gervase Mallory.

MELISANDE (*happily*). Ah!

(GERVASE *comes in, an apparently ordinary young man in a loud golfing suit.*)

GERVASE. How do you do?

MELISANDE (*looking at him with growing amazement and horror*). Oh!

(JANE *looks from one to the other in bewilderment.*)

GERVASE. I ought to explain. Mr. Knowle was kind enough to lend me some petrol last night; my car broke down; he was good enough to say I might come this afternoon and see his prints. I am hoping to be allowed to thank him again for his kindness last night. And—er—I've brought back the petrol.

MELISANDE (*still with her eyes on him*). My father will no doubt be here directly. This is my cousin, Miss Bagot.

GERVASE (*bowing*). How do you do?

JANE (*nervously*). How do you do? (*After a pause*) Well, I'm afraid I must leave you now, as——

MELISANDE (*with her eyes still on* GERVASE, *putting out a hand and clutching at* JANE). No!

JANE (*startled*). What?

MELISANDE. Don't go, Jane. Do sit down, won't you, Mr.—er——

GERVASE. Mallory.

MELISANDE. Mr. Mallory.

GERVASE. Thank you.

MELISANDE. Where will you sit, Mr. Mallory? (*She is still talking in an utterly expressionless voice.*)

GERVASE. Thank you. Where are you—— (*he indicates the sofa.*)

MELISANDE (*moving to it, but still holding* JANE). Thank *you*.

>(MELISANDE *and* JANE *sit down together on the sofa.* GERVASE *sits on a chair near. There is an awkward silence.*)

JANE (*half getting up*). Well, I'm afraid I must——
>(MELISANDE *pulls her down. She subsides.*)

MELISANDE. Charming weather we are having, are we not, Mr. Mallory?

GERVASE (*enthusiastically*). Oh, rather. Absolutely top-hole.

MELISANDE (*to* JANE). Absolutely top-hole weather, is it not, Jane?

JANE. Oh, I love it.

MELISANDE. You play golf, I expect, Mr. Mallory?

GERVASE. Oh, rather. I've been playing this morning. (*With a smile*). Pretty rotten, too, I'm afraid.

MELISANDE. Jane plays golf. (*To* JANE) You're pretty rotten, too, aren't you, Jane?

JANE. Bobby and I were both very bad to-day.

MELISANDE. I think you will like Bobby, Mr. Mallory. He is staying with us just now. I expect you will have a good deal in common. He is on the Stock Exchange.

GERVASE (*smiling*). So am I.

MELISANDE (*valiantly repressing a shudder*). Jane, Mr. Mallory is on the Stock Exchange. Isn't that curious? I felt sure that he must be directly I saw him.
>(*There is another awkward silence.*)

JANE (*getting up*). Well, I'm afraid I must——

MELISANDE (*pulling her down*). Don't go, Jane. I

suppose there are a great many of you on the Stock Exchange, Mr. Mallory?

GERVASE. Oh, quite a lot.

MELISANDE. Quite a lot, Jane. . . . You don't know Bobby—Mr. Coote?

GERVASE. N—no, I don't think so.

MELISANDE. I suppose there are so many of you, and you dress so much alike, and look so much alike, that it's difficult to be quite sure whom you do know.

GERVASE. Yes, of course, that makes it more difficult.

MELISANDE. Yes. You see that, don't you, Jane? . . . You play billiards and bridge, of course, Mr. Mallory?

GERVASE. Oh yes.

MELISANDE. They are absolutely top-hole games, aren't they? Are you—pretty rotten at them?

GERVASE. Well——

MELISANDE (*getting up*). Ah, here's my father.

Enter MR. KNOWLE

MR. KNOWLE. Ah, Mr. Mallory, delighted to see you. And Sandy and Jane to entertain you. That's right.

(*They shake hands.*)

GERVASE. How do you do?

(ALICE *comes in with tea.*)

MR. KNOWLE. I've been wasting my day at a sale. I hope you spent yours more profitably. (GERVASE *laughs pleasantly.*) And what have you been doing, Sandy?

MELISANDE. Wasting mine, too, Father.

MR. KNOWLE. Dear, dear. Well, they say that the wasted hours are the best.

MELISANDE (*moving to the door*). I think I will go and—— (MRS. KNOWLE *comes in with outstretched hands.*)

MR. KNOWLE. My dear, this is Mr. Mallory.

MRS. KNOWLE. My dear Mr. Mallory! (*Turning round*) Sandy, dear! (MELISANDE *comes slowly back.*) How do you do?

GERVASE (*shaking hands*). How do you do?

MRS. KNOWLE. Sandy, dear! (*To* GERVASE) My daughter, Melisande, Mr. Mallory. My only child.

GERVASE. Oh—er—we——

MELISANDE. Mr. Mallory and I have met, Mother.

MRS. KNOWLE (*indicating* JANE). And our dear Jane. My dear sister's only daughter. But dear Jane has a brother. Dear Harold! In the Civil Service. Sandy, dear, will you pour out tea?

MELISANDE (*resigned*). Yes, Mother. (*She goes to the tea-table.*)

MRS. KNOWLE (*going to the sofa*). I am such an invalid now, Mr. Mallory——

GERVASE (*helping her*). Oh, I'm so sorry. Can I——?

MRS. KNOWLE. Thank you. Dr. Anderson insists on my resting as much as possible. So my dear Melisande looks after the house for me. Such a comfort. You are not married yourself, Mr. Mallory?

GERVASE. No. Oh no.

MRS. KNOWLE (*smiling to herself*). Ah!

MELISANDE. Jane, Mother's tea. (JANE *takes it.*)

GERVASE (*coming forward*). Oh. I beg your pardon. Let me——

JANE. It's all right.

(GERVASE *takes up a cake-stand.*)

MR. KNOWLE. Where's Bobby? Bobby is the real expert at this.

MELISANDE. I expect Mr. Mallory is an expert, too, Father. You enjoy tea-parties, I expect, Mr. Mallory?

GERVASE. I enjoy most things, Miss Knowle. (*To* MRS. KNOWLE) What will you have?

MRS. KNOWLE. Thank you. I have to be careful. Dr. Anderson insists on my being careful, Mr. Mallory. (*Confidentially*) Nothing organic, you understand. Both my husband and I—Melisande has an absolutely sound constitution.

MELISANDE (*indicating cup*). Jane. . . . Sugar and milk, Mr. Mallory?

GERVASE. Please. (*To* MR. KNOWLE) Won't *you* have this, sir?

MR. KNOWLE. No thank you. I have a special cup (*He takes a large cup from* MELISANDE). A family tradition, Mr. Mallory. But whether it is that I am supposed to require more nourishment than the others, or that I can't be trusted with anything breakable, History does not relate.

GERVASE (*laughing*). Well, I think you're lucky. I like a big cup.

MR. KNOWLE. Have mine.

GERVASE. No, thanks.

BOBBY (*coming in*). Hallo! Tea?

MR. KNOWLE. Ah, Bobby, you're just in time. (*To* GERVASE) This is Mr. Coote. Bobby, this is Mr. Mallory.

(*They nod to each other and say, "How do you do?"*)

MELISANDE (*indicating a seat next to her*). Come and sit here, Bobby.

BOBBY (*who was making for* JANE). Oh—er—righto. (*He sits down.*)

MR. KNOWLE (*to* GERVASE). And how did the dance go last night?

JANE. Oh, were you at a dance? How lovely!

MELISANDE. Dance?

MR. KNOWLE. And a fancy dress dance, too, Sandy. *You* ought to have been there.

MELISANDE (*understanding*). Ah!

MRS. KNOWLE. My daughter is devoted to dancing, Mr. Mallory. Dances so beautifully, they all say.

BOBBY. Where was it?

GERVASE. Collingham.

MR. KNOWLE. And did they all fall in love with you? You ought to have seen him, Sandy.

GERVASE. Well, I'm afraid I never got there.

MR. KNOWLE. Dear, dear. . . . Peters is in love just now. . . . I hope he didn't give you cider in mistake for petrol.

MRS. KNOWLE. You have a car, Mr. Mallory?

GERVASE. Yes.

MRS. KNOWLE. Ah! (*To* MELISANDE) Won't Mr. Mallory have some more tea, Sandy?

MELISANDE. Will you have some more tea, Mr. Mallory?

GERVASE. Thank you. (*To* MRS. KNOWLE) Won't you——

(*He begins to get up.*)

MRS. KNOWLE. *Please* don't trouble. I never have more than one cup. Dr. Anderson is very firm about that. Only one cup, Mrs. Knowle.

BOBBY (*to* MELISANDE). Sandwich? Oh, you're busy. Sandwich, Jane?

JANE (*taking one*). Thank you.

BOBBY (*to* GERVASE). Sandwich?

GERVASE. Thank you.

BOBBY (*to* MR. KNOWLE). Sandwich?

MR. KNOWLE. Thank you, Bobby. Fortunately nobody minds what *I* eat or drink.

BOBBY (*to himself*). Sandwich, Mr. Coote? Thank you. (*He takes one.*)

MRS. KNOWLE (*to* GERVASE). Being such an invalid,

Mr. Mallory, it is a great comfort to me to have Melisande to look after the house.

GERVASE. I am sure it is.

MRS. KNOWLE. Of course, I can't expect to keep her for ever.

MELISANDE (*coldly*). More tea, Jane?

JANE. Thank you, dear.

MRS. KNOWLE. It's extraordinary how she has taken to it. I must say that I do like a girl to be a good housekeeper. Don't you agree, Mr. Mallory?

GERVASE. Well, of course, all that sort of thing *is* rather important.

MRS. KNOWLE. That's what I always tell Sandy. "Happiness begins in the kitchen, Sandy."

MELISANDE. I'm sure Mr. Mallory agrees with you, Mother.

GERVASE (*laughing*). Well, one must eat.

BOBBY (*passing plate*). Have another sandwich?

GERVASE (*taking one*). Thanks.

MRS. KNOWLE. Do you live in the neighbourhood, Mr. Mallory?

GERVASE. About twenty miles away. Little Malling.

JANE (*helpfully*). Oh, yes.

MRS. KNOWLE. Well, I hope we shall see you here again.

GERVASE. That's very kind of you indeed. I shall love to come.

MELISANDE. More tea, Father?

MR. KNOWLE. No, thank you, my love.

MELISANDE. More tea, Mr. Mallory?

GERVASE. No, thank you.

MR. KNOWLE (*getting up*). I don't want to hurry you, Mr. Mallory, but if you have really finished——

GERVASE (*getting up*). Right.

MRS. KNOWLE. You won't go without seeing the garden, Mr. Mallory? Sandy, when your father has finished with Mr. Mallory, you must show him the garden. We are very proud of our roses, Mr. Mallory. Melisande takes a great interest in the roses.

GERVASE. I should like very much to see the garden. (*Going to her*) Shall I see you again, Mrs. Knowle. . . . Don't get up, *please*.

MRS. KNOWLE (*getting up*). In case we don't—(*she holds out her hand*).

GERVASE (*shaking it*). Good-bye. And thank you so much.

MRS. KNOWLE. Not good-bye. *Au revoir.*

GERVASE (*smiling*). Thank you. (*With a bow to* JANE *and* BOBBY) Good-bye, in case——

BOBBY. Cheero.

JANE. Good-bye, Mr. Mallory.

MR. KNOWLE. Well, come along. (*As they go out*) It is curious how much time one has to spend in saying "How do you do" and "Good-bye." I once calculated that a man of seventy. . . .

[MR. KNOWLE *and* GERVASE *go out.*

MRS. KNOWLE. Jane, dear, would you mind coming with me to the drawing-room, and helping me to—er——

JANE (*resigned*). Of course, Aunt Mary.

[*They go towards the door.*

BOBBY (*with his mouth full*). May I come too, Mrs. Knowle?

MELISANDE. You haven't finished your tea, Bobby.

BOBBY. I shan't be a moment. (*He picks up his cup.*)

MRS. KNOWLE. Please come, dear Mr. Coote, when you have finished.

[MRS. KNOWLE *goes out.*

(JANE *turns at the door, sees that* MELISANDE *is*

not looking, and blows a hasty kiss to BOBBY.)

MELISANDE. More tea, Bobby?

BOBBY. No thanks.

MELISANDE. Something more to eat?

BOBBY. No thanks. (*He gets up and walks towards the door.*)

MELISANDE. Bobby!

BOBBY (*turning*). Yes?

MELISANDE. There's something I want to say to you. Don't go.

BOBBY. Oh! Righto. (*He comes slowly back.*)

MELISANDE (*with difficulty, after a pause*). I made a mistake yesterday.

BOBBY (*not understanding*). A mistake? Yesterday?

MELISANDE. Yes. . . . You were quite right.

BOBBY. How do you mean? When?

MELISANDE. When you said that girls didn't know their own minds.

BOBBY. Oh! (*With an awkward laugh*) Yes. Well —er—I don't expect any of us do, really, you know. I mean—er—that is to say——

MELISANDE. I'm sorry I said what I did say to you last night, Bobby. I oughtn't to have said all those things.

BOBBY. I say, that's all right.

MELISANDE. I didn't mean them. And—and Bobby —I *will* marry you if you like.

BOBBY (*staggered*). Sandy!

MELISANDE. And it was silly of me to mind your calling me Sandy, and to say what I did about your clothes, and I *will* marry you, Bobby. And—and thank you for wanting it so much.

BOBBY. I say, Sandy. I say! I say——

MELISANDE (*offering her cheek*). You may kiss me if you like, Bobby.

BOBBY. I say! . . . Er—er—(*he kisses her gingerly*) thanks! . . . Er—I say——

MELISANDE. What is it, Bobby?

BOBBY. I say, you know—(*he tries again*) I don't want you to—to feel that—I mean, just because I asked you twice—I mean I don't want you to feel that—well, I mean you mustn't do it just for *my* sake Sandy. I mean Melisande.

MELISANDE. You may call me Sandy.

BOBBY. Well, you see what I mean, Sandy.

MELISANDE. It isn't that, Bobby. It isn't that.

BOBBY. You know, I was thinking about it last night—afterwards, you know—and I began to see, I began to see that perhaps you were right. I mean about my not being romantic and—and all that. I mean, I'm rather an ordinary sort of chap, and——

MELISANDE (*sadly*). We are all rather ordinary sort of chaps.

BOBBY (*eagerly*). No, no. No, that's where you're wrong, Sandy. I mean Melisande. You *aren't* ordinary. I don't say you'd be throwing yourself away on me, but—but I think you could find somebody more suitable. (*Earnestly*). I'm sure you could. I mean somebody who would remember to call you Melisande, and who would read poetry with you and—and all that. I mean, there are lots of fellows——

MELISANDE. I don't understand. Don't you *want* to marry me now?

BOBBY (*with dignity*). I don't want to be married out of pity.

MELISANDE (*coldly*). I have told you that it isn't out of pity.

BOBBY. Well, what *is* it out of? I mean, after what

ACT III]　　THE ROMANTIC AGE　　241

you said yesterday about my tie, it can't be love. If you really loved me——

MELISANDE. Are you under the impression that I am proposing to you?

BOBBY (*taken aback*). W-what?

MELISANDE. Are you flattering yourself that you are refusing me?

BOBBY. I say, shut up, Sandy. You know it isn't that at all.

MELISANDE. I think you had better join Jane. (*Carelessly*) It *is* Jane, isn't it?

BOBBY. I say, look here—— (*She doesn't*) Of course, I know you think I'm an awful rotter. . . . Well . . . well—oh, *damn*!

MELISANDE. Jane is waiting for you.

MRS. KNOWLE *comes in*.

MRS. KNOWLE. Oh, Mr. Coote, Jane is waiting for you.

BOBBY. Oh—er——

MELISANDE. Jane is waiting for you.

BOBBY (*realising that he is not quite at his best*). Er—oh—er, righto. (*He goes to the door and hesitates there*) Er—(*Now if he can only think of something really good, he may yet carry it off.*) Er—(*something really witty*)—er—er, righto! (*He goes out—to join* JANE, *who is waiting for him.*)

MRS. KNOWLE (*in a soft gentle voice*). Where is your father, dear? In the library with Mr. Mallory? . . . I want to speak to him. Just on a little matter of business. . . . Dear child!

[*She goes to the library.*

MELISANDE. Oh! How horrible!

(*She walks about, pulling at her handkerchief and telling herself that she won't cry. But she feels that she is going to, and she goes*

242   THE ROMANTIC AGE   [ACT III

to the open windows, and stands for a moment looking out, trying to recover herself.)

GERVASE *comes in.*

GERVASE (*gently*). Princess! (*She hears; her hand closes and tightens; but she says nothing.*) Princess!
(With an effort she controls herself, turns round and speaks coldly.)

MELISANDE. Please don't call me by that ridiculous name.

GERVASE. Melisande!

MELISANDE. Nor by that one.

GERVASE. Miss Knowle.

MELISANDE. Yes? What do you want, Mr. Mallory?

GERVASE. I want to marry you.

MELISANDE (*taken by surprise*). Oh! . . . How dare you!

GERVASE. But I told you this morning.

MELISANDE. I think you had better leave this morning out of it.

GERVASE. But if I leave this morning out of it, then I have only just met you.

MELISANDE. That is what I would prefer.

GERVASE. Oh! . . . Then if I have only just met you, perhaps I oughtn't to have said straight off that I want to marry you.

MELISANDE. It is unusual.

GERVASE. Yes. But not unusual to *want* to marry you.

MELISANDE. I am not interested in your wants.

GERVASE. Oh! (*Gently*) I'm sorry that we've got to forget about this morning. (*Going closer to her*) Is it so easy to forget, Melisande?

MELISANDE. Very easy for you, I should think.

GERVASE. But not for you?

MELISANDE (*bitterly*). You dress up and amuse yourself, and then laugh and go back to your ordinary life again—you don't want to remember *that,* do you, every time you do it?

GERVASE. You let your hair down and flirt with me and laugh and go home again, but *you* can't forget. Why should I?

MELISANDE (*furiously*). How dare you say I flirted with you?

GERVASE. How dare you say I laughed at you?

MELISANDE. Do you think I knew you would be there when I went up to the wood?

GERVASE. Do you think *I* knew you would be there when *I* went up?

MELISANDE. Then why were you there all dressed up like that?

GERVASE. My car broke down and I spent the night in it. I went up the hill to look for breakfast.

MELISANDE. Breakfast! That's all you think about.

GERVASE (*cheerfully*). Well, it's always cropping up.

MELISANDE (*in disgust*). Oh! (*She moves away from him and then turns round holding out her hand*) Good-bye, Mr. Mallory.

GERVASE (*taking it*). Good-bye, Miss Knowle. . . . (*Gently*) May I kiss your hands, Melisande?

MELISANDE (*pathetically*). Oh, don't! (*She hides her face in them.*)

GERVASE. Dear hands. . . . May I kiss your lips, Melisande? (*She says nothing. He comes closer to her*) Melisande!

(*He is about to put his arms round her, but she breaks away from him.*)

MELISANDE. Oh, don't, don't! What's the good of pretending? It was only pretence this morning—what's the good of going on with it? I thought you were so different from other men, but you're just the same, just the same. You talk about the things they talk about, you wear the clothes they wear. You were my true knight, my fairy Prince, this morning, and this afternoon you come down dressed like that (*she waves her hand at it*) and tell me that you are on the Stock Exchange! Oh, can't you see what you've done? All the beautiful world that I had built up for you and me —shattered, shattered.

GERVASE (*going to her*). Melisande!

MELISANDE. No, no!

GERVASE (*stopping*). All right.

MELISANDE (*recovering herself*). Please go.

GERVASE (*with a smile*). Well, that's not quite fair, you know.

MELISANDE. What do you mean?

GERVASE. Well, what about *my* beautiful world—the world that *I* had built up?

MELISANDE. I don't understand.

GERVASE. What about *your* pretence this morning? I thought you were so different from other women, but you're just the same, just the same. You were my true lady, my fairy Princess, this morning; and this afternoon the Queen, your mother, disabled herself by indigestion, tells me that you do all the housekeeping for her just like any ordinary commonplace girl. Your father, the King, has obviously never had a battle-axe in his hand in his life; your suitor, Prince Robert of Coote, is much more at home with a niblick than with a lance; and your cousin, the Lady Jane——

MELISANDE (*sinking on to the sofa and hiding her face*). Oh, cruel, cruel!

GERVASE (*remorsefully*). Oh, forgive me, Melisande. It was horrible of me.

MELISANDE. No, but it's true. How could any romance come into this house? Now you know why I wanted you to take me away—away to the ends of the earth with you.

GERVASE. Well, that's what I want to do.

MELISANDE. Ah, don't! When you're on the Stock Exchange!

GERVASE. But there's plenty of romance on the Stock Exchange. (*Nodding his head*) Oh yes, you want to look out for it.

MELISANDE (*reproachfully*). Now you're laughing at me again.

GERVASE. My dear, I'm not. Or if I am laughing at you, then I am laughing at myself too. And if we can laugh together, then we can be happy together, Melisande.

MELISANDE. I want romance, I want beauty. I don't want jokes.

GERVASE. I see what it is. You don't like my knickerbockers.

MELISANDE (*bewildered*). Did you expect me to?

GERVASE. No. (*After a pause*) I think that's why I put 'em on. (*She looks at him in surprise.*) You see, we had to come back to the twentieth century some time; we couldn't go on pretending for ever. Well, here we are—(*indicating his clothes*)—back. But I feel just as romantic, Melisande. I want beauty—your beauty—just as much. (*He goes to her.*)

MELISANDE. Which Melisande do you want? The one who talked to you this morning in the wood, or the one who—(*bitterly*) does all the housekeeping for her mother? (*Violently*) And badly, badly, badly!

GERVASE. The one who does all the housekeeping for her mother—and badly, badly, badly, *bless* her, because she has never realised what a gloriously romantic thing housekeeping is.

MELISANDE (*amazed*). Romantic!

GERVASE (*with enthusiasm*). Most gloriously romantic. . . . Did you ever long when you were young to be wrecked on a desert island?

MELISANDE (*clasping her hands*). Oh yes!

GERVASE. You imagined yourself there—alone or with a companion?

MELISANDE. Often!

GERVASE. And what were you doing? What is the romance of the desert island which draws us all? Climbing the bread-fruit tree, following the turtle to see where it deposits its eggs, discovering the spring of water, building the hut—*housekeeping*, Melisande. . . . Or take Robinson Crusoe. When Man Friday came along and left his footprint in the sand, why did Robinson Crusoe stagger back in amazement? Because he said to himself, like a good housekeeper, "By Jove, I'm on the track of a servant at last." There's romance for you!

MELISANDE (*smiling and shaking her head at him*). What nonsense you talk!

GERVASE. It isn't nonsense; indeed, indeed it isn't. There's romance everywhere if you look for it. *You* look for it in the old fairy-stories, but did *they* find it there? Did the gentleman who had just been given a new pair of seven-league boots think it romantic to be changed into a fish? He probably thought it a confounded nuisance, and wondered what on earth to do with his boots. Did Cinderella and the Prince find the world romantic after they were married? Think of the endless silent evenings which they spent together, with nothing in common but an admiration for Cinderella's feet—do you think *they* didn't long for the romantic days of old? And in two thousand or two hundred thousand years, people will read stories about *us*, and sigh and say, "Will those romantic days never come back again?" Ah, they are here now, Melisande, for *us*; for the people with imagination; for you and for me.

MELISANDE. Are they? Oh, if I could believe they were!

GERVASE. You thought of me as your lover and true knight this morning. Ah, but what an easy thing to be! You were my Princess. Look at yourself in the glass—how can you help being a princess? But if we could be companions, Melisande! That's difficult; that's worth trying.

MELISANDE (*gently*). What do you want me to do?

GERVASE. Get used to me. See me in a top-hat—see me in a bowler-hat. Help me with my work; play games with me—I'll teach you if you don't know how. I want to share the world with you for all our lives. That's a long time, you know; we can't do it on one twenty-minutes' practice before breakfast. We can be lovers so easily—can we be friends?

MELISANDE (*looking at him gravely*). You are very wise.

GERVASE. I talked with a wise man in the wood this morning; I've been thinking over what he said. (*Suddenly*) But when you look at me like that, how I long to be a fool and say, "Come away with me now, now, now," you wonderful, beautiful, maddening woman, you adorable child, you funny foolish little girl. (*Holding up a finger*) Smile, Melisande. Smile! (*Slowly, reluctantly, she gives him a smile.*) I suppose the fairies taught you that. Keep it for *me*, will you—but give it to me often. Do you ever laugh, Melisande? We must laugh together sometimes—that makes life so easy.

MELISANDE (*with a happy little laugh*). Oh, what can I say to you?

GERVASE. Say, "I think I should like you for a companion, Gervase."

MELISANDE (*shyly*). I think I should like you for a companion, Gervase.

GERVASE. Say, "Please come and see me again, Gervase."

MELISANDE. Please come and see me again, Gervase.

GERVASE (*jumping up and waving his hand*). Say, "Hooray for things!"

MELISANDE (*standing up, but shyly still*). Hooray for things!

GERVASE. Thank you, Melisande . . . I must go. (*He presses her hand and goes; or seems to be going. But suddenly he comes back, bends on one knee, raises her hand on his, and kisses it*) My Princess!

[*Then* GERVASE *goes out.*
(MELISANDE *stays there, looking after him, her hand to her cheek. . . . But one cannot stand thus for ever. The new life must begin. With a little smile at herself, at* GERVASE, *at things, she fetches out the Great Book from its hiding-place, where she had buried it many weeks ago in disgust. Now it comes into its own. She settles down with it in her favourite chair. . . .*)

MELISANDE (*reading*). To make Bread-Sauce. . . . Take an onion, peel and quarter it, and simmer it in milk. . . .

(*But you know how the romantic passage goes. We leave her with it, curled up in the chair, this adorable child, this funny foolish little girl.*)

THE STEPMOTHER

A PLAY IN ONE ACT

CHARACTERS

Sir John Pembury, M.P.
Lady Pembury.
Perkins.
The Stranger.

The first performance of this play was given at the Alhambra Theatre on November 16, 1920, with the following cast:

Sir John Pembury	-	Gilbert Hare.
Lady Pembury	-	Winifred Emery.
Perkins	-	C. M. Lowne.
The Stranger	-	Gerald du Maurier.

THE STEPMOTHER

A summer morning. The sunniest and perhaps the pleasantest room in the London house of SIR JOHN PEMBURY, M.P. *For this reason* LADY PEMBURY *uses it a good deal, although it is not officially hers. It is plainly furnished, and probably set out to be a sort of waiting-room for* SIR JOHN'S *many callers, but* LADY PEMBURY *has left her mark upon it.*

PERKINS, *the butler, inclining to stoutness, but not yet past his prime, leads the way in, followed by* THE STRANGER. PERKINS *has already placed him as "one of the lower classes," but the intelligent person in the pit perceives that he is something better than that, though whether he is in the process of falling from a higher estate, or of rising to it, is not so clear. He is thirty odd, shabbily dressed (but then, so are most of us nowadays), and ill at ease; not because he is shabby, but because he is ashamed of himself. To make up for this, he adopts a blustering manner, as if to persuade himself that he is a fine fellow after all. There is a touch of commonness about his voice, but he is not uneducated.*

PERKINS. I'll tell Sir John you're here, but I don't say he'll see you, mind.

STRANGER. Don't you worry about that. He'll see me right enough.

PERKINS. He's busy just now. Well—— (*He looks at* THE STRANGER *doubtfully.*)

STRANGER (*bitterly*). I suppose you think I've got no business in a gentleman's house. Is that it?

PERKINS. Well, I didn't say so, did I? Maybe you're a constituent? Being in the 'Ouse of Commons, we get some pretty queer ones at times. All sorts, as you might say. . . . P'raps you're a deputation?

STRANGER (*violently*). What the hell's it got to do with you who I am. You go and tell your master I'm here—that's all you've got to do. See?

PERKINS (*unruffled*). Easy, now, easy. You 'aven't even told me your name yet. Is it the Shah of Persia or Mr. Bottomley?

STRANGER. The less said about names the better. You say, "Somebody from Lambeth"—*he'll* know what I mean.

PERKINS (*humourously*). Ah, I beg your pardon—the Archbishop of Canterbury. I didn't recognise your Grace.

STRANGER (*angrily*). It's people like you who make one sick of the world. Parasites—servile flunkeys, bolstering up an effete aristocracy. Why don't you get some proper work to do?

PERKINS (*good-naturedly*). Now, look here, young man, this isn't the time for that sort of talk. If you've got anything you want to get off your chest about flunkeys or monkeys, or whatever it may be, keep it till Sunday afternoon—when I'm off duty. (*He comes a little closer to* THE STRANGER) Four o'clock Sunday afternoon—(*jerking his thumb over his shoulder*)—just round the corner—in the Bolton Mews. See? Nobody there to interrupt us. See? All quite gentlemanly and secluded, and a friend of mine to hold the watch. See? (*He edges closer as he talks.*)

STRANGER (*retreating nervously*). No offence meant, mate. We're in the same boat—you and me; we don't

THE STEPMOTHER

want to get fighting. My quarrel isn't with you. You go and tell Sir John that there's a gentleman come to see him—wants a few minutes of his valuable time—from Lambeth way. *He'll* know. That's all right.

PERKINS (*drawing back, disappointedly*). Then I shan't be seeing you Sunday afternoon?

STRANGER (*laughing awkwardly*). There, that's all right. No offence meant. Somebody from Lambeth—that's what *you've* got to say. And tell 'im I'm in a hurry. *He'll* know what I mean.

PERKINS (*going slowly to the door*). Well, it's a queer game, but being in the 'Ouse of Commons, one can't never be surprised. All sorts, as you might say, *all* sorts.
[*Exit* PERKINS.

(THE STRANGER, *left alone, walks up and down the room, nervously impatient.*)

LADY PEMBURY *comes in. In twenty-eight years of happy married life, she has mothered one husband and five daughters, but she has never had a son—her only sorrow. Her motto might be, "It is just as easy to be kind"; and whether you go to her for comfort or congratulation, you will come away feeling that she is the only person who really understands.*

LADY PEMBURY. Oh! (*She stops and then comes towards* THE STRANGER) How do you do? Are you waiting to see my husband?

STRANGER (*taken aback at seeing her*). Yes.
(*He is not sure for the moment if this upsets his plans or forwards them.*)

LADY PEMBURY. I think he's engaged just now. But he won't be long. Perkins will tell him as soon as he is free.

STRANGER (*contemptuously*). His name is Perkins, is it?

LADY PEMBURY (*surprised*). The butler? Yes.

STRANGER (*contemptuously*). Mister Perkins, the Butler.

LADY PEMBURY (*with a friendly smile*). You don't *mind* our having a butler? (*She picks up some work from the table and takes it to the sofa.*)

STRANGER (*shrugging his shoulders*). One more parasite.

LADY PEMBURY (*interested*). I always thought parasites were much smaller than Perkins. (*Sitting down*) Do sit down, won't you? (*He sits down reluctantly.*) You mustn't mind my being here. This is really my work-room. I expect my husband will take you into his own room when he's ready.

STRANGER. Your work-room?

LADY PEMBURY (*looking up at him with a smile*). You don't seem to like our domestic arrangements.

STRANGER (*waving his hand at her embroidery*). You call that work?

LADY PEMBURY (*pleasantly*). Other people's work always seems so contemptible, doesn't it? Now I expect if you tried to do this, you would find it very difficult indeed, and if I tried to do yours—what *is* your work, Mr.—er—— Dear me, I don't even know your name.

STRANGER (*bitterly*). Never mind my name. Take it that I haven't got a name.

LADY PEMBURY. But your friends must call you something.

STRANGER. Take it that I haven't got any friends.

LADY PEMBURY. Oh, *don't* say that! How *can* you?

STRANGER (*surly*). What's it matter to you whether anybody cares about me?

LADY PEMBURY. Oh, never mind whether anybody cares about *you*; don't *you* care about anybody?

STRANGER. Nobody.

LADY PEMBURY. Poor, poor man! (*Going on with her*

work) If you can't tell me your name, I wish you would tell me what work you do. (*Winningly*) You don't mind my asking, do you?

STRANGER. I can tell you what work I'm going to do after to-day.

LADY PEMBURY. Oh, do!

STRANGER (*violently*). None!

LADY PEMBURY (*surprised*). None?

STRANGER. No more work after to-day.

LADY PEMBURY. Won't that be rather dull?

STRANGER. Well, *you* ought to know. I'm going to be one of the idle rich—like you and Sir John—and let other people work for me.

LADY PEMBURY (*thoughtfully*). I shouldn't have said my husband was idle. But there it is. No two people ever agree as to what is work and what isn't.

STRANGER. What do you know about work—you aristocrats?

LADY PEMBURY (*mildly*). My husband is only a K.B.E., you know. Quite a recent creation.

STRANGER (*not heeding her*). You, who've been brought up in the lap of luxury—never known a day's discomfort in your life——

LADY PEMBURY. My dear young man, you really mustn't tell a woman who has had five children that she has never known a day's discomfort in her life. . . . Ask any woman.

STRANGER (*upset*). What's that? . . . I didn't come here to argue with you. You began it. Why can't you let me alone?

LADY PEMBURY (*going to a side-table and taking up a photograph*). Five children—all girls—and now I'm a grandmother. (*Showing him the photograph*) There! That's my eldest daughter with her eldest son and my eldest grandchild. Isn't he a duck? He's supposed to be like me. . . . I never had a son of my own. (THE STRANGER *has taken the photograph in his hand and is holding it awkwardly.*) Oh, let me take it away from you. Other people's relations are so uninteresting, aren't they? (*She takes it away and puts it back in its place. Then she returns to her seat and goes on with her work.*) So you've made a lot of money? How exciting for you!

STRANGER (*grimly*). I haven't got it yet, but it's coming.

LADY PEMBURY. Soon?

STRANGER. To-day.

LADY PEMBURY. You're not married, are you?

STRANGER. You want to know a lot, don't you? Well, I'm not married.

LADY PEMBURY. I was thinking how much nicer it is when you can share that sort of news with somebody else, somebody you love. It makes good news so much better, and bad news so much more bearable.

STRANGER. That's what you and your husband do, is it?

LADY PEMBURY (*nodding*). Always. For eight-and-twenty years.

STRANGER. He tells you everything, eh?

LADY PEMBURY. Well, not his official secrets, of course. Everything else.

STRANGER. Ha! I wonder.

LADY PEMBURY. But you have nobody, you say. Well, you must share your good news with *me*. Will you?

STRANGER. Oh yes, you shall hear about it all right.

LADY PEMBURY. That's nice of you. Well then, first question. How much money is it going to be?

STRANGER (*thoughtfully*). Well, I don't quite know yet. What do you say to a thousand a year?

LADY PEMBURY. Oh, but what a lot!

THE STEPMOTHER

STRANGER. You think a thousand a year would be all right. Enough to live on?

LADY PEMBURY. For a bachelor, ample.

STRANGER. For a bachelor.

LADY PEMBURY. There's no one dependent on you?

STRANGER. Not a soul. Only got one relation living.

LADY PEMBURY. Oh?

STRANGER (*enjoying a joke of his own*). A father. But I shall not be supporting *him*. Oh no. Far from it.

LADY PEMBURY (*a little puzzled by this, though she is not going to show it*) Then I think you will be very rich with a thousand a year.

STRANGER. Yes, that's what *I* thought. I should think it would stand a thousand.

LADY PEMBURY. What is it? An invention of some sort?

STRANGER. Oh no, not an invention. . . . A discovery.

LADY PEMBURY. How proud she would have been!

STRANGER. Who?

LADY PEMBURY. Your wife if you had had one; your mother if she had been alive.

STRANGER (*violently*). Look here, you leave my mother out of it. My business is with Sir John—— (*sneeringly*) Sir John Pembury, K.B.E. If I want to talk about my mother, he and I will have a nice little talk together about her. Yes, and about my father, too.

(LADY PEMBURY *understands at last. She stands up slowly, and looks at him, horrified.*)

LADY PEMBURY. What do you mean?

STRANGER. A thousand a year. You said so yourself. Yes, I think it's worth a thousand a year.

LADY PEMBURY. Who is your father? What's your name?

STRANGER. Didn't I tell you I hadn't got a name?

(*Bitterly*) And if you want to know why, ask Sir John Pembury, K.B.E.

LADY PEMBURY (*in a whisper*). He's your father.

STRANGER. Yes. And I'm his loving son—come to see him at last, after all these years.

LADY PEMBURY (*hardly able to ask it*). How—how old are you?

STRANGER. Thirty.

LADY PEMBURY (*sitting down on the sofa*). Oh, thank God! Thank God!

STRANGER (*upset by her emotion*). Look here, I didn't want all this. I ask you—did I begin it? It was you who kept asking questions. I just came for a quiet talk with Sir John—Father and Son talking together quietly—talking about Son's allowance. A thousand a year. What did you want to come into it for?

(LADY PEMBURY *is quiet again now. She wipes away a tear or two, and sits up, looking at him thoughtfully.*)

LADY PEMBURY. So *you* are the son that I never had.

STRANGER. What d'you mean?

LADY PEMBURY (*almost to herself*). The son whom I wanted so. Five girls—never a boy. Let me look at you. (*She goes up to him.*)

STRANGER (*edging away*). Here, none of that.

LADY PEMBURY (*looking at him earnestly to see if she can see a likeness*). No—and yet—(*shaking her head sadly*) Poor boy! What an unhappy life you must have had!

STRANGER. I didn't come here to be pitied. I came to get my rightful allowance—same as any other son.

LADY PEMBURY (*to herself*). Poor boy! (*She goes back to her seat and then says*) You don't mind my asking you questions *now*, do you?

THE STEPMOTHER

STRANGER. Go on. There's no mistake about it. I can promise you that.

LADY PEMBURY. How did you find out? Did your mother tell you?

STRANGER. Never a word. "Don't ask questions, sonny——" "Father's dead"—all that sort of thing.

LADY PEMBURY. Does Sir John know? Did he ever know?

STRANGER (*feeling in his pocket*). *He* knew right enough. (*Bringing out letters*) Look here—here you are. This was how I found out. (*Selecting one*) There—read that one.

LADY PEMBURY (*taking it*). Yes—that's John's writing. (*She holds it out to him.*)

STRANGER. Aren't you going to read it?

LADY PEMBURY (*shaking her head pathetically*). He didn't write it to *me*.

STRANGER. He didn't write it to *me*, if it comes to that.

LADY PEMBURY. You're her son—you have a right. I'm—nobody.

STRANGER (*putting it back in his pocket*). Oh well, please yourself.

LADY PEMBURY. Did Sir John provide for your mother?

STRANGER. Well, why shouldn't he? He was a rich man.

LADY PEMBURY. Not in those days. . . . But indeed— why shouldn't he? What else could he do? I'm glad he did.

STRANGER. And now he's going to provide for his loving son. He's rich enough for that in these days.

LADY PEMBURY. He's never seen you?

STRANGER. Never. The historic meeting of Father and Son will take place this afternoon. (*With a feeble attempt at what he thinks is the aristocratic manner*)

Afraid the Governor will be in the deuce of a rage. Been exceedin' my allowance—what? Make it a thousand, dear old Gov.

LADY PEMBURY. Don't they call that blackmail?

STRANGER (*violently*). Now look here, I'd better tell you straight that there's no blackmail about this at all. He's my father, isn't he? Well, can't a son come to his father if he's hard up? Where are your threatening letters? Where's the blackmail? Anyway, what's he going to do about it? Put his son in prison?

LADY PEMBURY (*following her own thoughts*). You're thirty. Thank God for that. We hadn't met then. . . . Ah, but he ought to have told me. He ought to have told me.

STRANGER. P'raps he thought you wouldn't marry him, if he did.

LADY PEMBURY. Do you think that was it? (*Earnestly to him, as if he were an old friend*) You know men— young men. I never had a son; I never had any brothers. Do they tell? They ought to, oughtn't they?

STRANGER. Well—well, if you ask *me*—— I say, look here, this isn't the sort of thing one discusses with a lady.

LADY PEMBURY. Isn't it? But one can talk to a friend.

STRANGER (*scornfully*). You and me look like friends, don't we?

LADY PEMBURY (*smiling*). Well, we do, rather.

(*He gets up hastily and moves further away from her.*)

STRANGER. I know what *your* game is. Don't think I don't see it.

LADY PEMBURY. What is it?

STRANGER. Falling on your knees, and saying with tears in your eyes: "Oh, kind friend, spare me poor husband!" *I* know the sort of thing. And trying to work me up friendly before you begin.

LADY PEMBURY (*shaking her head*). No, if I went on my knees to you, I shouldn't say that. How can you hurt my husband now?

STRANGER. Well, I don't suppose the scandal will do him much good. Not an important Member of Parliament like *him*.

LADY PEMBURY. Ah, but it isn't the outside things that really hurt you, the things which are done to you, but the things which you do to yourself. And so if I went on my knees to you, it would not be for my husband's sake. For I should go on my knees, and I should say: "Oh, my son that might have been, think before you give up everything that a man should have. Ambition, hope, pride, self-respect—are not these worth keeping? Is your life to end now? Have you done all that you came into the world to do, so that now you can look back and say, 'It is finished; I have given all that I had to give; henceforward I will spend'?" (*Very gently*) Oh, my son that might have been!

STRANGER (*very uncomfortably*). Here, I say, that isn't fair.

LADY PEMBURY (*gently*). When did your mother die?

STRANGER. Look here, I wish you wouldn't keep on about mothers.

LADY PEMBURY. When did she die, proud mother?

STRANGER (*sulkily*). Well, why shouldn't she be proud? (*After a pause*) Two years ago, if you want to know.

LADY PEMBURY. It was then that you found out who your father was?

STRANGER. That's right. I found these old letters. She'd kept them locked up all those years. Bit of luck for me.

LADY PEMBURY (*almost to herself*). And that was two years ago. And for two years you had your hopes, your ambitions, for two years you were proud and independent. . . . Why did you not come to us then?

STRANGER (*with a touch of vanity*). Well, I was getting on all right, you know—and——

LADY PEMBURY. And then suddenly, after two years, you lost hope.

STRANGER. I lost my job.

LADY PEMBURY. Poor boy! And couldn't get another.

STRANGER (*bitterly*). It's a beast of a world if you're down. He's in the gutter—kick him down—trample on him. Nobody wants him. That's the way to treat them when they're down. Trample on 'em.

LADY PEMBURY. And so you came to your father to help you up again. To help you out of the gutter.

STRANGER. That's right.

LADY PEMBURY (*pleadingly*). Ah, but give him a chance!

STRANGER. Now, look here, I've told you already that I'm not going to have any of *that* game.

LADY PEMBURY (*shaking her head sadly*). Foolish boy! You don't understand. Give him a chance to help you out of the gutter.

STRANGER. Well, I'm——! Isn't that what I am doing?

LADY PEMBURY. No, no. You're asking him to trample you right down into it, deeper and deeper into the mud and slime. I want you to let him help you back to where you were two years ago—when you were proud and hopeful.

STRANGER (*looking at her in a puzzled way*). I can't make out what your game is. It's no good pretending you don't hate the sight of me—it stands to reason you must.

LADY PEMBURY (*smiling*). But then women *are* unreasonable, aren't they? And I think it is only in fairy-stories that stepmothers are always so unkind.

STRANGER (*surprised*). Stepmother!

LADY PEMBURY. Well, that's practically what I am, isn't it? (*Whimsically*) I've never been a stepmother before. (*Persuasively*) Couldn't you let me be proud of my stepson?

STRANGER. Well, you *are* a one! . . . Do you mean to say that you and your husband aren't going to have a row about this?

LADY PEMBURY. It's rather late to begin a row, isn't it, thirty years after it's happened? . . . Besides, perhaps you aren't going to tell him anything about it.

STRANGER. But what else have I come for except to tell him?

LADY PEMBURY. To tell *me*. . . . I asked you to give him a chance of helping you out of your troubles, but I'd rather you gave *me* the chance. . . . You see, John would be very unhappy if he knew that I knew this; and he would have to tell me, because when a man has been happily married to anybody for twenty-eight years, he can't really keep a secret from the other one. He pretends to himself that he can, but he knows all the time what a miserable pretence it is. And so John would tell me, and say he was sorry, and I would say: "It's all right, darling, I knew," but it would make him ashamed, and he would be afraid that perhaps I wasn't thinking him such a wonderful man as I did before. And it's very bad for a public man like John when he begins to lose faith in what his wife is thinking about him. . . . So let *me* be your friend, will you? (*There is a silence between them for a little. He looks at her wonderingly. Suddenly she stands up, her finger to her lips*) H'sh! It's John. (*She moves away from him.*)

SIR JOHN PEMBURY *comes in quickly; big, good-looking, decisive, friendly; a man who wears very naturally, and without any self-consciousness, an air of being somebody.*

PEMBURY (*walking hastily past his wife to her writing-desk*). Hallo, darling! Did I leave a cheque-book in here? I was writing a cheque for you this morning. Ah, here we are. (*As he comes back, he sees* THE STRANGER) I beg your pardon, Kate. I didn't see—— (*He is making for the door with the cheque-book in his hand, and then stops and says with a pleasant smile to* THE STRANGER) But, perhaps you are waiting to see *me*? Perkins said something——

STRANGER (*coming forward*). Yes, I came to see you, Sir John.

> (*He stands close in front of* SIR JOHN, *looking at him.* LADY PEMBURY *watches them steadfastly.*)

PEMBURY (*tapping his cheque-book against his hand*). Important?

STRANGER. I came to ask your help.

PEMBURY (*looking at his cheque-book and then back with a smile at* THE STRANGER). A good many people do that. Have you any special claim on me?

STRANGER (*after a long pause*). No.

> (PEMBURY *looks at him, undecided.* LADY PEMBURY *comes forward.*)

LADY PEMBURY. All right, dear. (*Meaning that she will look after* THE STRANGER *till he comes back.*)

PEMBURY. I'll be back in a moment. (*He nods and hurries out.*)

> (*There is silence for a little, and then* LADY PEMBURY *claps her hands gently.*)

LADY PEMBURY (*with shining eyes*). Oh, brave, brave!

THE STEPMOTHER

Ah, but I am a proud stepmother to-day. (*She holds out her hand to him*) Thank you, son.

STRANGER (*not seeing it, and speaking in a hard voice*). I'd better go.

LADY PEMBURY. Mayn't I help you?

STRANGER. I'd better go.

LADY PEMBURY (*distressed*). You can't go like this. I don't even know your name, nor where you live.

STRANGER. Don't be afraid—you shan't hear from *me* again.

LADY PEMBURY (*gently*). Not even when you've got back to where you were two years ago? Mayn't I then?

STRANGER (*looking at her, and then nodding slowly*). Yes, you shall then.

LADY PEMBURY. Thank you. I shall wait. I shall hope. I shall pray. (*She holds out her hand again*) Good-bye!

STRANGER (*shaking his head*). Wait till you hear from me. (*He goes to the door, and then stops and comes slowly back. He says awkwardly*) Wish you'd do one thing for me?

LADY PEMBURY. Yes?

STRANGER. That fellow—what did you say his name was—Perkins?

LADY PEMBURY (*surprised*). The butler? Perkins—yes?

STRANGER. Would you give him a message from me?

LADY PEMBURY. Of course.

STRANGER (*still awkwardly*). Just to say—I'll *be* there—at the Mews—on Sunday afternoon. *He'll* know. Tell him I'll be there. (*He squares his shoulders and walks out defiantly—ready to take the world on again—beginning with* PERKINS *on Sunday afternoon.*)

(LADY PEMBURY *stands watching him as he goes. She waits after he has gone, thinking her*

> *own thoughts, out of which she comes with something of a shock as the door opens and*
>
> SIR JOHN *comes in.*

PEMBURY. Hallo! Has he gone?

LADY PEMBURY. Yes.

PEMBURY. What did he want? Five pounds—or a place in the Cabinet?

LADY PEMBURY. He came for—a subscription.

PEMBURY. And got it, if I know my Kate. (*Carelessly*) What did he take from you?

LADY PEMBURY (*with a wistful little sigh*). Yes; he took something from me. Not very much, I think. But just—something. (*She takes his arm, leads him to the sofa, and says affectionately*) And now tell me all that you've been doing this morning.

> (*So he begins to tell her—just as he has told her a thousand times before . . . But it isn't quite the same.*)

A NOTE ON THE TYPE IN WHICH THIS BOOK IS SET

This book is set in a type called Scotch. There is a divergence of opinion regarding the exact origin of this face, some authorities holding that it was first cut by Alexander Wilson & Son, of Glasgow, in 1837, while others trace it back to a modernized Caslon old style brought out by Mrs. Henry Caslon in 1796. Its essential characteristics are sturdy capitals, full rounded lower case letters, the graceful fillet of the serifs and a general effect of crispness.

SET UP, ELECTROTYPED, PRINTED
AND BOUND BY THE HADDON
CRAFTSMEN, CAMDEN, N. J.
PAPER MADE BY TICONDEROGA
PULP AND PAPER CO., TICON-
DEROGA, N. Y.